beauty of the broken

beauty of the broken

of the

broken

Tawni Waters

Simon Pulse
NEW YORK LONDON TORONTO SYDNEY NEW DELHI

SIMON PULSE
An imprint of Simon & Schuster Children's Publishing Division
1230 Avenue of the Americas, New York, NY 10020
First Simon Pulse hardcover edition September 2014
Text copyright © 2014 by Tawni Waters
Jacket photograph copyright © 2014 by Mark Owen/Trevillion Images
All rights reserved, including the right of reproduction
in whole or in part in any form.
SIMON PULSE and colophon are registered trademarks of
Simon & Schuster, Inc.
For information about special discounts for bulk purchases,
please contact Simon & Schuster Special Sales at 1-866-506-1949 or
business@simonandschuster.com.
The Simon & Schuster Speakers Bureau can bring authors to your live event. For more
information or to book an event contact the Simon & Schuster Speakers Bureau at
1-866-248-3049 or visit our website at www.simonspeakers.com.
Jacket designed by Regina Flath
Interior designed by Hilary Zarycky
The text of this book was set in Berling.
Manufactured in the United States of America
2 4 6 8 10 9 7 5 3 1
Library of Congress Cataloging-in-Publication Data
Waters, Tawni.
Beauty of the broken / by Tawni Waters.—First Simon Pulse hardcover edition.
pages cm
Summary: As if her parents' heavy drinking and her father's abuse—which nearly killed
her half-brother, Iggy—were not enough, fifteen-year-old Mara is caught kissing her
girlfriend, Xylia, by the preacher's son and becomes terrified that her own life is at risk.
ISBN 978-1-4814-0709-0 (hc)
[1. Family problems—Fiction. 2. Brothers and sisters—Fiction. 3. Child abuse—Fiction.
4. Alcoholism—Fiction. 5. Lesbians—Fiction. 6. Christian life—Fiction.] I. Title.
PZ7.W264359Be 2014
[Fic]—dc23
2014006632
ISBN 978-1-4814-0710-6 (eBook)

For my precious parents,
who taught me the way of love

CHAPTER 1

MOMMA AND WILLY MACYNTIRE MADE
Iggy in a barn. It was an act of passion, I heard
my momma say to her cousin. She was on the
phone at the kitchen table while Daddy was off on some
hunting trip. Why she was baring her heart to this relative
she sees maybe once every five years, I don't know. She
says she's like a sister to her, but I don't understand how
because they almost never talk. Then again, Daddy never
did let Momma have friends, and he thinks Momma's family is a herd of Godless heathens. He keeps us away from
them, and Momma lets it happen. Momma lets Daddy do
whatever the hell he wants. Why wouldn't she? He'd bust
her wide open if she didn't. Plus, my guess is she's trying to

make up for cheating on him all those years ago when they were engaged. As far as I can tell, it's not working. Daddy still hates Momma most days.

When I heard about how Iggy was made in a smelly barn and not a sacred marriage bed, it made me want to throw up. It's been almost a year, and I still feel like barfing at the thought of Momma and this man humping away in the hay, their bare, pasty skin all covered in goose pimples and sweat. I can't stop thinking about it though, even when the sick taste is in my mouth, and my throat is as tight as a fist full of quarters. I think about it before I go to bed, as the floorboards are creaking and Daddy is grunting and Momma is making no noise at all. I think about it in science class when Mr. Farley talks in his deep, garbled voice about stamens and pistils, and shouldn't we all know not to giggle at these lessons by now, shouldn't we think of flower reproduction as a gift from the good Lord and not fodder for dirty, hell-spawned thoughts? I think of it when Iggy wonders why Daddy hates him. But I never tell Iggy what I know.

Sometimes when I imagine Willy Macyntire, he looks like Bugs Bunny, buck teeth and all. Sometimes he looks like a movie star. Sometimes he looks like the devil. I've never seen him, and I never will, because Momma said even before she knew she was pregnant, Daddy took his rifle to Willy's house and told him to leave town or he'd kill him. Willy left. When Daddy says he'll kill you, you believe him. His eyes get flat and shiny, like asphalt on a hot day. They go dead.

Sometimes knowing is torture. You wish you could hide your secret away in a dark, cobwebby shed, shut the door, and break the key in the lock so no one can ever get in again. You wish that you could go to sleep and have your last thought be anything but the buttery light of the New Mexico moon sneaking in through the cracks of an old barn's walls. But you can't erase the knowing, and you can never tell your secret. If there is one thing this world has taught me, it's that no matter how bad things get, they can always get worse. Secrets should stay secrets. It keeps them tolerable. Telling secrets turns them into full-on hell.

I think all this as I stare at Iggy. We're lying under the porch. It's so hot, sweat is trickling from the sandy tips of Iggy's hair and zigzagging over his freckles, mixing with the tears that keep sneaking out of his rust colored eyes. He's trying not to cry, I can tell. He never cries anymore. Not even in front of me. But today Daddy said he was gonna kill him, and today we believe him.

"He'll never find us here," I whisper. When I touch Iggy's arm, I notice how small and white my hands look. My fingers tremble at my bold-faced lie. Still, I say it again. "He'll never find us here, Iggy." I lie partly for Iggy, partly for me. Maybe Daddy won't find us. You never know. But deep down I know the truth. Daddy always finds us.

Iggy only cries harder. He squeezes his eyes shut to make the tears stay in his head. We can hear Daddy in the house, calling for us in his thunder voice.

"Mara! Iggy!" The way he says our names makes them sound like cusswords. If we were close enough, we would smell the whiskey on his breath and see the bulging vein in his forehead.

But we aren't that close. We're under the porch praying Daddy won't find us and take the belt to Iggy. Bars of sunlight fall like slices of heaven between the slats of the porch above us. Dust swirls in the light. To me it looks like a golden cloud. When I try to catch it like I would a firefly, it slips through my fingers. I try again. You gotta try to hold on to beauty when you find it.

"I'm just gonna do it, Sis," Iggy says. "I'm just gonna go out there and knock the shit out of him."

"No, Iggy. No," I whisper, because last time Iggy tried that, Daddy nearly killed him. He was out of school for two weeks. Granted, Iggy was six inches shorter then and had a lot less muscle, but still. The thought of losing my brother scares me more than anything in the world. He's my only safe place. I'd die without him.

"Don't go, Iggy," I say, and he thinks for a minute.

I grab Iggy's hand, and we catch some dust between our fingers. After a moment he says, "Fine." The sweet smell of the corn that's ready to be harvested and the musty smell of the mist rising from the river on the other side of the fields waft in on the breeze. We just lie there staring at the sunlight falling over our hands, noticing the way they fit together so perfectly. I watch my skin glow, thinking maybe I'm an angel sent from God to protect Iggy because God knew what a screwed-up family he lived in. I always thought that Iggy was my angel, but today I wonder if it's the other way around.

When I was little, in Sunday school, they told us that the angels have big strong hands and fiery swords that they use to vanquish all their foes. They told us that no man on earth or demon from hell can stand up before the power of those flaming swords. But I feel like an angel with small hands and no sword.

"I didn't lose the fucking hammer, Sis," Iggy says. Of course he didn't. I know that. Who doesn't know that? What would he want with Daddy's old hammer anyway, for God's sake? I squeeze his hand.

He shakes his head. "Then why the hell is he after me again? I hate that crazy son of a bitch." I think like mad. How can I explain Daddy's anger without lying? I'm two full years younger than Iggy, and he's usually the one explaining things to me. Iggy has see-clear-through-you eyes, eyes that see everything. He taught me just about all I know. He taught me about science and math and verb conjugations. He taught me how to gut a fish. Iggy's the smart one, but today I'm the explainer, because I know what I know. I know he's a bastard, and that's why Daddy hates him. I know Daddy proposed to Momma because in those days she was movie-star pretty, with soft blond-white curls and legs as long as the railroad tracks between Barnaby and Santa Fe. And I know he married her even after he found out about Willy because no way in hell was he going to let her shame him with her whoredom. Momma said so on the phone, and now I know Daddy hates Iggy because he's a walking sin, and that's that.

But I can't tell my secret, so I say, "Iggy, you're not the reason Daddy gets mad. He was born mad. I hate him for not seeing how good you are. Someday, I'm gonna leave this town. Leave all those dresses he buys me so he'll miss me when I'm gone. I swear, I'm gonna make him cry the way he makes you cry."

beauty of the broken

We huddle there on the musty earth, sweating, our palms pressed together, listening to the whisper-whisper of our breathing and the stomp of Daddy's boots as he searches heaven and hell and everywhere in between for the sad likes of his wife's bastard son.

"Someday," whispers Iggy, "I'm gonna leave too, and I'm gonna do something great. I'll become a pilot or a president, and then he'll know what I am. He'll look at me and say he's sorry, and I'll tell him to go straight to hell."

I don't say anything to that. Momma once told me, "Sure enough, your brother is a gentle giant." She took a long drag off her cigarette. "But someday, you mark my words, your brother is gonna snap. Someday, when your Daddy gives him what for, he's gonna give it back to him. You just watch out for that day." She seemed hopeful when she said it. Smiled a little secret smile. Remembering her words now, I feel anything but hopeful. I pray today isn't that day. Above us, the screen door slams.

"You hear that, Sis?" Iggy asks me. When he talks, his breath is low and raspy, like he's swallowed a swarm of bees.

Daddy's thunder gets closer. He's outside now, and his footsteps pound on the porch. "Iggy, is that you?" he bellows, and we can see the waffle prints of his boot soles overhead. Iggy holds my hand tighter.

"Get out here now, boy, or I'll whip you double good!" shouts Daddy. Iggy looks at me, and I kiss his cheek. My eyes beg him to keep his mouth shut.

"I'm under here," he says. He starts to roll away from me.

"No, Iggy. No!"

Daddy looks under the porch. I'm not sure whether he is a man or a demon as he stares at Iggy. That blue vein is bulging. "You been hiding from me, boy?" When he grabs Iggy by the arm and yanks him from his hiding place, I wish that I had a fiery angel sword. I have only my small hands, so I crawl out and stand there trembling while Daddy stares Iggy down, breathing hot and heavy and slow. Daddy's holding a warped two-by-four.

"You hiding from me, boy?" he asks again.

Iggy balls up his fists. He stares right back at Daddy, into his dead eyes. I can't believe how brave he is. The bees are still buzzing in Iggy's throat, long and low. "I didn't take your hammer, Daddy," he says.

Daddy lifts the two-by-four. "Come again?"

Iggy has never been in a fight before. Not really. He tried to stand up to Daddy that one time, but other than that, Momma's right. He's a gentle giant. He fishes. Chops the heads off the chickens so I won't have to. But mostly he hates to hurt anything. Right now though his face has that hard look, the one he had the day he fought back. He raises his fist, and I almost feel hopeful, almost think it's going to knock Daddy straight into forever.

The two-by-four slams into the side of Iggy's head. He groans, stumbles backward, falls to the ground in a crumpled heap, like a pile of dirty old laundry. Daddy drops the two-by-four.

"You wanna repeat yourself, boy?" Daddy's fists whistle and whip through the air, finding Iggy's face and his back and his freckled arms when he holds them up to stop the blows. Everything is happening so fast. I can't see what part of Iggy Daddy is gonna hit next, and I can't remember which part of him he hit last. I can't tell where the blood is coming from, and I can't tell who's screaming no—me or Iggy.

And then Daddy's footsteps fade into the house, and he's gone. Iggy's curled up in the grass. I wonder if he's dead.

My scream gets caught in my throat. Finally it breaks through my lips, coming out a hoarse whisper. "Iggy." I stare at my brother's bloody face, his twisted hands, the stillness of his eyelids. "Iggy!"

His body lurches, and he starts to shake and sob. He's not dead. The blood that's pumping down his cheek is hot, fresh, alive. I'm thankful for that, so thankful my chest almost explodes. I race to his side and hold him and say,

"I hate you, Daddy. I hate you, Daddy." Daddy's back in the house so he can't hear me, but Iggy tells me not to hate because it will eat me up like the Hansel and Gretel witch, and I wonder where in God's name he comes up with this stuff anyway. Why does Iggy suddenly care if I hate Daddy when ten minutes ago Iggy was saying he hated him too? How can he *not* hate Daddy after what he just did?

We huddle together until the sun falls behind the low, rolling hills, casting orange light over the cornfields and golden grass. Daddy's boots stop stomping, and we know he's hiding in his room now, the way he does when his hitting is done. We know he will pass out soon. We know he won't come out until morning.

The summer heat still rages. I worry that we will get ticks behind our ears from lying in the grass for too long, especially with the smell of Iggy's blood to attract them. Some of the blood is coming from Iggy's eye, which is purple and swollen halfway shut. I know ice is the thing for bruises and swelling, so I take Iggy's hand and help him up. We tiptoe into the house and into Momma's kitchen.

She's sitting there at the table, her delicate, clean hands folded neatly in her lap. She stares at the pink roses embroidered on her white lace tablecloth. She doesn't look up when we walk in.

"We need ice, Momma," I say, and she nods, standing slowly, as if she's a beauty queen being called to the microphone to talk about starving children and how she'd love to fill their bellies with nice, warm milk. Momma smooths the wrinkles in her apron. I wonder how her candy-apple-colored lipstick stays so perfect, not a bit of it gummed on her straight, white teeth in this humidity.

"You okay, sport?" she asks Iggy. She reaches up to tousle his wheat-colored hair and dabs at the clotted blood with the corner of her starched apron.

Iggy nods, and she smiles and says, "That's my boy." She opens the freezer and a breath of winter comes whooshing out, cooling us down a little bit. Fanning her face with her manicured fingertips, Momma slowly presses her breath out through her big lips, the way she does when she's smoking cigarettes. "It was a hot one out there today." She laughs and takes the ice trays from the freezer as if she intends to plop the cubes into a glass of fresh-squeezed lemonade.

"I swear, Mara, I was never meant to be a farmer's wife. That much I know." She sighs, folding a checkered dishcloth around the ice cubes. "I shoulda gone to Albuquerque with my cousin. When Wanda went off to that cosmetology school, I shoulda gone there too. She makes forty dollars an hour now. Did I tell you that?"

I shake my head no.

"Well," she goes on, "she does. And I'm not sure this life is suited to me."

I think she's right. She has a magazine-girl hairstyle and white, oval fingernails. She should be one of those women in the television ads that click-clack around their city houses in fancy shoes and designer jeans, dusting things and declaring that they could never live a moment without their Swiffer mop. She presses the dishcloth to Iggy's eye. He raises a hand to hold it, and when she sees the way his pinky finger sticks straight out to the side, her face crumples like she's gonna cry. Instead she pulls it together and says, "I do declare, Iggy, the scrapes you boys get yourselves into sometimes."

If I had my angel sword, I'd hit her over the head with it for being so dumb and blind. She knows how Iggy got hurt. Maybe a good whack with a fiery sword would get her thinking and talking straight. I cross my arms and stare hard at her, knowing that she's trying to make up for what Daddy did.

She wipes at Iggy's eyes until the blood is gone, and she kisses him on the cheek and says, "You're the boy I always wanted, Iggy. If I could have any boy in the whole world for my pick, it'd be you."

His eyes flare like the August sun, like he has been waiting all his life to hear someone say this, even though Momma says it every time Daddy beats him.

Momma takes Iggy by the hand and leads him up the stairs and tucks him into his bed. He lets her, mostly for her sake. That's how Iggy is. Always taking care of me and Momma. Always trying to make Momma believe she's a good momma even though she fucking sucks. If she needs to treat him like he's four to make up for what Daddy did, Iggy'll let her. But it's not bringing him comfort.

I know Momma expects me to go to bed too, though she's so busy making up for Iggy's bloody eye and busted finger that she doesn't have time to say so. She knows I'll do what's right without being asked, because that's what angels do best. I huddle in my bed, listening to Momma trying to sing Iggy to sleep, even though he's a full seventeen years old. When her shoes click-clack down the stairs, I tiptoe across the hall and crawl into Iggy's bed.

"Hey, Sis," he whispers, and his hand finds mine in the dark. We lie there together, side by side, watching the window as the moon rises into the sky like a lost lemon meringue pie. We don't talk. Iggy will cry if he tries, and if I talk, I'll tell my secret for sure, and how will that fix anything? So I don't say a word.

We fall asleep with our hands still stuck together and

me thinking that everything will be all right in the morning. Momma will cook us breakfast and sing about clowns with their pants falling down and how the world is a stage of entertainment. The pancakes will be warm and just the right kind of brown. Daddy won't be drunk anymore, and he'll call me his rosebud and send me off to school with a kiss on the cheek. And there I'll learn that flies carry so many germs it's a miracle that any of us filthy hooligans are still alive, and scientists think that cell phones might cause cancer, and the lark's on the wing and the snail's on the thorn and God's in His heaven, and all's right with the world.

Iggy wakes up in the middle of the night barfing, making this awful, roaring sound. It scares me. I switch on the lamp just as he finishes. Vomit is everywhere. On his bed, on the walls, on the rainbow-colored rug Momma bought him at Walmart. It has even splattered on some of the drawings I made for him, which he has pinned to the wall. The whole room smells sour. It might piss me off if Iggy didn't look so scared. So different.

"You okay, Iggy?" I ask.

He just sits there shivering, his arms wrapped around his knees, staring at the ceiling.

"Iggy," I say, "let's go to the bathroom, okay?" But he doesn't. He just pukes again, right on his bed. "Momma!" I holler, and half a minute later she comes running in, tying her bathrobe.

"What is it?" Her hair is a mess. Her eyes are wild. Seeing the barf, she stumbles toward Iggy. "My baby," she says. "You feeling sick, honey?"

Iggy just stares.

It goes on like that for a long, long time. Momma and me asking Iggy questions. Iggy answering by barfing and staring. Daddy must still be too drunk to hear anything, because we're making enough noise to raise an army of dead men, but he never comes in. Thank God. The last thing we need is to deal with his ugly face.

It seems like forever before Momma says, "Get dressed, Mara."

"Why?" I ask. Something tells me I should remember her words. Something in me knows they will change everything. Nothing will ever be the same again.

"We're going to the hospital," she says, and chokes a little, like she's going to cry, but doesn't. She takes the afghan Grandma made Iggy from the chair in the corner and wraps it around him. "Come on, baby," she says. "Let's get you to the doctor."

She doesn't tell Daddy we're going. I worry. I wonder what Daddy will do when he finds us gone. I wonder if he'll kill us all. Never in our lives has Momma ever done anything without Daddy's permission. Iggy stumbles to his feet, shuffles along beside Momma as she leads him down the stairs, her arm around his shoulder.

"If I could pick any boy in the world, it'd be you," she keeps saying.

He never stops staring.

I follow them, watching Iggy's head nod like one of those bobbers on a fishing pole. "Momma, I'm scared," I say.

She says nothing.

CHAPTER 2

GGY IS LYING IN A HOSPITAL BED. SITTING IN A chair beside him, I wonder what he's looking at. The yellow walls? The bluebird hopping on his window sill? The gauzy curtains? Whatever it is, it must be interesting. He never stops staring.

He's been like this for twenty-seven hours and six minutes. That night he got sick, Dr. Groves said he had a bad concussion.

"What happened?" he asked, looking at Iggy's bruises, his busted finger.

When Momma said Iggy fell out of a tree, Dr. Groves didn't bat an eye. I wondered if Dr. Groves just went along with Momma's story because he and Daddy played high school football together. Either way, no one called the cops. But Dr. Groves was serious and sad. He said Iggy might not live. I started to cry when he said that. Iggy was the one light in my whole world. Without him, everything would be dark.

"Someone has to watch him, make sure he doesn't sleep. If he goes into a coma, he may never come back to us."

When Dr. Groves said that, I jumped right up. "I'll watch him," I said.

And so here I am. Momma and me have been taking turns watching Iggy. It's my turn now. Momma went home a few hours ago to get some rest. Daddy never showed up, even though Momma called and told him that Iggy might die.

I try to talk to Iggy, but he doesn't answer.

"What does a blue jay sound like, Iggy?" I ask. He's real into birdcalls. Usually he'd be all over that question. But he just stares.

Momma comes stumbling in. With one glance I can tell she's drunk. She's wearing a pair of Daddy's overalls, which is strange. Usually she's dressed up like she's ready to be interviewed for the five o'clock news.

"Hey, Momma," I say.

She smiles. Too big. Gleeful, almost. "Why, hello, darling," she says, and she wanders to Iggy. "How you doing, sport?" she asks, rumpling his hair.

Iggy stares.

She's holding two paper bags. "I made you both sack lunches," she says. "This hospital food is shit."

I jump a little at that. It's the first time in my whole life I have ever heard my momma cuss. All the cussing I know I learned from school. And Daddy. Daddy can cuss up a blue streak when he's mad. I take both lunches and set Iggy's on the table beside him.

"Thanks, Momma," I say. My voice sounds flat.

I open my sack and peer inside. A sandwich. Bologna, by the smell of it. An apple. Cookies. Home baked. They look like chocolate chip, Iggy's favorite. I squeeze the sack shut, hating Momma for thinking she can fix this mess with lunch. Iggy might die, and she thinks cookies will make it better. I want to strangle her.

She goes to Iggy's bed and sits on the edge, brushes his hair from his bruised face. "I love you, Iggy," she whispers. "So fucking much."

Twice. She cussed twice in one day. Heck, twice in five *minutes*.

Hearing her swear scares me. It scares me more than the way Iggy is staring. It scares me more than Dr. Groves did when he told me Iggy might die. Iggy is gone, and now so is my momma. I need her the same as she's always been. Messed up as she is, she's all I got.

I go sit down by Momma, wrap my arms around her, bury my head in her shoulder. She smells dirty, like she hasn't showered in days. Most times she smells perfume-y and sweet. My broken heart almost explodes. It hurts so bad, I start to cry. Momma wraps her arms around me, whispers, "Mara, Jesus, Iggy, I'm sorry." Her breath smells like rum, but in that moment, I need her to be the good guy, so I forgive her anyway.

"It's not your fault," I say.

"It's not your fault," Iggy says.

Me and Momma jump.

"Iggy!" Momma screams.

"Iggy!" I scream it too.

We turn toward him. We're the ones who are frozen now, staring. He looks at us, and for a minute his eyes are the way they used to be, see-clear-through-you. Smart. "Nothing is anyone's fault," he says.

"Iggy, you're back," I say, laughing and crying at the same time. I throw myself on his chest, tasting my salty tears and snot, feeling the safe beating of his heart.

Finally I pull away and hold his face between my hands. I get scared again. He's not staring anymore, but his eyes aren't see-clear-through-you either. They're somewhere between here and there, somewhere far away.

"Iggy?" I ask.

He smiles, lopsided. "Hey, Sis," he says, but it doesn't sound like him.

"Iggy?" Momma says.

"Hey, Momma," he answers back. His words are too slow.

"Dr. Groves!" Momma yells. "Nurse! Someone! Iggy's back!"

A minute or so later Dr. Groves runs in.

"He doesn't seem right," I tell Dr. Groves. I sound desperate, even to me, but I'm hopeful. Maybe Dr. Groves is a miracle worker. Doctors know things, right? They have pills and fancy machines and stuff. They can make people better.

Dr. Groves does his magic. Shines lights in Iggy's eyes, asks him to count, stuff like that. After a minute I can't watch. It's hard for Iggy to count. He can't remember his birthday. "We're both Pisces, Iggy. Remember?" I say, hoping to prod him into recollection. Dr. Groves gives me a look that says I'm not helping.

I glance out the window. A raven is pecking at something dead in the parking lot. I read once that the only difference between crows and ravens is that ravens are loners. They'll kill anything that gets close to them. If you see a gaggle of black birds, you know they're crows, because a raven would be running alone.

I look back to Dr. Groves.

"Your boy has been in one too many scrapes," he says to Momma. "These concussions can be cumulative."

"What does that mean?" Momma asks. She balls up her fists, looking mad, as if Dr. Groves is being confusing on purpose.

I look back at the raven. It pulls something long and stringy from the dead thing. *Dead things are made of string,* I think. It sounds crazy, even to me. But I'm often crazy inside my own head. I wonder if everyone is.

Dr. Groves rustles around in the pocket of his lab coat, looking for answers. "What it means is that your son has suffered multiple concussions, and this time, he has . . . sustained quite an injury."

"He fell out of a tree," Momma says, too quick.

"I understand that," Dr. Grove says. "Whatever the case, his brain has been injured badly. Now, usually after a concussion, the brain goes back to normal. Within days. Sometimes weeks. Sometimes months." He's silent for a moment. He looks at Iggy, who is fidgeting with the hem of his hospital gown. Dr. Groves clears his throat. "Sometimes never."

"Never." The word explodes like a grenade.

That is the moment my whole wide world goes black.

CHAPTER 3

"NEVER." IT WAS A BIG WORD. I NEVER FORGOT it. Dr. Groves was right. Iggy was never the same. Once in a while his see-clear-through-you eyes would come out and you'd think for a second the old Iggy was back, but he'd always leave again. I hated Daddy even more after that day. It's been six months since our trip to the hospital, and Iggy still isn't Iggy.

As if things couldn't get worse, Daddy drowned my kittens this morning. He took our barn cat Rapunzel's babies to the river in a sack. Said there's enough strays running around these hills without us adding our passel to the fray. I'd already given them names: Mary Magdalene, Simon, Garfunkel, Picasso, and Elvis. Now they're pushing up daisies at the bottom of the river, even though I'm well aware that daisies don't grow at the bottom of rivers. It's just an expression, and my kittens are dead. Don't expect me to think too clear right now. I've been crying since I woke up, and Rapunzel keeps coming to the door and meowing, asking where her kittens are. I don't know what to tell her.

I guess I sorta think they're coming home too. I keep glancing out the window, looking for them. Instead I see the corn plants cut to the ground and shivering in the frost. I button the black silk dress I borrowed from Momma's closet, the one she bought for her aunt's funeral. Three days before my sixteenth birthday, and I'm going around mourning those poor cats, wearing black up to my chin like a nun or something. Just call me Sister Mary Mara, for God's sake. I don't think Momma would like it if she knew I was wearing her dress, but what she doesn't know won't kill her. She's always asleep when we leave for school these days, so there's not much chance of her finding out. I slide into my hiking boots and plod down the stairs.

My party invitations are stacked on the table by the front door, right by the change jar Daddy keeps filled to the top with quarters. For a rainy day, he always says. I dream about stealing those quarters and buying myself something nice, but not today. Today all I can see are those invitations waiting for me to take them off to school and give them to my friends.

Most of the kids in school send e-vites, but Daddy won't let me use the computer, so Momma made my invitations with her scrapbooking kit. *Sweet Sixteen* they say on the front. There's a picture of birthday cake underneath. I'm kinda embarrassed, but what am I supposed to do? Tell my momma I won't use her invitations? That will send her on a bender for sure.

Mostly I just want Xylia to like the invitations. I think about the way her upper lip is just a tiny bit bigger than her lower one. The way she lisps a little when she talks, not enough so everyone would notice, but enough that people catch on if they're paying attention. I notice because I'm always paying attention to Xylia, even if she doesn't know I'm alive, which I'm pretty sure she doesn't.

I reach out to grab the stack of envelopes when I see Momma sitting at the kitchen table, staring out the window, floating in a cloud of smoke. My first thought is that she'll kill me if she sees me wearing her dress, but the way she looks, I know she won't care about anything. Her hair is mussed, and her nightgown is bunched around her waist, revealing lumpy thighs. She clasps a glass of something brown in one hand, a cigarette in the other. A piece of pink paper lies on the table beside her. It smells like rosewater, even from far away. This is what I'll be someday, I think, and it scares me so much, I forget all about Xylia.

"Good morning, Momma." My voice is quiet, even though I don't mean for it to be.

When she looks at me, her eyes are empty as ghost towns.

"I do these things," she says, and she wads up the paper. "I do these things, and I don't even know why."

"Do what, Momma?" I move toward her, reaching for the paper.

"Don't you dare, missy," she says. "Don't you dare pry into my secret dreams."

I stop short.

She uncrumples the paper and reads it, her lips silently forming the words. I watch them moving, but I can't make out what she's saying, except that she repeats "Iggy" over and over again. "I meant it when I said it," she whispers. "I meant it, but now, I don't know what I mean." She crosses her arms on the table and plops her head on them.

"Let's get you to bed, Momma."

She sits up, her head tilting to one side, like it wants to fall off. "It's just now morning. See, the sun's coming up." She points at the window, at the eyelet-lace curtains glowing gold with the sun's first light.

She's right. The bright orange sun is peeking up over the hill. Naranja, I think. I learned the word in Spanish class. I'm crap when it comes to verb conjugations, but I'm okay with vocabulary words.

She looks back at me. "You should do something with your hair. It's as rebellious as you are." She has said this to me a billion times. She knows I can't do anything with my hair. It does what it wants.

"Momma, you're sick," I say. This is what we call it when Momma gets like this. Sick. Though she has never been sick this early in the morning. Usually we find her this way at midnight, wandering in the yard, muttering secrets to the moon. "You should sleep."

She nods. "I am sick, sweet thing," she agrees. "Sicker than a frog in heat."

This perplexes me. As I help Momma out of her chair, I wonder if frogs do go into heat. And if so, do they get sick from it? I don't know. Whatever the case, I give her points for originality, the way Mr. Farley did on career day, when I told the class I wanted to be a painter, but not the kind that has caterpillar eyebrows, like Frida Kahlo. I was trying to make people laugh, but no one ever laughs at my jokes. No one ever talks to me, really. I'm pretty much invisible. Well, except to Elijah Winchell, who is the preacher's kid. He is the last person in the whole world I want to notice me.

"Come on, Momma."

She stands, wobbling a little, but doesn't fall. I take her by the arm.

As we pass Daddy's picture in the hallway, she whispers, "Damn that man."

"Damn that man," I whisper too, hoping my words are a magic curse that will send Daddy straight to hell for all eternity. Even though I know he's in the barn, I'm scared he'll hear me when I say it. I take her to her room and tuck her beneath the rose-covered comforter. "Night, Momma." I kiss her on the cheek.

She has that bitter smell again, the one that comes from the rum. "Night, lover girl," she says, slurring her words.

The sick taste comes into my mouth as I watch her lying there, face slack, eyes staring but seeing nothing.

"Sweet thing, bring me my glass," she tells me.

"'K, Momma," I say. I won't, but she'll forget she even asked. I head back to the kitchen and the note Momma was writing.

"You don't have to be cruel to rule my world!" Iggy shout-sings behind me.

I startle so hard, I drop the paper. It falls by my feet. "For God's sake, Iggy," I snap, picking it up. "You scared the crap out of me." I know the paper is important and probably says something ugly, since that's the way things are going for me these days. I uncrumple it. *Dearest William*, I start to read. I get nervous. William. Who's William?

"Don't have to be cruel to rule my world!" Iggy scream-sings again.

"It's 'you don't have to be *cool* to rule my world,'" I say, shoving the note in my pocket. I'll read it later when Iggy isn't so busy being an asshole. I hate the way he always sings the stupid songs Momma listens to on the radio, songs from the eighties that sound like idiots wrote them. He used to hate them, but ever since his brain broke, he's all about them.

"I got you," Iggy squeals, laughing until he doubles over and a little line of snot slips out of one nostril. All six feet two inches of him quiver with joy. "I scared you good. Twice!"

"Don't hyperventilate," I tell him. He doesn't stop. "For God's sake, you sound like a donkey braying."

He gulps and wipes at his nose with his fist, still smiling. "I got you good, Mara."

When my heart stops pounding, I don't feel mad anymore. "Yeah, sport, you got me good." I reach up and rumple his hair.

Iggy laughs again, but this laugh is too tiny for his big, lanky frame.

"Did you pack a lunch?" I ask. I remember when I didn't have to remind Iggy about anything. It was only six months ago, but it feels like a million years. It's as if my big brother turned into my baby brother.

Iggy looks at the floor and shuffles his feet. "I forgot."

"Of course you did." For a second I hate him. I hate him for being what he is now instead of who he used to be. I stomp to the fridge and pull out the bread.

"Rena's family don't keep the bread in the fridge," Iggy says. Rena is a girl from his special-ed class, his only friend, as far as I can tell.

"It keeps better that way." I pull the peanut butter and honey from the cabinet and slap a sandwich together.

"Did you make me a double-decker?" Iggy asks as I shove the sandwich into a baggie. Iggy loves double-decker sandwiches—three pieces of bread, two layers of peanut butter and honey.

"No, Iggy. We don't have time. We're already about to miss the bus." I dump the sandwich and an apple into a plastic grocery bag and hand it to him.

"I want a double-decker," he whines.

"Too bad," I say.

He looks inside the bag. "No dessert?"

I bite back a swear and go to the cookie jar. "Here." I pull out two store-bought chocolate chip cookies and push them into the bag, not even bothering to wrap them to keep them fresh.

Iggy grins.

"Don't have to be cruel to rule my world!" Iggy screams behind me.

"Don't have to be *cool*," I say, spinning toward him. The smear of chocolate on his chin tells me he's already eaten one of the cookies. I think about getting him another for lunch, then decide he doesn't deserve it. "Can we just go now?" I head for the door, and Iggy follows.

We walk to the bus stop in silence, except for the bumping of Iggy's lunch, which he holds over his head and shakes like a tambourine. The bus is just pulling up as we arrive, and we file on with the other kids. Elijah Winchell manages to get behind me, as usual. I can feel his hot breath on the back of my neck and his blue eyes staring at my backside. I turn around and glare at him. He sneers.

Iggy and I walk to the back of the bus and slide into a tattered seat. As the bus rattles onto the road, Iggy smiles. "Elijah's got the hots for you," he says.

I slap him on the arm. "No he doesn't."

"He does. Rena said so."

"Well, Rena can shove it."

Even from the front of the bus, Elijah hears Iggy. His head snaps back and he laughs. In my aisle seat I can see his perfect teeth, bleached white and approved by the American Dental Association. He got his braces off last year. I suppose he'd be handsome if it weren't for all his freaking pimples.

"Mara and Elijah sitting in a tree. K-I-S-S-I-N-G."

"Shut up, Iggy," I say. He doesn't, so I punch him.

"Ow!" He rubs his arm. "Why'd you have to hit me?"

"'Cause you won't leave well enough alone," I say, turning to look past him and out the window. Cedars and cactus plants whiz by, as if trying to outrun the blue mountains looming in the distance.

"You don't like Elijah?" Iggy asks.

"No."

"Why not?" he asks.

"He's a boy, and boys suck."

"Oh." Iggy starts to laugh.

"What?"

For a second his eyes get see-clear-through-you. "You like girls."

My face flushes red-hot. "Kiss my butt, Iggy." I turn to stare out the window again. My eyes sting. I blink, remembering the things Reverend Winchell says about women burning for other women, giving up the natural order.

And I remember Daddy sitting in his easy chair, reading aloud from a magazine about how some gay boy got tied to a fence and shot. "Good," Daddy snorted. "It's a damned abomination. If I ever found a faggot in this town, I'd do the same thing."

I believed Daddy when he said it. Once a man at Al's Roadhouse grabbed Daddy's butt, and Daddy beat him so bad, the guy was in the hospital for a week. In his report, Sheriff Perkins called it "self-defense," and Daddy didn't have to spend one minute in jail. Daddy can get away with anything he wants, seems to me. He bragged about that man's smashed-in face for months.

I write the word "abomination" on the seat in front of me with my fingertip, one letter on top of the other, so no one but me knows what I'm spelling. When we get to the school, Iggy's see-clear-through-you eyes are gone, and his foggy eyes are back. He leaves his lunch under the seat.

"Iggy." I pick the bag up and shove it into his hand as we file off.

"See you later, alligator," he says. He smiles, revealing that one crooked tooth he has up front, which always makes me love him. I feel bad for being mad at him all morning.

"After a while, crocodile," I say, and kiss him on the cheek. He heads to the little red building where the special classes meet, tripping on the curb as he goes, making bird-calls—*caw, caw*, whistle, warble, so on and so forth. I head off for the big school where the regular kids go, where Iggy went too until six months ago. He was going to be valedictorian of his class. Now he can hardly count to fifty. If we went to the public school, we'd probably ride different buses, but since we're in Christian school, all the classes are in one place. There are 172 kids, counting the kindergarteners and special eds.

The morning stumbles by. Since there are only a few people in my grade, we don't change classes. We have the same damned teacher all freaking day. I have to listen to Mr. Farley drone on all morning about x squared and y cubed, and how Missy Larington is home with a busted kneecap, and how verbs and adverbs go hand in hand, like husbands and their wives. But none of it matters with the lightning zinging around in my brain. I feel like my head is making a voice-over track, going on behind everything I do. All I hear is Iggy saying, "You like girls." It even echoes a little, the way bad thoughts echo in the movies.

I hand out my invitations. Although none of the kids like me much, they seem happy to have a party to go to. There isn't much to do in Barnaby, unless you're into hanging out at the Dairy Queen. Everyone asks if Elijah Winchell is invited. I tell them of course he is. His daddy is the preacher. They all ask, "Can't you tell Elijah Winchell is hot for you?" I tell them I don't give a rat's ass if Elijah Winchell is hot for me. They say I'm lying, but I'm not.

I catch Mr. Farley's questions though, even through the lightning in my head.

"Have you finished your paper on Leonardo da Vinci, Mara?" (I haven't.)

"Who caught Rush Limbaugh's broadcast yesterday?" (Elijah Winchell says he did.)

"What is the largest Great Lake?" (I have no freaking idea. Geography is not my strong suit.)

Even though I hear things, my brain is so full of lightning, it doesn't have room to hold on to any thoughts for very long.

Until I see her. Xylia's wandering down the hallway, staring straight ahead with wide, dark eyes. She moved from San Francisco two months ago, and she's one grade higher than me. She wears clothes like nothing I've ever seen. Not just jeans and T-shirts, but fashion statements, like a magazine girl. Some of the kids laugh at her hippie skirts and bangles, but I love the way she looks. And I love her name, too. She's not a Lisa or a Rebecca or a Michelle, but Xylia. Doesn't that have a nice ring? It starts with an X, even though it sounds like it should be a Z. I know because her papers are always plastered all over the school bulletin boards with big, fat A+'s at the top. She's smart, like Iggy used to be.

"Xylia," I say. My voice comes out too quiet, but she stops, looking surprised.

"Yeah?" she says nervously. I never see her talking to anyone. Maybe she's shocked someone knows her name.

This is the first time I've spoken to her. I almost throw up. "I'm having a birthday party. I thought you might want to come, is all." I hold out an invitation, and she reaches for it, smiling shyly. As she takes it, our hands touch for a second. Warmth floods through me.

"Thanks. I'd like that." She opens the invitation. "Wow," she says. "This is really cool. You must have worked hard on these."

"No," I say, thinking maybe she is making fun of me. "My momma made them."

"You must have an awesome mom," she replies. She's not making fun of me. She's serious.

"She has her moments," I manage.

We stare at each other, trying to find things to say. All the words that live in my head get jumbled up. I always thought Xylia was pretty, but I never noticed just *how* pretty until now. Her beauty stabs at my heart, makes the lightning crackle even louder between my ears. Her skin is the color of the white sand beaches on tropical islands that I've seen in books. Pale and perfect. Her black hair is long and stick straight. It looks soft. I wish I could touch it.

"Well, I'll see you Friday," I say finally. "The address is on the invitation."

"Okay," she says. "See you then." She smiles again, and then continues down the hallway, her sparkly sandals click-clacking.

All through lunch all I can think of are Xylia's eyes, and that makes everything worse. I want to go home, and I want to never go home again.

At the beginning of science class I try telling Mr. Farley I'm sick. He looks up from the papers he's grading, scrawling big *X*'s everywhere with his ugly, red ink.

"Are you now?" He removes his thick glasses and squints at me. The clock on the wall ticks. I manage a feeble little cough. He rolls his eyes. "You're no sicker than I am, Mara Stonebrook," he pronounces finally. "Sit down."

I go to the back of the room and slump into a desk. These two girls, Hannah and Keisha, are having a grape fight, and one hits me.

"Watch it," I snap.

Hannah and Keisha laugh in this hyena-meets-SpongeBob way that makes my skin crawl. Their hair is brown with orange stripes, like they tried to do highlights themselves. They wear tons of makeup, and both sport bright red press-on nails. They smell like armpits. Especially Hannah. They've been torturing me, and anyone else who isn't cool, since sixth grade. It's not that they're popular, they're just more popular than me. I don't know why anyone likes them. I suppose because they're Elijah's buddies. They all sing in the choir at church on Sundays, so I guess they bond while singing "glory hallelujah" together. Hannah throws another grape, and it hits me in the eye. Clearly, she did it on purpose this time.

"Go to hell," I say. Hannah and Keisha laugh.

I stare at the front of the class, hating the sight of the dusty blackboards. Every school in the United States of America upgraded to whiteboards years ago, if TV is to be believed, but our school is stuck in the fifties. I put my head on my desk. My stomach really is feeling rumbly. I wasn't lying when I said I was sick.

Someone swats the back of my head. I sit up fast. Elijah's standing there, leering. Hannah and Keisha squeal gleefully. Mr. Farley doesn't even look up from the papers he's grading.

"Screw you," I whisper.

Elijah just keeps grinning and slides into the desk beside me. I glance at him out of the corner of my eye, thinking how stupid it is for a kid his age to wear his hair all slicked back like an old man. I let my gaze drift to his feet. His black shoes shine, the way they always do the day after he polishes them. Which is every day.

Elijah slips a piece of paper onto my desk. I open it. *Give me ur digits.* But it's a command, not a request, which pisses me off. I've had just about enough of that from my daddy, thank you very much. Elijah's handwriting is messy. And he doesn't have the wherewithal to write out "your"? Give me a break.

"Digits?" I whisper. "You think you're a rapper or something?"

"I think you like me," he says back.

"Well, I don't."

"Come on. Give me your number."

"I don't *have* a number," I say. "My daddy won't let me have a cell phone. And even if I did have one, I wouldn't give my *digits* to your sorry ass."

Elijah looks like he's going to say something mean, but Mr. Farley interrupts him. "Invertebrates," he says, letting the word hang in the air like it's a cliffhanger. I guess he imagines we are all sitting there holding our breath, waiting to hear the big news about animals with no spines. He takes off his glasses and taps them against the back of his veiny hand. Finally he launches into some speech about earthworms. He walks around the room while he talks, stopping to lay a hand gently on his worm farm, encouraging us to take the time to get to know our soil-saving friends. "Were it not for the existence of earthworms," he says slowly, weighing each word carefully, "we might not very well exist either." He says eye-ther, not ee-ther, and it gets to me. When he's done singing the praises of worms, he slips out to get coffee from the teachers' lounge. Mr. Farley does that a lot. I think it's mostly to get away from us "hooligans," which is what he calls us. I wonder, sometimes, if his heart will explode from too much caffeine. When he goes on and on about worms, I hope it will.

"I'm going to get to know my soil-saving friends," Elijah says. A few kids laugh, and everyone watches as he struts over to the terrariums. Elijah's the most popular kid in school. It's not like in the movies, where people are popular because they are good-looking or funny or the quarterback on the football team. In our town Reverend Winchell's family is royalty. Pimples or no pimples, Elijah is the prince.

"Here wormy, wormy, wormy," he says. He removes the

screen over the worm farm and digs into the dark, wet soil with his fingertips.

"Gross," a girl whispers.

He laughs. "Can't find one." I know he could if he really wanted to. Through the glass I can see segmented purple bodies everywhere, nestled in their little tunnels.

"Some big man you are," I snort. "Scared of a scrawny little worm."

Elijah's eyes widen, and he thrusts his hands into his pockets. "What did you say?" He reminds me of my daddy, the way he always makes you repeat yourself if you say something he doesn't like.

"I said, you're a wimp." I march over to the terrarium and bury my hand in the dirt. Seconds later I pull out a writhing, pink squiggle.

Elijah's frozen, fists clenched, huffing and puffing. I can tell he's trying to come up with a way to put me in my place. Finally, he yanks the worm from my hand, drops it on the floor, and brings his shiny black shoe down on its tender little body.

Normally I wouldn't cry over a worm. I fish regularly, for God's sake, bait my hook with worms practically every day. But somehow this worm reminds me of my kittens dying, and tears burn my eyes. "No!" I shout, but it's too late.

Elijah grinds his foot back and forth until the worm is nothing but a smear on the tile. All the pain in the whole wide world rushes over me. I think about all the innocents being drowned in bags or squashed by folks like Elijah. Worms and kittens and even people. People like Iggy. I think about that two-by-four and about the blood oozing out of Iggy's head. I sink to the floor and touch the worm's remains.

"Asshole," I say to Elijah.

"Freak," he says, going back to his chair. The other kids start to giggle, and when Mr. Farley comes back, all he sees is me sitting on the floor, trying not to cry while the rest of the class goes wild.

"Mara Stonebrook," he says. "I am not even going to ask what you are up to. Get back to your seat."

Slowly I stand, saying "I'm sorry" inside my head over and over to the dead worm, wishing I'd never been so stupid as to call Elijah Winchell a wimp.

As I'm sitting down, Mr. Farley says, "I look forward to seeing you at lunch detention tomorrow, Ms. Stonebrook. Our blackboards could use some industrious scrubbing."

I nod.

The rest of the day is a blur, and me and Iggy are sitting at the back of the bus again. Thank God he doesn't say much. When I get home, Momma is in the kitchen, cooking up a storm like she was never sick at all. The smell of frying chicken fills the house.

"Hi, Momma," I say, heading straight for her bedroom. I hang her funeral dress back in her closet, making sure the new stain on the elbow faces the wall.

After homework and chores I have dinner with Iggy, Momma, and Daddy. Fried chicken is my favorite, but I can't eat much for the churning in my stomach. There are also biscuits and garden green beans, which Momma reveals she got in trade from Nancy Witherspoon for some fresh-baked bread and six eggs. Daddy sings "I've Been Working on the Railroad" at the table and even smiles when Iggy says he has a joke.

Daddy says, "Tell us."

"A duck walks into a bar," Iggy starts.

"Yeah?" Daddy asks through a mouth full of beans.

"And the duck says, 'Got any grapes.' The bartender says no."

Daddy nods, chewing forcefully.

"So, um, the duck goes to the guy again and says, 'You got any grapes?' And the guy says no. And then the duck asks again, and the guy says, 'Listen, duck, if you ask me for grapes again, um, I will nail your feet to the floor. So the duck says, 'Got any nails?' and the guy says no. And the duck says, 'Good. Got any grapes?'" Iggy starts to laugh, spewing little bits of chicken over the table.

"Good one, sport," Daddy says. He laughs for real, and I think it's probably because he likes the idea of a duck getting its feet nailed to a floor. I hate that man. I think that if someone walked past our window right now, they would never know what our daddy really is. Sure, they would see the green beans trapped between his teeth, and maybe that'd gross them out, but otherwise they'd think he was a decent human being. The kind of human being who sings "I've Been Working on the Railroad" all the time, the kind of person who never stops smiling green-bean smiles, the kind of husband who never raises a hand to his pretty wife, even when she does talk a little too long with the handsome checkout boy at the grocery store. The kind who probably would never tie a gay kid to the fence and shoot him to death if he had half a chance. They would think that someone can't be so good and so bad at the same time, and they would never believe the stories that I have to tell.

During times like this I used to forget why I was scared of my daddy. I'd look at him and think: He's nice. He smiles and laughs, so how can he be bad? It's not like he ever hits *me*. Iggy, sure, and Momma, too, but maybe they *really do* deserve it. *You're crazy, Mara*, I'd think. *You're crazy to hate him; you're crazy not to love him; you're crazy to make up those stories about the terrible things he does.* And then I would love him, just for a minute. I'd look at him and imagine what he must have been like when he was a little boy, getting picked on at school or winning at Monopoly or playing fetch with his puppy. Sometimes I'd start singing right along with him, because it's so much nicer to have a daddy who sings and smiles and pats Iggy on the back and calls me rosebud. But my singing never made it true.

I stare at Daddy as he pats Iggy on the shoulder. Daddy's teeth are really ugly. With those bug eyes of his, he looks like a giant praying mantis. I think about how much I hate the sound of his voice and how much I hate the way he laughs. I think that someone as ugly as him should never be allowed to laugh like that, and I consider taking the issue up with God in my bedtime prayers. I tell myself that I will never forget that my daddy is a monster. Iggy and his broken brain will never let me.

I excuse myself from the table, and Momma asks if I'm feeling ill.

"Why, yes, I am, thank you for asking," I reply, and she raises her eyebrows and shakes her head and reminds me that it is church night, and if I think I am getting out of it by playing sick, I've got another thing coming.

Church night. As if this day could get any worse.

· · ·

The sun is just starting to sink low over the hills when we enter the little white church we've gone to for forever. Momma and Daddy got married here, but of course I wasn't there for that. Several hundred of Barnaby's residents attend, though attendance on Tuesdays is a lot lower than on Sundays. Sometimes Reverend Winchell gives sermons about not forsaking the assembling of yourselves together, but it doesn't seem to do any good. Most people stay home on Tuesdays. But not us.

Reverend Winchell is at the door, shaking hands and smiling, wearing that same ugly striped suit he wears every time he preaches. Daddy leads us to the pew where we always sit, third row back, out of the "splash zone," as Daddy likes to joke. Reverend Winchell has a tendency to spit when he gets riled up, which is often. We file into our seats, Daddy first, then Momma, then me, then Iggy.

"My collar itches," Iggy complains.

"Hush, Iggy!" Daddy snaps.

"Hush, Iggy," I whisper. "You don't wanna make Daddy mad."

Thankfully, the choir starts to sing, distracting Iggy. Iggy loves the church songs, and so do I. "I'll fly away, oh glory. I'll fly away!" Me and Iggy belt it out, big grins on our faces.

When the song is over, Reverend Winchell, puffing and red, heads for the pulpit, like the walk to the front of the church is killing him. He takes his place and starts in on some long-winded prayer that I don't hear. I bow my head while he's talking, but I don't close my eyes. Instead I study my hands and the chipped, dirty nails. The dry patches on my knuckles. The nicks I have from whittling wood sculptures. Then Reverend Winchell launches into his sermon.

"New Orleans," he says, and lets the words just hang there. Some lady behind me says, "Ummm hmmm," in a meaningful way, like she knows what's coming. Reverend Winchell explains (for those of us who have been living under rocks) that what happened in New Orleans was that a hurricane wiped it out, and now it is just bones stripped bare, a skeleton of sin. He says it's Sodom and Gomorrah all over again, filled up with dykes and fairies and faggots. While I hate Reverend Winchell, I appreciate his alliteration. I'm addicted to poetry. Sometimes I memorize it just for fun. I love that language can sound so musical even when the words are so mean.

The only pretty thing about the church is the stained glass window, which sits just over the pulpit. A crying Mary Magdalene kisses the feet of Jesus. You'd never think tears could be so pretty, but in that picture they are. It's like Jesus is wearing diamonds on his toes. He looks at her, smiling softly, as if he loves her. There are angels all around, little, fat ones, not the fierce, fiery ones I hear about in Sunday school. The angels look mostly sad and some of them, bored. Seems to me angels—real angels—would never be bored with someone else's pain.

When Reverend Winchell starts talking about abominations, my mind slips away into the scene in the colored glass. If I could, I'd kiss Jesus's feet with Mary. Reverend Winchell once said she kissed his feet because she was anointing them for burial, and I feel sorry for Mary, knowing those beautiful feet were gonna get holes in them soon.

Studying her soft, brown eyes, I wish I could tell Mary the rest of the story. "It's okay," I'd say. "He'll get nailed to a cross, but then he'll be back." I wouldn't tell her the part about folks like Reverend Winchell turning Jesus into a reason to hate and kill people. I wonder, looking at the Jesus in that window, how he has anything to do with the hateful hypocrites who go around wearing his cross on their necks. They're so mean. He looks so gentle. Why's this world gotta put nails in everything that's beautiful? Why's the ugly gotta take all the pretty and swallow it whole?

"God hates homosexuals!" Reverend Winchell shouts. He

smiles, like it is good news. Little bits of saliva spray in every direction when he says it, and my daddy shouts, "Amen!" and slaps his knee.

I look back up at Jesus, thinking I'd like to introduce myself to him, explain my side of the story, let him know how nice I am. I can't imagine those gentle eyes looking at me with anything but love, no matter what Reverend Winchell says.

"Abominations!" Reverend Winchell says, pounding the pulpit, and again Daddy shouts "amen," along with fifty other people. Old Mrs. Blackwell gets up in the corner and does a little dance, waving her lace handkerchief the way she always does when the spirit moves her.

The pew is digging into my back. Reverend Winchell opens his Bible. "Who brought their Bible?" he shouts. Reverend Winchell can't just talk. He always has to shout. Some people get ear damage from going to rock concerts, but I'm the lucky girl who is going to go deaf from listening to this old, fat fart with his slick hair, shouting about "the damned." Reverend Winchell waves his Bible in the air enthusiastically. "What, you didn't bring your Bibles to church? That's like showing up to army training camp without your gun!" His reprimand complete, Reverend Winchell starts in. With every breath he takes, his fat belly strains under his shirt. I watch the buttons, hoping one will pop. Now that would be entertainment.

"This story is about a vipers' nest called Sodom and Gomorrah. It was a den of depravity. A sanctuary for sinners." Again his alliteration isn't lost on me, but my heart's pounding now. I'm starting to sweat. I feel like I'm going to be marched up to a bonfire and burned at the stake. Barnaby hasn't had any witch hunts lately, but I wouldn't put it past them.

He pauses for effect, letting his beady eyes sweep the room. "And what kind of sin was it?" he asks. Apparently it's not a rhetorical question, because he waits for an answer.

Finally someone in the back calls out. "It was a town full of faggots and dykes!"

And Reverend Winchell points a fat, quivering finger at the back row. "Yes! A town full of deviants overtaken by the demon of lust—so much so that when the angels came to their town, all the people could think about was raping them."

I examine the angels in the stained glass, wondering why anyone would want to rape them. They look like those fat, plastic dolls you can buy at Walmart, only with wings. The angels from Reverend Winchell's story must have been the tall, sexy, fiery ones we learned about in Sunday school.

Reverend Winchell continues. "Every man and woman

and child in Sodom and Gomorrah had been infected with the disease of sin. All, save one. A righteous man named Lot."

The preacher goes on to say how Lot and his whole family were actually good, and I have to wonder why he used the phrase "all, save one," when clearly Lot had quite a few people in his family, which is more than one. But in the Bible only the people with manhoods (that's what Momma calls boy parts) win the prizes. Girls don't count, except when they eat apples and screw paradise up for everyone. That much I learned a long, long time ago.

"So Lot took the angels in and fed them, as we should—as we would—were angels to come to our town," Reverend Winchell says. Sweat pours down his fat face, and he mops it away with the yellowed handkerchief he keeps in his pocket. "But these homosexuals, they go to Lot's door, and they pound on it." Reverend Winchell pounds his microphone against the pulpit twice, and the noise is so loud I jump.

I look up at Jesus's beautiful feet, think about the two nails being driven in. *Bang. Bang.*

"Lot tries to cut a deal with them. He says, 'Look, my daughters are beautiful virgins. Do whatever you want with them. Spare the angels.' Now, any normal man would be enticed by this offer." Reverend Winchell gives a sneaky smile, and some of the men in the church make hooting noises. "But these deviants are not men, never mind the color of their blood. They are cancer."

I stare again at the window, at the crying Mary with her long, shiny hair. Suddenly she reminds me of Xylia. I wonder why raping women is any better than raping angels, but it must be, because the reverend says so. Lot is a good man, and here he is, offering his daughters to save the angels. I wonder if my daddy would offer me up to rapists if it came down to me or the angels. I don't think so. Even he couldn't be that bad. But Lot is supposed to be *good*.

This is what the Bible stories do to me: get me all mixed up in my head, because what seems really wrong is supposed to be good, and what seems right is wrong. The confusion hurts me inside. Why is Lot good, and I'm bad, even though I'd never let anyone get raped? I'm so busy trying to figure this out that I miss what Reverend Winchell has to say. When I tune back in, fire and brimstone are raining down on Sodom and Gomorrah, and the one good man, Lot, (and his good family that doesn't count) are running as fast as they can out of town.

"God tells them not to look back!" Reverend Winchell shouts. "But Lot's wife is weak willed, as women are, and she does the unthinkable. She has pity on the objects of God's wrath and looks back. This, my brothers and sisters, is a sin just as vile as sodomy. And for this sin, Lot's wife is punished along with the homosexuals. She is turned into a pillar of salt. And the city burns. And the children scream. And the deviants die in their fiery beds, finally understanding, too late, the ways of the good Lord.

"Do not sin, as Lot's wife did. Do not pity them. When you see the news footage of devastation and destruction, fall to your knees and thank God for removing a pocket of disease from our planet. Let us pray."

I close my eyes, hoping not to cry. I try to imagine Jesus from the window looking at me with love, but instead I see Xylia's eyes. My sinful thoughts make me sure Reverend Winchell is right about me, and after that all I can see is fire raining down on me in my bed. All I can think is I deserve whatever hell I've got coming.

We drive home, all squished together in the cab of Daddy's truck, and I look out the window, watching Barnaby pass me by. I make myself stop thinking about eternal punishment and lose myself instead in the familiar landscape around me. We drive by the boarded-up Friendly Store, where Momma used to buy her groceries until the new supermarket moved in and shut it down. Miss Mattie, who used to run the

Friendly Store, works at the supermarket as a checker now. "If you can't beat 'em, join 'em," she always says, shrugging. I admire her spunk.

Down the road is the new McDonald's and the ancient Dairy Queen, which has a big sign advertising that they have live rattlesnakes. But the sign is faded and peeling, and there haven't been rattlesnakes at the Dairy Queen for a good ten years.

Then comes the town's one bar. Al's Roadhouse. The parking lot is filled to bursting, and I figure Reverend Winchell will notice too and give some sermon on Sunday about drunkards who value their sin more than God. Daddy spends enough nights at Al's for me to agree with Reverend Winchell on this particular subject. Whiskey *is* the devil's brew, and if you don't believe me, just look at my brother's broken brain.

Town turns to farmhouses and horses and cactus, and in the distance I see the beautiful, black outline of the mountains, which somehow feel sacred to me, even though Reverend Winchell says it's a sin to worship the creation and not the creator. All the farms are surrounded by barbed wire, and I wonder about the rest of the world beyond these barbed-wire fences, those majestic mountains. I wonder about places where fairies and faggots and deviant dykes live, where the roads are mostly asphalt instead of dirt, and cows are never seen.

I'd like to see all that someday. I'd like to cut through the wires, scale the mountains, go somewhere where there are other people like me. Hell, I'd run off to New Orleans today, hurricane or no hurricane, if only it weren't for Iggy. But I know I can't go. I can't leave my broken brother, who sits next to me picking his nose, humming "I'll Fly Away."

The stairs are cold, and my room is so icy dark, I almost knock over the lamp in my hurry to switch on the bulb.

The ghosts are out tonight. I thought they went away when I grew up and stopped believing in monsters, but I can feel them hovering, hissing, slipping through my skin and into the marrow of my bones, filling me with fear. I don't take off my clothes. I don't want the ghosts to see me naked and eat my flesh, leaving me lying there on my quilted bed, nothing but a pool of blood. So I leap under my blankets and wait to hear the reassuring pound-stomp of Iggy's boots on the stairs.

I consider going back down and getting a glass of orange juice, but I hear Daddy's voice get loud, and even though it doesn't sound mad, I don't want to take the chance. I'm more scared of him than the ghosts, so I stay still and wait for Iggy. At last I hear his footsteps, and even though he's a retard now, with him is the one place I feel safe. As he passes by my room, I call out his name. Iggy's face peeks around the corner and chases the ghosts away.

"I'm scared, Iggy. Sleep on my floor."

He shrugs and smiles. When he disappears from my doorway, I feel the ghosts all over again. But he comes back quick, carrying an armload of blankets and his favorite pillow, the yellow one Momma made him when he was a first grader. He doesn't ask me why I'm scared, and I'm grateful for that. He throws the bedding on the floor and switches off the lamp.

"Did you have a good day at school?" I ask.

"Good as any," he says, copying the way Daddy answers when Momma asks him how his day was. Iggy's voice is sleepy.

"Missy Larington busted her kneecap," I say. He doesn't answer.

If you've ever been visited by ghosts, then you know that talking keeps them away, so I try again. "Mr. Farley gave us this stupid lecture about worms today." No answer. "Can you imagine that? Thinking we'd care about worms?" No answer again. "You asleep, Iggy?"

I judge from the quiet that he is asleep. I lie there silently, staring up into blackness so thick, it hurts my eyes. Finally

I reach out and touch Iggy's back, feeling his shoulders rise and fall with his slow, steady breathing. In the darkness Iggy's light still chases the ghosts away. My bones warm up, and my heartbeat slows. Momma and Daddy go to bed. There's no grunting tonight. I'm grateful for that. When Iggy starts to snore, I bury my fingers in his hair.

"I love you, Iggy," I whisper, and I do, because if it weren't for him, the ghosts would've eaten me alive on nights like tonight. I close my eyes and think about Xylia, about her pretty lips and her sparkling sandals.

"Iggy," I whisper, so quiet that he couldn't hear me even if he was awake. "I got a secret to tell you. Remember what you said on the bus today?"

He doesn't answer, so I decide to go ahead.

"I think you were right." Outside, a barn owl hoots and the corn plants whoosh in the wind. "Iggy, I think I'm an abomination."

CHAPTER 4

THERE'S A NEW FRESHMAN NAMED HENRY AT our school. He's an Indian who moved from the reservation. His father came here to work at the prison, not as a guard, but as a janitor. Henry has no mother. No one knows why for sure. Some people say she drowned herself when he was little, right after his baby brother drowned in the tub. But I don't know if that's true. People talk a lot, and only half of it has any basis in reality.

What I do know is that Henry has long braids, black and shiny like licorice whips. Daddy said Henry's father fought the school for Henry's right to keep his braids, and they agreed because they needed his tuition money. That pissed Daddy off so bad, he drank all night and punched out a window. "It's a disgrace for a man to have long hair!" he bellowed. "It says right there in the first Corinthians. They call that place a Christian school? The little fucker probably worships rocks and trees and wolves and shit."

Daddy isn't alone in his convictions. All the boys at school hate Henry. Especially Elijah Winchell. I heard that in the bathrooms, they shove him up against the wall and call him gay. Also, people say he wears tighty-whities, which is weird because, apparently, most boys wear boxers these days. Not that I'd know from personal experience, but everyone seems to agree on it.

It makes me mad the way people treat Henry. Most days he eats his lunch alone, staring down at his ugly pile of white-brown mashed potatoes. If I ever saw people call him names, I'd probably punch them, but I'm never in the boys' bathroom.

Today, as always, Henry is by himself in the corner of the lunch room. I watch him, wondering why his brown shirt has white spots all over it. He looks sad, but also smart. His thick glasses have black rims, and beneath the lenses, his small eyes shine deep brown.

I wonder if he's really gay. It makes me happy to think he might be, that maybe I'm not alone. It's not like I'm the most popular kid in school either. Maybe I should make a friend. So

I pick up my green tray, with my corn dog, French fries, and banana pudding, and I walk to Henry.

"Mind if I sit here?" I ask.

He looks stunned. "Um, yes, yes," he says, and he moves aside his books. "Of course. Sit."

He talks funny, more slowly and carefully than most teenagers I know. "I'm Mara," I say, and I stick out my hand.

He shakes my hand, but his grip is loose, like he isn't too sure about me yet. No wonder. He probably thinks I'm gonna start saying "how" and calling him "chief" any second now. That's what most of the kids do. "I'm Henry," he replies. "Henry Begay."

Begay. Poor kid. As if those braids weren't bad enough.

He must know what I'm thinking because he says, "It's a pretty normal last name on the reservation." He says it defensively, like I've made an accusation.

I shrug. "I didn't say anything. And hey, I mean, even if you were gay, I wouldn't care." I try to sound casual as I say it, but I wait for his answer, my heart pounding. I set my tray down and sit beside him.

"Well, I'm not," he says.

I try not to look disappointed. "That's cool."

We sit there moving our pudding around with our spoons until finally I feel like I gotta say something. "So, why does your shirt have white spots?" *Great opening line,* I think. But he doesn't seem offended.

"My dad bleaches me," he says.

I smile, confused. "Bleaches you?"

"Yeah." He smiles back. "Father's afraid of germs, so he carries bleach everywhere in a little spray bottle. He bleaches tables and chairs and sofas. Everything in our house is freckled with white bleach spots. Once Father even bleached a chicken that pecked its way into our yard. Ever since then, no chicken has come near our house. He bleaches me all the time. He doesn't mean anything bad by it. He'd bleach you, too, if you came over."

I laugh. I like this Henry kid. "Well, remind me not to wear my best dress if I ever come to your house."

"Don't wear your best dress if you come to my house." Henry grins. His teeth are too big for his face.

"Speaking of coming over," I say, "I'm having a birthday party tomorrow. You should come. I don't have any more invitations, but I can write down our address."

"That'd be great," Henry says, grinning so wide now, his face looks like it might break.

And that's when everything goes bad. Elijah, Hannah, and Keisha come sauntering over.

"Hey, Ringworm," Elijah says. Elijah calls Henry

"Ringworm," because apparently he got it from nursing a sick, stray dog, but like I said, who knows what's true and what's not?

"Hey, Ringworm," Hannah repeats.

Sometimes when I ask Daddy if I can do something, and he says no, I say, "But so-and-so is doing it." He says, "If so-and-so was running off a cliff, would you do it too?" Well, if Elijah was running off a cliff, Hannah would be two steps behind him. I think she has a crush on Elijah, but you can tell he'd never date her. She's kinda fat, which he points out sometimes. Once he called her the Pillsbury Doughgirl. She looked like she wanted to cry, but she didn't.

"Hey, Ringworm," Keisha says too. She's skinny and short. I think without Elijah and Hannah for friends, she'd probably be shy.

"It's starting to sound like an echo chamber in here," I say.

Henry doesn't say anything, just looks down at his tray.

"We got something to show you," Elijah says.

"Leave him alone," I snap.

"What? We just wanna show him something," Hannah says, all innocent. She juts out her fat hip and puts her hand on it.

"What? Your big ass?" It's not nice, I know, but I kinda have my daddy's temper. Elijah laughs. I glare at him. Shouldn't he at least stick up for his friend?

"No," Hannah says, all pissed off. She looks me over for a few seconds. People say I'm pretty, but I'm tough-looking, too. You grow up with a daddy like mine, and you get an angry way about you, a touch-me-and-you're-dead attitude.

"This." Elijah whips a magazine out of his backpack: It's a *Playboy*. He opens it up and shows Henry a picture inside. "So, what do you think?"

"Where'd you get that, preacher boy?" I ask.

Elijah pretends he doesn't hear me.

Henry stares at the picture for a few seconds. "That's nice." He looks away.

The lady in the picture has bleached blond hair. I'm pretty sure her boobs are fake. They sit oddly on her chest, round like mini basketballs. Her skin is tan, too tan. Almost orange. I like girls, and *I* think she's weird-looking. I can understand why Henry is unimpressed.

Elijah isn't pacified. "What's wrong, Ringworm. Not interested in women?"

Henry looks back at the picture, and then he surprises everyone, including me, by barfing on Elijah's shiny shoes, which I'm gonna guess cost more than my own, or anyone's in this cafeteria.

"Ew!" Hannah and Keisha shriek in unison, and run away, still screaming.

"Idiot!" Elijah yells. He grabs my napkin, upending my chocolate milk onto my tray. My corn dog is swimming. So much for lunch. Elijah swipes at his shoes, but the mess on his feet just gets worse.

Looking embarrassed, Henry dabs at the corners of his mouth with a napkin. I put my hand over his.

"Might wanna get to the bathroom and wash that off before it soaks in," I tell Elijah. "Otherwise, you'll never be able to wear your fancy shoes again." My words are nice on the surface, but there's an edge to them.

Elijah picks up on it. He narrows his eyes. "I think my daddy's right about you."

"Oh yeah?" My heart pounds. I wonder if his daddy knows I'm an abomination.

"He says you have a Jezebel spirit," Elijah replies.

I think I'm supposed to have my feelings hurt, but I have no idea what he's talking about. Jezebel was the queen who killed all God's prophets in the Bible. I don't know what a Jezebel spirit is though. I must have missed that sermon. "Sounds like a cool band name," I say. "Barnaby, please welcome *Jezebel Spirit*!"

Henry still looks kinda sick, but he laughs anyway.

"It's not funny!" Elijah screeches like a girl. "It's when a woman doesn't know her place!"

"My place? Like where I live?" It's fun to rile him.

"You were born as a helpmeet for man!"

"Is a helpmeet like a swap meet?" I ask innocently.

Elijah breathes heavy. "I hope you end up like Jezebel, eaten by dogs." He finally leaves, taking his stupid porn with him.

Elijah doesn't know it, but that zinger hits home. I was bitten by a German shepherd when I was two. I'm still scared of dogs. Touching a tiny scar on my lip, I turn toward Henry. "You okay?" I ask. His eyes are misty behind his glasses. Everyone is looking at us. This incident isn't going to help his reputation one bit.

"Yeah," he whispers.

"Hey," I say, really quiet, so no one but him can hear me. "It's okay if you don't like girls. I don't like boys."

He stares at me, and then speaks so softly I have to get closer to hear him. "My stomach hurt when I saw the magazine girl's sharp nipples. They looked like arrows." Then he adds. "But I don't think that makes me gay. I don't like boys, either. Naked people, in general, hold no interest for me."

"Well, that's okay too," I say.

The lunch ladies come over with mops and a bucket, all pissed off because Henry puked on their clean floor. They say stuff to each other in Spanish, and even though I'm still in my first year of language classes, and I'm not very good, I know what they're saying isn't nice. The lunchroom has been silent since Henry puked, but now everyone starts talking again. The fun is over.

I smile at Henry. "That was pretty cool."

Henry grins back. "You think?"

"Hell, yeah," I say. "It's about time someone put him in his place. Maybe vomit is your superpower."

Henry laughs and adjusts his glasses. "Bwwwaaahaaahaaa!" he says with his best sinister laugh.

I grin. Henry is funny. "So anyway, will you still come to my party?"

"Will Hannah and Keisha be there?"

"No way."

"Elijah?"

"I pretty much *had* to invite him. He's the preacher's kid, but don't worry," I say. "Elijah messes with you, I'll punch him in the face."

Henry looks up at me and smiles. "All right," he says.

And that is how I end up with a genuine Indian coming to my birthday.

CHAPTER 5

DADDY IS PISSED WHEN HE FINDS OUT I'VE invited a "heathen" to my party, but Momma says, in her sweet, sex-me-up voice, "For God's sake, it's her birthday. Don't spoil it." Then she kisses Daddy's cheek. They go upstairs, and I can hear the grunting. I try not to picture what they're doing, but I can't help it. It makes me sick. When they come back, Daddy seems happy and doesn't say anything more about Henry except, "I don't like it, but I suppose you had to invite everyone just to be fair."

I don't mention I didn't invite Hannah and Keisha.

"I heard you invited Elijah," Daddy says.

"You told me I had to."

"Good," he says. He puts his hand on my shoulder and

winks at me. Then he sweeps his finger along the edge of the frosting bowl, which Momma is holding. She slaps playfully at his hand. "You! Stop it!" she says, but she doesn't mean it, and Daddy chuckles.

"If you need me, I'll be in the barn."

The door slams behind him. Friday. It's Friday. I'm having my very first real birthday party. Momma and Daddy usually just do a family dinner, but Daddy said sweet sixteen was special. It's not the first time Daddy's done something special for me. I'm his rosebud, and he makes sure I know it. Buys me presents. Dolls when I was little, now dresses. He never buys Iggy anything. This party is the biggest present he's ever given me. And really, the only one I've ever liked. I'm so excited, I can't stop dancing around, the way Momma does when she listens to her Ethel Merman. Not because of the cake or the streamers or even the presents. Because of *her*. Xylia will be at my house tonight. We'll smile at each other and talk about smart things. Her papers are always on the bulletin boards with nice words at the top. Excellent. Fantastic. And once, Wondrous. That's the perfect word for her. "Wondrous."

It's 4:44 when I glance at the clock, which feels lucky. Guests will arrive at five. Momma's flouncing around the kitchen in her apron, putting sausage on the homemade pizzas and frosting things. When Momma finishes, she gives me the bowl, and I lick it, thinking about all the times in my life she's made me cakes. Sometimes Momma can be all right, even when she's drunk. I'm so full of joy and anticipation, I throw my arms around her waist. "Thanks, Momma."

She hugs me back. "It's a special day, baby. You're sweet sixteen. Never been kissed." She pulls away from me, her hands still on my shoulders, a gleam in her eye. "You haven't, right?"

"Haven't what?"

"Been kissed?"

I feel myself blushing. "No. Why would I?"

She laughs. "Oh, Mara. Boys aren't so bad." She takes my hand, pulls me to the table, and sits down. I don't join her. Finally she pats the chair beside her. My belly fills with cold dread. This is going to be like the time she told me how babies were made when I was twelve. She called boy parts "manhoods." It sounded like the hood on a boy's coat. She said the manhood would be ugly and scary at first, but it wouldn't hurt too much, and after a while, I'd grow to like it. I ran out of the room crying.

She pats the chair beside her again. "Sit down."

Reluctantly I do. The chair feels harder than usual.

"So, who is he?" she asks.

"Who is who?" I look at my hands. Why are my finger-nails always so dirty? I should take care to make them pretty. Xylia's nails are always painted red.

"You know," Momma says. "You've been walking around mooning all day. You look just like I did when I fell in love with . . . your daddy." She brushes my hair from my forehead.

"I'm not in love."

"Oh, Mara. You can tell me. I'm your mother, for God's sake. Who is it? Elijah Winchell?"

"That pimply freak?" I yank my hand away. "No way."

Momma laughs again, as if I have just told a great joke. "Fine then," she says. "Keep it a secret."

I can smell the sweet frosting from my cake, which sits at the center of the table. *Sweet Sixteen!* it says. For a second I wish I could tell her. I wish I could say, "Momma, I think I'm in love with Xylia," but I know what will happen if I do. She'll cry, and then Daddy will come in and ask why. Momma will try to protect me, but at some point she'll get drunk, and the whole sad story will come tumbling out. Daddy will get that ugly look in his eyes, the one he got when he went after Iggy with that two-by-four, the one he must've had when he beat that gay man in the bar. Even though I'm the only family member Daddy has never hit, he'll have no mercy for me. And I'll end up brain damaged like Iggy. Or worse. If Daddy finds out what I am, chances are I'll end up dead.

"I'm not in love with anyone," I say, glaring at Momma. "You think I wanna end up stuck in some hellhole marriage like you?"

It's too mean, and I know it as soon as the words come out of my mouth. Momma looks like I just slapped her. After a moment she stands. "Well, in any case," she says, smoothing her apron, "your daddy and me will take a walk after the party starts. He thinks you're sweet on Elijah. He wants you two to have a little time alone." She walks to the stove and starts stirring a pot with a wooden spoon. I watch her for a minute, hating myself for making her sad, trying to find the words to make it up to her.

"I'm sorry, Momma," I finally say. I walk up behind her and put my arm around her waist. "It's not your fault Daddy's the way he is."

She smiles her fake smile she gets when she wants to cry. "Imagine my little girl, a preacher's wife." The doorbell rings, and I don't care anymore that she thinks I love Elijah. I straighten the front of my yellow dress. I almost never wear dresses, but I spruced up, since Xylia always does. My heart pounds her name. *Xylia. Xylia. Xylia.*

I open the door. It's Elijah. It's sorta like expecting a

kitten for Christmas and getting a box of dog shit. He holds a fancy present with red wrapping paper and white ribbons.

"Oh, hey, Elijah. Come on in."

He smiles. "Don't mind if I do." He presses the box into my hands and sweeps past me.

"Momma!" I shout. "What do I do with the presents?"

"Just put them on the table by the door," Momma calls back.

As I'm doing so, I hear a voice. "Hi," it says, like music.

I spin, and there she is, wearing these cool jeans with holes in them and a tube top with a long, black jacket. High heels. She looks like a rock star.

"Hi, Xylia." I can hardly get the words out, my throat is clamped so tight.

She's holding a handful of wildflowers. "I didn't have money for a present, so I picked these for you," she says. She sounds embarrassed.

Jesus Christ. This is the first time I have ever taken the name of the Lord in vain, even inside my head, but Xylia picked me flowers. I will press them into my favorite book, the one with the poem about the Highwayman, and save them forever.

I take them. "Thank you so much. It's the prettiest thing I ever got." It sounds stupid, but I mean it.

"Nice outfit," Elijah says, sneaking up behind me, ruining my perfect moment. "You look hot, Xylia."

Xylia looks as annoyed as I feel. "Thanks," she says curtly.

"If you're hungry, there are snacks in here," Momma calls from the kitchen. "Come and get 'em." Elijah barrels down the hall, a dog hearing a dinner bell, but Xylia and I walk slower.

"I really do like the flowers," I say. There seem to be hundreds of them. An explosion of color, like fireworks.

"I tried to get at least one of every kind," she says back. She has a little freckle underneath her right eye. It makes me love her more.

"They're beautiful. And Elijah was right. Your outfit is cool." I'm searching for things to say, so that by the end of this conversation, she and I are fast friends. We stop walking and stand there in the hallway, under the head of the deer that Daddy killed a few years back.

"Thanks. This is the way everyone dresses in San Francisco."

I look down at my yellow dress, which seems stupid and old-fashioned now. "This is the way everyone dresses here."

"I think it's beautiful," she says. "Kinda retro. This whole town is retro. It's like I stepped into a time warp or something."

Just then a bunch of people stream through the door, all bearing gifts, and that's the end of our private conversation.

Henry arrives, and I give him a weird, little hug, to make him feel more comfortable.

"Hey, Henry," I say. "I'm glad you could come."

"Me too." He pushes his glasses up on his nose.

"Do you know Xylia?" I ask.

"No," Xylia answers. "We've never met." She holds out her hand. "Xylia Brown."

Henry takes it in both of his and shakes it emphatically. His eyes light up. I'm not sure I like it. "Henry Begay."

"Henry's new this year too," I say, hoping Xylia will look at me. She doesn't.

"So where'd you come from?" Xylia asks.

"My father and I moved here from the reservation," Henry says. "You?"

"San Francisco."

"I've always wanted to go there," Henry says. "I've seen pictures of that red bridge."

"It's exquisite," Xylia says. "When you drive over it at sunset, it feels like you're flying."

"That sounds amazing," I say.

Xylia turns to me. "It is. Maybe I'll take you there someday."

I almost fall over dead, I'm so happy.

In the kitchen, Momma turns on the radio. "Married, buried," Kurt Cobain starts to sing, and I think he's got a point. Everyone wants to know where to put the presents, and I tell them. Everyone wants to know where the food is, and I show them. They gobble up the pizza so fast, it's like a swarm of locusts descending on a field. They talk loud and make dirty jokes and flirt, and all of that is just background noise, because for me, the only one in the world right now is Xylia. My chest burns. I want to touch her so much it hurts.

By the time I'm done showing everyone where everything is, Henry and Xylia are sitting in the corner of the living room, chatting and eating chips. She laughs at something he says, and I get a little jealous. She probably likes Henry, not me. I mean, for God's sake. Not every girl is like me. I'm almost too shy to talk to her again, but I know that two hours from now she'll be gone, and she may never sit in my house again. Time opens doors once, then it slams them shut forever. So I muster all the bravery I can. "Hey, wanna see my room?" I ask them. I wish I could only ask Xylia, but I don't see how without hurting Henry's feelings.

"Sure," Xylia says.

"Sure," Henry echoes.

I take them upstairs. I cleaned my room for the first time in like ten years, so it looks pretty good.

"Wow," Xylia says, glancing at my books tucked into their shelves and my wood carvings on the dresser and my drawings hung up everywhere.

"Wow," Henry says. I hate the way he's copying her.

"You're an artist, huh?" Xylia asks.

I shrug. "Someday."

She grins. Those teeth. So white. "You are already." She goes to one of my drawings, a mouse, and studies it. "This has beautiful lines," she tells me. "It makes me wanna cry. I don't know why, but it does."

I walk up behind her. I can smell her. Not thick like Momma's perfume—soft, sweet. Like flowers. "I was really sad when I drew it," I say. "I get sad when I draw little things. They seem so . . ."

"Vulnerable?" she asks.

"Exactly." *Jesus Christ.* Twice I have taken the name of the Lord in vain. That's how much I love this girl. She knows everything about me without knowing me at all. She feels like home.

"Mice *are* vulnerable," Henry says. I'd forgotten he was there.

"How do you know?" Xylia turns toward him, interested.

"It's hard to explain," Henry says. "I feel what others feel."

"You're psychic?" Xylia asks, her eyebrows raised high.

"I don't know if I'd call it that."

"Sounds like it to me," Xylia says. "You have a gift. You should develop it."

Henry beams. I want to smack him.

"Mara Stonebrook," Momma says from the doorway, and I whirl toward her. "Here you are. Neglecting the rest of your guests. It's time you started the party games. Your father and I are going to take a walk." She gives me a meaningful look, which I'm meant to interpret as, "Now go and get Elijah Winchell to propose marriage," or some such bullshit. I have no idea what party games she's talking about, because we never discussed party games. Are we in first grade? What the hell does she want from me? *Jesus Christ.* This time I think the Lord's name in vain because my mother is an idiot.

"All right," I say, and we all follow Momma downstairs. Before long I'm sitting in the living room with my guests, trying to figure out how not to neglect them. Everyone's being really quiet and staring at the walls, which, let's be frank, are not all that interesting. I know I'm supposed to liven things up, but I don't know how.

"Maybe we should dance," Xylia suggests.

Everyone looks at her like she just suggested we cut off our right boobs, the way the Amazons did.

"Or not . . ." she adds, eyeing me like, *What the hell is wrong with these people?*

I shrug apologetically.

"I have an idea," Elijah Winchell says. He's sitting on the couch with his feet on the coffee table. Daddy would kill him if he saw it.

"Elijah has an idea," Iggy echoes.

"How about we play spin the bottle?"

The girls start to giggle.

"What's that?" I ask.

Then everyone does more than giggle. They laugh at me hard.

"You don't know what spin the bottle is?" Elijah taunts.

"Neither do I," says Xylia, and she grabs my hand defensively. Right there on the damned carpet, I almost melt into a mess of blood and bones and love. Xylia's touching me. I don't give a shit what the game is now, until Elijah explains it.

My heart pounds. I love this. I will spin that bottle until it breaks or I kiss Xylia. Her hand in mine is soft and hot.

Before I know it, we're all in a circle. There's a bottle, and Xylia is sitting right next to me. I wonder if I can spin the bottle just a little so it will land on her.

"I'll go first," Elijah says. He gives the bottle a hefty spin, and I swear to God, when he's done, it's pointing right at Henry.

"It landed on Missy," Elijah says.

"No, it didn't," someone says. "It landed on Henry."

The laughter starts again.

"That's sick," Elijah says. "No freaking way am I kissing that faggot."

I look over at Henry. He's frozen, staring at the bottle, as if no one will see him if he doesn't move.

Even though I was mad at him two minutes ago, I feel sorry for him, especially since Xylia's still holding my hand, not his. "He's not a faggot," I say. "He's just smart enough not to go all crazy for fake boobs. I mean, who's stupider? The people who get all hot and bothered about lumps of silicone, or the people like Henry, who hold out for the real deal?"

My party is quiet. I'm not sure if that means I'm making my point, or if they just hate me. "And anyway, he's my friend. If you make fun of him in my house, I'll punch you in the teeth."

Xylia squeezes my hand. Henry looks up and smiles at me. Elijah's acne burns.

"Why wouldn't you kiss him?" Xylia shrugs. "In San Francisco, guys kiss guys all the time. Nothing wrong with it."

Elijah turns so red, his head might blow up. "That's an abomination."

Xylia laughs scornfully, like he's a world-class loser. "Whatever," she says. "You're stuck in the Stone Age."

Henry looks like he's about to bolt. But before anyone

can do anything, Elijah leans across the circle, grabs Missy's face with both hands, and kisses her hard on the mouth. Her eyes go wide. She wasn't quite ready for it. When he pulls away, she makes a face. I would be grossed out too, his pimply face so close to mine.

"You used your tongue," Missy says angrily. She swipes her mouth with the back of her hand and rubs it on the carpet.

"So?" Elijah says. "That's how you kiss. Who's next?"

Someone says, "Let's just go around the circle." Which means that my brother is next, since he's sitting next to Elijah.

He spins, and it lands on Christa, who's sitting next to Xylia. She's one of the ugliest girls in school. She has an extra row of teeth. It's weird. Iggy leans in to kiss her, and she jerks back. "No way," she says. "I'm not kissing that freak."

Iggy's face falls, like he isn't sure what's going on, but he's pretty sure he's going to cry. That's when Xylia makes me love her forever and ever and ever.

"Freak?" she says. "He's the hottest guy here." And she leans across the circle and gives my brother with the broken brain a long, wet kiss.

CHAPTER 6

MY PILLOW IS WARM, BUT MY SHEETS ARE cool when I move my legs. My party's over. Has been for hours. But the barn owl outside my window has been screeching all night. Maybe that's what's keeping me awake.

Wrapping my pillow around my head, I try to make my brain shut up, but it won't stop talking. It says things about Xylia, about the flowers she gave me and the way she held my hand. It reminds me that I never got to kiss her.

As soon as she kissed Iggy, Elijah said the game was stupid and threw away the bottle. I tried to suggest playing again, but no one listened. They just went back to talking and eating.

I opened my presents, and I have to say I got some pretty cool stuff. Henry gave me a hawk feather, which he explained was his totem and would bring me good luck. He gave it to me after everyone left, so no one would laugh at him. I kissed him on the cheek and hung the feather over my bed.

Elijah gave me a book about Shakespeare, which I'll admit I liked. But nothing was as good as the flowers from Xylia, who kissed my broken brother. As jealous as I am, she saved him. And I love her even more for it. I keep seeing the way she smiled when she declared him "hot." I hope someday she says I'm hot. But maybe she won't. I can't tell if she likes boys or girls. Probably boys. Doesn't everyone but me like boys?

Something wails. At first I think I'm dreaming, but I sit up, and I hear it again, a gurgling cry coming from outside my window. My stomach knots up. I creep over and part the curtains, afraid of what I might see, but too curious not to look. I peep out into moon-wrinkled night.

My momma's hunched over a pile of pea pods on the picnic table. Her hands are shaking, but she's busy. Break the pod. Pull back the string. Drop the peas in the pot. *Ping!* Put the pod on the pile. As if it's an instinctive behavior, the same as nose picking or butt scratching. She doesn't know I see her. She thinks she's alone.

I'm frozen, wanting to run from and to my momma at the same time.

Momma picks up the glass I knew would be beside her, even though I couldn't see it behind the pot, and takes a swig. I admire her ladylike insistence on drinking from a glass, even at night when she thinks no one is watching.

She mumbles something I can't understand. Then she says louder, "Damn him." I know she's talking about my daddy. Her cool eyes stare up at the ghost-stone moon, and she says it over and over. "Damn him. Damn him. Damn him."

I want to be angry that she's drunk, but I only feel sorry for her. Maybe she never loved my Daddy. She always says she did. My, wasn't he handsome in his football uniform? My, didn't his eyes sparkle just so? But when I see her tears, I can tell that Momma has rewritten her story, made love out of necessity, Romeo out of Frankenstein. She's had to lie to survive. She had to lie to herself, to Daddy, to us. But she can't lie to the pea pods.

There's something hopeful about pea pods, isn't there? I've always thought so. The way they look so full, so young. I can understand why the pregnant pods made Momma feel empty enough to weep.

Still, my world goes topsy-turvy with my momma's

sobbing, the way it always does, no matter how many times I see her cry. There's something cold about a mother's tears, colder than any murder you read about in the news, more chilling than all the wars of the world put together.

Momma should be safe. Momma should be warm. Momma should be happy, happy, happy, ready to mend your scrapes with the Band-Aids in her apron pocket. Ready for anything that comes along. She irons out wrinkles. She combs out tangles. She bakes peanut butter cookies, even when it's 102 degrees outside, with no thought for the rivers of sweat that run along her hairline and down that hollow place between her boobs. Momma shouldn't cry. Momma crying is like God crying. It makes the walls of the whole world come crumbling down.

I want to go to her, bury my head in her lap, tell her everything will be all right, but what I really need is for her to tell me she is fine so the world can go back to being a safe place. She will tell me, won't she? I tiptoe down the stairs.

When the screen door swings open, Momma jumps up so fast, she knocks over the pot of peas, and they go rolling on the ground like a thousand little ants. She swipes the tears from her cheeks and straightens her nightgown. It's so cold, my teeth are already chattering, but she doesn't notice. She falls on her knees and begins to retrieve the peas, one at a time. *Ping. Ping. Ping.* The brown outline of her nipples shows through the flimsy fabric, and it scares me that her boobs are not as neat and pointed as they are when she traipses around the house wearing her fancy brassiere and her starched blouses.

"I heard you crying," I whisper, staring at her drooping chest.

She manages a weak smile. I wait. I want her to say that it's just her allergies, or that she's crying for the sheer joy of being alive. Say something, for God's sake!

She doesn't. She stares at me with eyes that seem tiny without their makeup. I fall to my knees and bury my face in her shoulder. Her skin's soft and warm. I want her to be the momma she might have been once upon a time, before my daddy started breaking Iggy. She begins to cry again, softly this time, like the whispering of the river at the first spring thaw.

"It's just so cold here, Mara," she whispers. "Why does it have to be so damn cold?" It is cold. It's so cold, the grass blades are frozen spears. But I know she isn't talking about the weather.

"Yeah, Momma," I whisper. "It's cold."

She smiles wanly. "Well, then." She gets to her feet, wiping at her face with the back of her hand. "We should get inside. You're barefoot. Haven't I raised you better than that?" She sighs. "Of course I haven't. I mean, I tried." She picks up the pot of peas. There's only a handful now. They look lonely. She picks up her glass. "God knows, I tried."

She heads for the house, and I have no choice but to follow. I pick my way across the frosty ground, listening to my Momma's lament. "I mean, you always were barefoot, even when you were a baby. Did you know that?"

"Yes, Momma."

"You were a hurricane in a handbasket, Mara Stonebrook. I'd put your shoes on, and the second you left my sight, you'd have them off. Even in the snow. Even in the snow, you and Iggy had to go barefoot. I thought you'd catch your death of cold." She laughs weakly. "I did try, though."

We slip inside, and she heads for the kitchen. I wiggle my toes on the soft, warm rug. Momma switches on the pantry light.

"Aren't you going to bed, Momma?" I ask.

She turns, and her ghost eyes are still there. They scare me.

"These peas need attention." Momma sets the pot and her glass on the table and slumps into the chair.

When she sits like that, I'm reminded of when I found her writing that letter. I see it clear as day. That paper, all pink and poisoned with rosewater. *Dearest William*. I've been so busy dreaming about Xylia and getting ready for my party, I forgot all about it. My heart bangs. It's hard to swallow. *What happened to the letter?* I remember shoving it into my pocket. But what pocket?

"Night, Momma." I rush upstairs, taking the steps two at a time, wondering what that letter said, knowing it couldn't have been anything good. I flip on my bedroom lamp and rush to my closet, rooting around in the pockets of all my jeans, swearing like Daddy each time I come up empty.

My closet and my dresser are gutted, and still no letter.

I slouch against the wall. I wish I had some pea pods to talk to the way Momma does, but I don't. I just have me and my empty pockets and maybe God, who Reverend Winchell says will always listen to a good woman, like the "Proverbs 31 woman" who always takes care of her husband. I'm sure I'm not a good woman, but God is my only shot, so I take a chance and whisper a prayer.

"God, if you're listening, I'm sorry for all my mistakes and for liking Xylia and all that. But the thing is, I gotta find that letter. If you could help me, I'd appreciate it." I don't know what else to say, so I just whisper, "Yours truly, Mara Stonebrook." Then I bury my head in my hands.

Outside the window, our barn cat yowls. I get even sadder, thinking Rapunzel's still weeping for her dead kittens. I picture them writhing in that burlap sack as Daddy carries them off to the river, and myself standing at the window, all dressed up in funeral garb, crying for them. And then I remember. That was the day Momma wrote the letter.

My heart bangs in my throat as I tiptoe down the hallway, past Iggy's room, to Momma and Daddy's bedroom. From the other side of the door, I can hear Daddy snoring.

"God," I say inside my head. I'm on a roll with this prayer thing. "I just need to ask for one more thing: Don't let my daddy wake up, or he'll kill me." I reach for the doorknob, then realize God may need more of an explanation. "I know it's a sin to steal, but it's a bigger sin to kill, and I'm guessing whatever is in that letter will get Momma killed." I imagine God asking me how I know that, and I say, "I just know."

The door squeaks a little, and the dark lump that is Daddy rolls over. I freeze, coming up with excuses to tell him, like, "I had a bad dream," even though I know he'll just get irritated and tell me to get off back to bed, I'm sixteen years old, for God's sake. But Daddy doesn't move again.

I tiptoe past the bed, where I can safely say I was just looking for comfort, to the closet door, where all my excuses fly right out the window.

Please God, please God, please, I think. Then I open the closet door. I slip inside, closing it gently behind me. I wait, listening for signs that Daddy's finding a weapon to use to kill me. A shoehorn. A pair of scissors. Anything. The only sound, though, is Daddy's deep snoring. Holding my breath, I rustle around in Momma's dresses, trying to figure out which one is her funeral dress. They all feel the same in the dark.

Please God.

More fabric, scratchy and cool, and then I feel buttons, the round, pearly ones.

I thrust my hand into the dress's pocket—one, then the other. My fingertips meet paper. I grasp the letter and try to shove it into my pocket, but my nightgown doesn't have a pocket. I fumble around, stuffing it down the front of my panties. I feel like throwing up. Daddy's still snoring, and I have to walk past him again. If he catches me this time, he'll kill me twice. But if he finds me here in the closet tomorrow, it'll be worse.

I open the closet door again. Daddy mutters something and rolls over. I wait. He returns to snoring. I tiptoe past him, breathing a sigh of relief when I get to the side of his bed, knowing I can use my bad dream excuse again. I make it all the way out of the bedroom. As I close the door, the bed creaks.

"Cora?" Daddy mumbles. "Is that you?"

I wait, scared.

"Cora?"

Momma hears him. "Just shelling some peas, honey," she calls from downstairs. Her voice is quiet, but I can make out her words. "Couldn't sleep."

"Damn woman," I hear Daddy say. The bed creaks some more, and his snoring starts again.

I almost run back to my bedroom. I hold the door shut, gasping. Then out comes the letter. I would never know Momma had written it, had she not told me herself. The handwriting is jumbled and splotchy, not clean and slanted, the way Momma usually writes. Still, I can make out the words if I squint.

Dearest William,

I don't blame you for running away. I know what happened. He told you to run or he'd kill you. He admitted that to me when he was drunk. He said he made you run. So I don't blame you a bit.

Sometimes I remember the way you put that yellow flower in my hair and told me I was pretty by the river. I think about how you looked at me, your eyes shining blue as the sky. You must have really loved me. You must have, right?

The thing is this: I know he told you I'd be better off with him, but I'm not. He hits me. Worse than that, he hits Iggy, Willy. Sometimes I am afraid he will kill him, and what will I ever do? How will I ever live knowing my husband killed my son, and I stood by and did nothing?

So this is my way of doing something. Come for us, Willy. Me and Iggy. Save us. We're still at the old farm. If you come, we will go with you. We'll leave everything.

I lie awake at night thinking about my wasted life. It wouldn't be wasted if I'd married you. Maybe it wouldn't be so wasted if we were all a family. You, me, and Iggy. Come for us, Willy. We will wait.

All my love,

Cora

The pink paper trembles in my hands. I stare at the letters, hoping they will change, say something else. I tell myself she didn't mean it. My stupid Momma who couldn't keep her skirt down with stupid Bucktoothed Willy didn't mean a thing she wrote.

After crumpling up the letter, I open the door and throw it as hard as I can into the hallway. It lands behind a potted plant. I close the door and bury my face in my pillow and scream.

I've lost my mother. In her mind, she's run away with her true family, leaving me to be damned with him.

CHAPTER 7

ENRY'S TELLING ME WHY HE DOESN'T LIKE tater tots. Apparently, when he was four, he bit into a rotten one. Not that his story isn't scintillating, but I still can't help but watch the cafeteria door, waiting for Xylia.

"My father says I should get back on the horse, so to speak, but I just haven't been able to do it," he tells me, shaking his head sadly as he stares at his little brown mound of tater tots. "You can have mine if you want them."

"Thanks." I grab my spoon and scoop his tater tots onto my tray.

It's the first day back at school after my party. Henry just sat down next to me like it was the way things were supposed to be. Which is okay, though I'm not sure I like the idea of him horning in on my time with Xylia. I intend to ask her to sit with me the minute she walks into the cafeteria. But I guess Henry will be sitting with us too.

"What about you?" he asks, wiping his mouth with his napkin.

"What about me?"

"Do you like tater tots?"

"I wouldn't have taken yours if I didn't."

"Good point." Henry takes a gulp of milk. "What foods don't you like?"

Dear God, will he shut up? I mean, I like Henry, but I'm afraid that if I look away from the door, I'll miss Xylia. "I hate peas." Which wasn't actually true until the other night, but he doesn't need to know that.

"That's a common one," he says, like he's taking a survey or something. The kid is weird.

Finally, there's Xylia. She's wearing these tight black pants with tall boots. She reminds me of the Highwayman, the way the poem talks about his boots being up to his thighs. She has on jangly silver earrings and about a million bracelets. Like a maniac, I wave my hand in the air. "Xylia!"

She smiles and waves back. She doesn't look like a maniac though.

"I saved a place for you!"

Grinning, she gives me a thumbs-up and steps in line to get her tray. Henry drones on about something, but I can't really hear him. It's like there is no room inside my head for anything but Xylia. Definitely not for whatever Henry's saying.

Xylia moves as gracefully as the deer in the forest by our house. People ignore her, and I wonder what the hell is wrong with them. It's like being unimpressed by the Taj Mahal.

Finally she comes to sit with us. She's close enough that I can feel the warmth from her body. It's a miracle, having her beside me. It's like the way Mary in the church window must have felt kissing Jesus's feet. I would kiss Xylia's feet. I'd kiss her everything.

"Holy frijole, Batman," she says as she piles pickles onto her hamburger. "What a day."

"Do you read comic books?" Henry pipes in, and I want to smack him.

"No, but I used to watch reruns of Batman when I was a kid."

"Why has it been a bad day?" I ask, resisting the urge to reach out and brush a stray strand of hair from her eyes.

"We started trigonometry," she says. "I suck at it."

"I can't imagine you sucking at anything," I say.

"Yeah," says Henry.

Don't make me kill you, short one. Inside my head, I sound like a ninja.

"Oh, you'd be surprised," Xylia says. "Don't get me wrong; I'm good at some stuff. I'm an English whiz. It's in my blood, for fuck's sake. My dad's a writer."

"Really?" I ask. She just said "fuck." No one in this school ever says "fuck" right out loud. I mean, maybe they whisper it in the bathrooms or whatever. But in the cafeteria? Never.

"Yep," she says. "His third novel just came out last year."

"Are you rich?" asks Henry.

She laughs. "Hardly. Being a writer isn't as exciting as you'd think. We could barely keep the lights on." She pops a tater tot into her mouth. She's wearing a big ring on her pointer finger. It has a shining woman painted on it.

"I like your ring," I tell her.

"Thanks," she says. "My mom got it for me in Mexico. It's the Virgin of Guadalupe."

"She's beautiful." The Virgin of Guadalupe's smile reminds me of Xylia's.

"Yeah, I dig her. I'm not Catholic or anything, but I love the idea of the feminine divine, you know?"

I don't know. "Is that like a girl God?" The idea is so weird to me, I can't even pretend not to be surprised.

"Yeah," she says. "It's the female half of God."

"The female half," I repeat.

"My tribe believes God is both male and female," Henry says. Through his thick glasses, his eyes are earnest.

"Really?" I ask, still stunned.

"Sure," Henry says. "Why not? Look around you. People. Animals. Insects. Even flowers are all male and female. Why wouldn't God be both?"

I don't know what to say.

Xylia leans in close and puts her hand on my knee. Her touch makes me dizzy. "You don't mean to tell me you seriously buy all this big, white, pissed-off-guy-in-the-sky stuff they peddle around here?"

"I guess I just never thought of God as being any other way." I wonder if I should put my hand on her knee too. Her hair smells fresh, like shampoo.

She takes her hand off my knee, picks up her fork, and moves the green beans around on her tray. The place where her hand was feels cold now. "I was lucky, I guess. My parents always encouraged me to think of God as too big for one definition. My mom collects images of goddesses, but the Virgin of Guadalupe is definitely her favorite."

"Well, if you wanted, I could come over to help you with your math," I offer. "And maybe you can show me your mom's goddess collection." I feel like a sinner for wanting to see her goddesses. I'm pretty sure they stoned people in the Bible for stuff like that, but I'd do anything to visit Xylia's house.

"That would be cool," she says. "My mom would love to show them off."

"Well, I'd love to see them," I say. I wonder if the others in her mom's collection are as pretty as the one on Xylia's finger. "And trigonometry's pretty easy once you get the hang of it," I add.

"Doesn't surprise me that you're good at it," Xylia says. "That's why my mom sent me here. She said this school has the best test scores in the state."

"We do," I say too quickly.

"Well, then, it's a date! You sure you don't mind?"

"It's no big deal," I say. "It'll be fun." But all I can hear is her calling it a date.

"Math just isn't my thing, you know?"

"What *is* your thing?" Henry asks.

"Wow," she says, leaning back a little, really thinking about the question. "Well, poetry, for one. I just love the music of the words, you know? Like, when you hear a really good phrase, it's so beautiful, so visceral, like an *orgasm* or something." I almost die when she says "orgasm." I can't help but picture her having one. My face gets so hot, I think the whole cafeteria must notice how red I am. "And music. I love music, too. The older stuff. The Doors, Janis Joplin, Bob Dylan."

I nod. I vaguely remember that the Doors sang, "I'm gonna love you till the heavens stop the rain." I know right then I will love Xylia that long. I can't explain how I know it. It's as if something inside me has known Xylia for a million years. Maybe reincarnation is real, and I feel like this because I've known her since the beginning of time.

"I love dancing, too," she says. "I took ballet most of my life, but there's no studio here, so I practice on my own."

"I'd love to watch you dance sometime," I tell her.

"Maybe when you come over to tutor me, we can dance together."

I shake my head. "I don't dance."

Xylia throws back her head and laughs. "Of course you dance! Everyone dances."

"I'm really bad," I say.

Xylia looks into my eyes, like she's delivering the secrets of the universe. "Listen to me, Mara," she says, and my name sounds like music coming from her lips. "There's *no such thing* as a bad dancer."

CHAPTER 8

MOMMA, REMEMBER THAT GIRL, XYLIA, from my party?" I ask over dinner—pot roast, buttered corn, and green Jell-O salad. Momma has burned the roast, so the house has taken on a charred smell, but Daddy just cut off the edges of his meat and told her it was the best roast he'd ever had. Daddy's good like that when he's not mad.

"Xylia?" Daddy chews his meat like a cow chewing cud. "What kind of a name is that?"

"A pretty one," I say defensively, and then I worry that he will know right then that I want to kiss her and will take a two-by-four to my head.

"It's weird if you ask me" is all he says.

"Anyway, Momma." I turn away from Daddy, who I want to poke with my knife for insulting Xylia. "She invited me over on Thursday to help her with trigonometry."

"Is she paying you?" Daddy asks.

"I don't want her to." I reach for the salt so I won't have to look at Daddy. "She's my friend."

"Russ." Momma uses her sexy voice and touches her cleavage. "A lady doesn't ask a friend for money. It's not proper."

Daddy snorts, "You women and your pansy-ass friendships." But he sounds pacified. "Pansy-ass!" Iggy repeats, laughing.

"It's good that Mara's making friends," Momma says quickly. "She's never had friends before."

I clear my throat. "Why are you talking about me in the third person? I'm right here."

Momma smiles apologetically. "Xylia sounds wonderful, honey. Tell me about her."

"She's smart." My cheeks flush. I could talk about Xylia all day. "And she's a dancer."

Momma leans in, interested. "What kind of dance?"

"Ballet," I say.

"Did I ever tell you I took ballet when I was young?"

"Was it hard?" I ask.

"Oh yeah. Bar work alone was enough to knock me out."

"Bar work?"

Momma nods. "An hour of bar work before we even started dancing."

"Were you any good?"

Momma tries to look modest. She fails miserably. "Let's just say Miss Eva was not easily impressed, but she certainly thought I showed promise."

"Can you teach me some moves?" Maybe Momma can give me a quick lesson so I won't feel so stupid when I dance with Xylia.

Momma looks like she just won the lottery. "Of course!" She stands and puts her hand on the back of her chair. "This is plié," she says, squatting low and moving her hand gracefully in front of her. "You try."

I stand and mimic Momma.

"Good!" she says. "But turn your toes out a bit."

Daddy grabs Momma's butt. She squeals. So does Iggy.

Momma slaps playfully at Daddy. "Russ!"

Daddy roars, as if Momma's protest is the best joke he has ever heard. I can see my ballet lesson is over. I sit down. So does Momma, her face red. "Well, that was nice of you to offer to tutor your friend, sweetie, but you'll have to do it another night. Thursday's Iggy's birthday."

Iggy grins, wriggling in his chair. "My birthday!" Clearly he didn't realize his birthday was approaching. It makes me sad for a minute. Last year, when he was turning seventeen, he planned his birthday for weeks, not a party, because that was out of the question, but private activities. Reading poems about the meaning of life. Sitting under the stars until midnight and wishing on the moon as the next year of his life began. This year he's legally an adult, and he's a little less smart than he was in fourth grade.

I'd feel bad about not remembering his birthday, but since he didn't even remember himself, it doesn't seem like that big a deal. I'm disappointed I can't see Xylia Thursday, but I don't want to hurt Iggy's feelings. "Eighteen." Grinning, I punch Iggy in the arm. "My big bro is getting old."

Iggy laughs.

Iggy and I are both Pisces. Last year, when I read our horoscope aloud over breakfast, Momma sent me to my room for studying astrology, which is apparently a sin. I still read my horoscope in the newspaper sometimes. Today it said I should expect wonderful surprises. It was pretty right on, with Xylia inviting me over to her house, so I don't care what Momma says. From now on I'm reading my horoscope.

Daddy looks at Momma with that hungry-wolf look he gets sometimes. I know what he wants, and it makes me sick, but I'm also happy he wants it, because wanting it and getting it both seem to put him in a good mood. I feel like he needs to be in a good mood just now, as we are discussing Iggy's birthday, and anything that has to do with Iggy is always a danger zone. I'm pretty sure Momma waited until Daddy was looking at her like that to bring up the subject. Momma's smarter than I give her credit for.

Grabbing Momma's butt seems to have worked its magic on Daddy. He clears his throat, staring at Iggy with a half smile. "The boy is almost a man."

Iggy gets so proud and red, I think his face is going to spontaneously combust, the way Mr. Farley said can happen when there's a demonic influence. Iggy touches the tines of his fork to the little yellow flowers on his plate, smiling.

"Practically a man," Momma echoes, plopping another load of Jell-O on Iggy's plate. Little dabs of it land on her embroidered tablecloth. "I think this calls for a celebration. Excuse me, please." She pushes away from the table and saunters to the kitchen. I wonder if she's going to give Iggy a party too. I hear her rustling around in the cupboard where she keeps her cookbooks. "What kind of cake would you like, Iggy?" she calls.

Iggy giggles. "I don't know."

Daddy grimaces. "It's a simple question." He takes a bite

of roast and chews it loudly. I hate the way Daddy can go from glad to mad in two seconds flat. It's probably the worst thing about him, which is saying something, considering all the things that are wrong with him. I hate being in the same room with him, even when he's happy. You never know what's gonna set off his temper. I'm pretty sure Iggy isn't getting a party.

"Come on, Iggy," I prod. "Just tell Momma what kind of cake is your favorite. Chocolate, right?"

"Chocolate!" he yells, raising his fork in the air as if he is brandishing a spear.

"Keep your voice down," Daddy snaps. Iggy lowers the fork. I can feel Daddy's mood changing the way old men sense weather changes in their bones.

"Chocolate?" Momma's voice tinkles. "Why, wouldn't you know my boy's favorite cake is also my own? I'm going to make you a chocolate cake, Iggy. I'm going to make it special, from scratch."

I poke at my pot roast, praying. *Just let us get through this conversation without anyone getting hurt.* I look at Daddy. He's staring at the table, his face blank. He's deciding how to feel. It could go either way. *Come on, Momma,* I think. *If there was ever a time to flash some cleavage, it's now.*

"I get a cake," Iggy informs me. He takes a gulp of milk,

and when he pulls the glass away, he has a thin white mustache.

"Yep," I say. "That's cool." I move my fork around on my plate, making ugly scraping noises.

"Momma's gonna make it special," he says, shoving a spoonful of green Jell-O into his mouth.

"Don't talk with your mouth full," I say, trying to beat Daddy to the punch.

"For God's sake, listen to your sister. Keep your mouth closed when you chew." Daddy helps himself to another slab of meat and shakes his head at me, as if we're the only adults in the house.

"Just three more days," Iggy says, holding up three fingers.

I wonder if Iggy has a manual inside his head called *How to Piss Off Daddy with Every Move You Make*. He's acting like a two-year-old. It's making Daddy mad, never mind that he's the one who broke Iggy's brain. I'm starting to get really scared, when Momma waltzes in. She takes these short little ballet steps and then pliés right in front of Daddy, so her butt is in his face.

I watch Daddy, waiting to see what he'll do. "Now that's what I call a rump roast," he says with a guffaw.

I have never, ever been happier to see my daddy grope my momma's ass.

• • •

Three days later Iggy and I come home from school to find the house all decorated with blue streamers. In the doorway Momma has hung a handmade sign, made from a piece of butcher paper. *Happy birthday, Iggy!!!!* it says in bubble letters. Momma's favorite Ethel Merman CD is playing.

Dropping his backpack, Iggy starts to laugh. "Momma, look! A birthday poster! For me!" He runs his finger under his name on the sign. "Iggy," he pronounces proudly.

"Iggy," I sigh. "Pick up your mess. I'm not your maid."

Ignoring me, he throws his coat on the floor and runs to the kitchen. I pick up his backpack and lug it to the table. It's heavy. I remind myself that it's his birthday, that I should be extra nice to him today. It's hard because I could be at Xylia's, and instead, I'm here. Tomorrow I will be at Xylia's though, looking at her momma's goddess collection, telling her about the Pythagorean trigonometric identity. This makes me happy again. I pick up Iggy's coat and hang it on a hook by the door. Then I follow him into the kitchen. He's standing there wrapped in Momma's arms, while Momma beams, saying, "My gosh, baby. You grew faster than a bedbug."

As I go to the refrigerator for a snack, I wonder how fast a bedbug grows. Probably pretty quickly, considering Mr.

Farley's recent insect lecture. Egg, larva, pupa, adult. I wonder which stage Iggy would be if he were a bug. Stuck somewhere between larva and pupa, I guess.

Iggy sings along with Ethel.

"You like this?" Momma asks.

Iggy nods.

She starts to dance, and Iggy follows, more or less, stepping on her feet. I pull out a bag of grapes and pop a couple in my mouth.

"Mara, wash those first," Momma scolds. "You have no idea what kind of germs are on them." I take a cluster to the sink and rinse it.

Finally Momma releases Iggy. "Would you help me decorate Iggy's cake?" she asks me.

"Sure." Iggy's birthday cake sits on the counter, a three-layer, lopsided monstrosity. "Nice Leaning Tower of Cake," I want to say, but I'm pretty sure it would hurt Momma's feelings. Instead I say, "The cake's pretty, Momma. Better than Martha Stewart."

"Thanks." Momma beams as I carry the cake to the table.

"She made me a cake," Iggy says. He sits at the table, eagerly watching me, as if cake decorating is an Olympic event. "From scratch," he adds.

I smile. "That's 'cause you're the bee's knees," I say.

Momma laughs. "What does that even mean, you crazy girl?"

"It means he's the best brother ever." I glue the crumbly layers together with frosting as best as I can. Then I slap another layer over the outside.

"Very nice," Momma says, holding a baggy with a hole cut in the corner. It's filled with sunny yellow frosting. "It's time for the finishing touch." *HAPPY BIRTHDAY IGGY*, she writes in squiggly letters.

Then she adds an exclamation point. Pause.

Another exclamation point.

Exclamation point.

Exclamation point.

Four exclamation points.

I try to remember how many I had on my cake. Now that I know Momma would leave me here with Daddy, I can't help but think she loves Iggy more.

Iggy holds up the red bowl Momma used for the frosting. "Can I lick the bowl, Momma?"

"Of course."

I stick my finger in the bowl. Iggy jerks it away. "Momma said I could have it."

"You have to share," I say. "Family rules."

Momma sighs. "Mara, it's his birthday. Could you let

him have one little treat without making an issue of it?"

I want to tell her that I'm tired of being nice to Iggy. I want to tell her that when it comes to her, he always gets the treats. I want to tell her that last I checked, she was pretty much ready to run off with the kid she actually loved and leave me here to rot with Daddy. Instead I mumble, "Sorry, Iggy."

I must look really apologetic because Iggy says, "Here." He tries to give me the whole bowl, but I just take one lick and give it back. Then I stare out the window, watching a falcon spin and swoop in the sky. It makes me feel better.

I think about Henry's hawk feather hanging over my bed, bringing me good luck. It must be working. I'm going to Xylia's tomorrow. "Thanks, Henry," I whisper.

Breathing in the sweet smell of cake, I think about how things have been since Henry gave me his feather. As much as I get sick of Iggy acting like a toddler, Daddy is being nice, and Momma seems mostly happy. I wonder if there really is something to Henry's magic. I wonder if he really does have a gift, like Xylia says.

Soon Daddy comes home. When he calls for Momma, there's a smile in his voice. "Cora, come see this."

I hear the click-clack of Momma's shoes and a little gasp. "Oh, Russ. It's beautiful."

"What is it?" Iggy calls, running toward the front door.

"Not now, Iggy," Daddy says. "March right back into that kitchen. It's a birthday present." His words are stern, but his voice is still cheerful.

"Mara," Momma calls. "Come see what Daddy got Iggy." Her voice is full of happiness, like a piñata stuffed with sweet candy. Daddy has never, ever gotten Iggy a present in his whole life. Not once.

Daddy's standing in the front hall holding a brand-new rifle. I know it must have cost a lot of money. I'm stunned. Most times Daddy has to be pestered to buy school supplies for Iggy. A heavy feeling lifts off my back. Today Daddy loves Iggy. Tomorrow he'll probably be back to acting like a spit wad with legs, but at least for now he's nice.

I touch the polished metal of the gun barrel. "It's the prettiest thing I've ever seen." I think of the beauty of the Highwayman's twinkling pistol, finally understanding that part of the poem.

Tonight we're just like a real family. We laugh at the table, long and loud, and Daddy laughs loudest of all. He is twitchy and excited, and I'm anxious with him.

"I can't wait to see the look on Iggy's face," I whisper when Iggy goes to put his plate in the sink.

Daddy winks. "You just wait, Rosebud. This is gonna be his best birthday ever."

Momma brings out the cake, blazing with eighteen candles. She sets it in front of Iggy.

"Momma made it from scratch," Iggy says.

"Ready to sing?" Momma starts, but her voice comes out too high. Daddy imitates her, and we all start to laugh so hard, we can hardly finish the song. Then Daddy shouts, "Blow out your candles, boy, and make a wish!"

Iggy sucks in a deep breath, and *whoosh*, out go the candles. Every single one.

I feel like I got a wish too. This day is magic. Some white witch must've wandered into Barnaby and replaced my daddy with another man. Or maybe it's Henry's hawk feather, making everything okay. It's like this when Daddy is nice. Every time it happens, it makes my head spin.

Tonight he claps Iggy on the back for blowing out the candles. He takes the time to wink at me before he leaves the room, returning with his hands behind his back. I can see the rifle butt through the space between his legs, but I guess Iggy can't, because when Daddy shows him the gun, Iggy's freckles light up like the Fourth of July.

"Holy cow, Daddy! Holy cow!" Iggy scoots away from the table and runs to Daddy, tripping over Momma's chair on the way.

He takes the gun in his hands and stares at it with wide eyes.

Daddy puts his hand on Iggy's shoulder. Daddy's voice is serious now. "When a boy gets his first gun, not an old BB gun, but a twenty-two-caliber rifle, it means he's not a boy anymore. He's a man."

Iggy stands up taller.

I watch, feeling a little choked up, hoping that this moment will change everything. I let myself believe it. We're going to be happy now. We're going to be a family. Me, Momma, Daddy, and Iggy. And all because of a stupid old gun.

"Maybe the liberals wouldn't go on so much about gun control if they saw Iggy's face right now," I call out, and Daddy smiles. He's proud, I can tell, that I know so much about politics.

"Maybe they wouldn't," he says.

Iggy takes the gun to his chest, presses it close. "Thank you, Daddy."

"So, how about some target practice?" Daddy asks.

It's only then that I remember what guns are used for. Iggy's not a killer. He never was, but since Daddy broke his brain, it's worse. He can't even chop the heads off soup hens anymore—can't stand the misery in the chickens' eyes. So I do it for him. I don't really like it, but I wait a whole hour to wash the blood off my hands, just so Daddy will think it's no big deal and won't punish Iggy for not doing his chore. But now that Daddy has given Iggy this gun, there's nothing I can do.

"Target practice?" Iggy asks.

Daddy shrugs. "Yeah, grab some of those soup cans from the trash, and let's have at 'em."

Iggy whoops, and I whoop right along with him. Soup cans! Daddy only wants Iggy to kill soup cans.

We gather our coats and run into the yard. Daddy sets a soup can on a stump, then shows Iggy how to hold the gun.

"Safety," Daddy says solemnly, "is your first concern when you use a firearm. You got that?"

Iggy nods.

"Repeat what I said," Daddy says, turning the gun this way and that, checking it out.

"Safety is your first concern." Twilight will fall soon, turning the whole world purple, but for now we can still see in the dimming light.

"You could kill a man with this. It's a weapon, not a toy. Now here. Put her up on your shoulder." He adjusts the gun so it's comfortable for Iggy, shows him how to aim, even helps Iggy pull the trigger the first time. There's a boom, and what's left of the soup can flies away from the stump.

"Hot damn!" Daddy shouts, clapping Iggy on the shoulder. "You're a regular sharpshooter, boy!"

Iggy laughs. "Hot damn!" he echoes.

I stand on the porch and wonder at the way all of Iggy and Daddy's problems seem to have melted into the icy evening. I rub my arms, trying to erase the chill bumps that have broken out all over them, even under my coat. When I'm sure that Iggy and Daddy are getting along fine, I sit on the porch and pull a piece of driftwood out of my pocket. I found it washed up on the shore while I was fishing last summer.

I pull out my pocketknife and ask the wood, "What are you?"

Then I start to whittle, helping it become what it was meant to be. A female figure. I give her hips and breasts, waves of hair falling over her forehead and shoulders. I carve compassionate, wide eyes. Xylia's eyes. When she is smooth and soft, I push her in my pocket. Daddy and Iggy are still getting along, so I go inside. By the porch, I stop and break an icicle from the window sill.

When I walk into the kitchen, Momma's at the sink, her arms buried up to her elbows in suds. She's scrubbing away, like always, but her eyes are bright blue, the way they were when I was little.

"Here, Momma," I say. "I got this for you."

Momma laughs. "Oh, Mara. How lovely." She kisses my cheek, and her velvety skin rubs my own. Then she dries her hands and places the icicle in a vase, as if it were a flower.

I look out the window, watching Iggy and Daddy take turns shooting the cans until Iggy's best birthday ever fades to moonlit blue.

CHAPTER 9

A FTER SCHOOL FRIDAY, XYLIA'S MOMMA picks us up in a bright red convertible. The top is down even though it's freezing out, and her wavy brown hair is a mess, but she's smiling. I think she's the prettiest grown-up I've ever seen. No wonder Xylia is so beautiful. She looks just like her momma, only her momma is a little plumper. Not fat, but curvy. She has little wrinkles around her dark eyes. I imagine that is what Xylia will look like when she's older. I hope I still know her then so I can see it.

As I approach the car, Xylia's momma says, "Hello, Mara," thrusting out her hand. As I shake it, she says, "I'm Juliette. Xylia's told me so much about you." My heart pounds. Xylia's told her momma so much about me?

"She's told me about you, too," I say.

Without opening the door, Xylia hops over the side of the car and plops onto the seat. "Jump in!"

I try to do what she did, but I trip and face plant beside her.

She laughs. "You're so cute," she says, helping me up.

"If it's too cold for you girls, I can put the top up," Juliette says.

Xylia looks at me, her eyebrows raised in a question.

"I like it," I say.

Xylia beams, as if I have just answered exactly the right way. "I knew you would."

Juliette pulls out of the parking lot, and I can feel myself blushing, both from the shame of falling and from the joy of having Xylia tell me I'm cute. We can't talk much on the way home because the wind is loud and Xylia's momma's music is even louder. Xylia sings along, her hair slapping around her face.

When we get to Xylia's house, Juliette shoves open the door, which she hasn't bothered to lock, and holds it for us. *"Mi casa es su casa."* Warm air wraps around me.

It's like I stepped into a fairyland. There are so many colors, it's dizzying. African masks and huge paintings in gold frames hang from the walls. Juliette must have a green

thumb, because everywhere I look, there's some sort of potted plant. The leaves of one wind all the way up the banister.

"That's Maury," Xylia says, pointing to the plant. "He's
mom's favorite philodendron. You wouldn't believe the
trouble she went through to make sure his arms didn't break
off during the move." I'm not sure if I should shake one
of Maury's many hands or not. Glass fairies and butterflies
and birds hang everywhere, dangling from doorways and
windows and lampshades. The whole place smells like cin-
namon. Outside, a million wind chimes jangle, making the
most beautiful music I've ever heard.

"I love your house so much!" I say, and I mean it. I've
never felt more at home anywhere.

"It's a little eclectic, but then, so are we." Juliette puts
her arm around Xylia's shoulder and squeezes. Eclectic? My
momma would call this place freaky, but I think it's breath-
taking.

Xylia smiles. "Mara's eclectic too. You should see her art,
Mom. She's amazing."

"Maybe you can bring it next time you come over?"
Juliette asks.

"Sure," I say, not really believing that a grown-up wants
to see my art.

"Xylia tells me you wanted to see my goddess collection."

I nod, feeling like I'm looking at a goddess already. Juliette's like no mom I've ever seen before. She leads us to a room that's almost all windows. Sunlight creates kaleidoscopes on the paintings and statues that are everywhere, surrounded by flowering plants and tiny fountains.

"Welcome to the goddess room," Juliette says, picking up a hand-size, clay statue of a fat lady. "I got this one in Malta. They worshipped the goddess there for thousands of years. Their temples are mostly gone, but the walls are still there."

She puts the Maltese goddess down and goes to the biggest statue in the room, an almost life-size version of the Virgin of Guadalupe. She looks exactly like the one on Xylia's ring, smiling serenely, her eyes dark and forever. She's the kind of God I could imagine loving, the kind of god who might even understand my love for Xylia. I feel like a heathen for doing it, but I send her a quick prayer inside my head. *Please, if you can hear me, I have to tell someone. I think I might love Xylia. Even if you don't approve, I had to say it anyway.* I study her face, watching for a reaction. A beam of sunlight falls over her lips, and it seems as if she smiles a little more, as if she doesn't think I'm an abomination at all.

After we are done looking at the goddesses, Xylia leads me to her room. It's small, but otherworldly, just like the rest of the house. It has Xylia's soft, flowery smell. "So, shall we dance first, or shall we do the trig?"

I still can't imagine dancing in front of Xylia, so I say, "We probably should get the work out of the way first."

"You're probably right," says Xylia, sighing as she unzips her backpack. "I mean, I don't get this shit *at all*. Putting letters in math? As far as I'm concerned, it's blasphemy." She laughs.

I laugh too, though I don't get the joke. I *like* trig. "I can show you how it works. Like I said, it's really easy, once you get the hang of it." I sit beside her.

She hands me her notebook and a pencil. Our fingers brush, and a shiver runs through me. "Okay," I say. "So let's start at the beginning."

Xylia leans in close. Just then a big orange cat wanders into the room. "That's Octavio Paws," she says. "Like the poet."

I shrug, confused.

"Octavio Paz was this Mexican poet. My dad was always making poetry jokes like that." She smiles wistfully.

She holds out her hand to the cat. "Here, Octavio," she coos. He comes and curls up in her lap. I've never in my life wanted to be a cat more than I do right now.

"He's so fat," I say.

"He is, isn't he? You're getting a gut on you, aren't you baby?" She pets his belly, and he purrs in response.

I explain the basics of trig to Xylia, all the while watching her stroke Octavio's fur, wishing I were him. She's as smart as I thought she was, and she picks up on trigonometry fast. Within an hour, she's become a pro.

"I totally get it," she says gleefully. "You're a miracle worker, Mara." She kisses me on the cheek. I swear, it feels like her lips burn a hole in my face. I don't know what to say.

Luckily I don't have to say anything. Juliette shows up in the doorway, wearing a kimono. "Would either of you girls like a beverage?"

A beverage? She sounds like someone in a movie.

Xylia asks. "Do you want something?"

"Sure, I'd love a beverage." I try to sound sophisticated, but I sound nervous instead.

Xylia's mom returns with two glasses of something that looks like wine. The crystal glasses are elegant, with slender stems. "Sparkling cider," Juliette says as she presses a glass into my hand. "No alcohol."

Xylia smiles. "Dad lets me drink wine on special occasions." She takes a sip of her cider. I worry for a second when she says this. I wonder if she's like my daddy when she gets drunk. But watching her glittering eyelids close as she takes a sip of the cider, I think she could never in a million years be anything like my daddy.

"Well, not on my watch," Juliette says. "Anyway, you'll have plenty of time to enjoy that when you're older. Like anything else, it's wonderful in moderation." She leaves Xylia and me alone with our drinks.

I take a sip. The bubbles tickle my nose.

"Do you like it?"

What a question. How do I answer that? How do I tell her that the day I met her, my world went from black-and-white to color? How do I tell her that everything I have said, seen, tasted, since I met her has been the best thing that ever happened to me? I can't say any of that, so instead I ask, "Does wine taste like this? I've never had it before."

"I've only had it twice. Once on my birthday, and once on New Year's Eve. If you drink it slowly, you can pick out the different flavors in it. My dad's a total wine snob. This is how you do it." She takes a drink of her cider and swishes it around in her mouth. "Hmmmm," she says in a snooty voice, "I taste raspberries with an underlying oaky flavor, and perhaps a hint of smoked salmon."

I laugh. "Smoked salmon?"

"Sure." She giggles. "It's really just bullshitting. You can say it tastes like whatever you want."

I take a sip and swish it around. "Well," I say slowly, "I think it tastes like rainbows and flowers and every other perfect thing in the world. That's what I think it tastes like."

Xylia smiles. "That's better than salmon."

As we drink our cider, Xylia's leg presses against mine. I feel close to her. I want to get closer. I want to tell her a secret.

"I've never drank alcohol before because it scares me. Both of my parents are drunks," I blurt out. As soon as I say it, I feel guilty. I backtrack. "I mean, it's okay. My momma is a nice drunk. The worst thing she's gonna do is cry."

"What about your dad?" Xylia asks. It doesn't feel nosy. It feels like she actually cares.

"My dad?" My throat tightens. "Watch out. He'll kill you." I can't believe I said it. This is the first time I've ever told anyone about Daddy.

"Does he hurt you?" Xylia asks quietly.

"Not me," I say. "Not yet, anyway. But my mom and my brother, yeah, he hits them. He'd hit me, too, if he knew what I was."

"What are you? Some kind of alien?" Xylia asks, trying to make me smile, but her eyes are still worried.

I think about telling Xylia that I like girls, and then I decide not to. What if she hates me? What if she gets up and leaves me here with my cider? Tears sting my eyes. The last thing I want to do is end up blubbering like my momma. "I think you should teach me how to dance," I say quickly.

Xylia stares at her glass, watching bubbles rise. "You know you can tell me anything, right?"

The heat from her leg seeps into mine. "I just told you more than I've ever told anyone," I whisper.

"Want to say more?" Xylia asks.

"Not really."

Xylia grabs my hand. "Okay." She lifts my fingers to her lips and kisses my knuckles. Then she puts her glass on her desk and stands up. As she pulls out her iPod and scrolls through the songs on her playlist, I watch her, feeling naked, wishing I'd said less and wishing I'd said more all at the same time. She holds out her hand to me. A man's scratchy voice sings, "'Come in,' she said, 'I'll give you shelter from the storm.'" Xylia sings along for a minute, still smiling, and then says, "May I have this dance?"

I should be nervous, but just being near Xylia makes me happy. I take her hand in mine.

"First, you have to feel the music." She grabs my other hand and pulls me to her. Her body bounces to the beat. "Feel that?" she asks. "Feel the rhythm?"

I whisper that I do. I feel the rhythm. I feel the pounding

drums and the gyrating air molecules and Xylia. Most of all, I feel Xylia. I feel her like she's a part of me. I feel her soft skin and her pounding heart and her gentle breath. I think I even feel her soul. I'm almost sure that's what the warmth wrapping around me is. She leans her head on my shoulder.

"See, dancing isn't so hard," she says.

"No," I say, putting my arms around her waist.

We stay like that for a long, long time, moving together, becoming the music. Becoming each other.

CHAPTER 10

I DREAM I'M TIPTOEING THROUGH A SUNLIT FOREST, smelling leaves, talking to deer and raccoons. Bob Dylan's voice sings to me from somewhere far away. I'm ten again and boobless, wearing only a pair of jeans. I used to love to go without a shirt, back when Momma said I had a good eternity before my boobs came in, and why in heaven's name should a little girl have to wear a shirt when there was no one to see her but God and the chickens, when the only men around were her daddy, who had held her naked since she was three hours old, thank you very much, and her brother, who couldn't care less to look at her even if she did have boobs. In my dream, I'm a child, and I'm happy.

But then the dream changes. The trees go black, and I see

a face peeking at me from the branches. It's bigger than the whole sky. It has slick hair and several chins. Its eyes burn with hate. "Reverend Winchell," I whisper. I glance down, and my boobs have come in. I'm still topless.

"Abomination," Reverend Winchell says. His booming voice echoes through the forest, and he shoots a flaming arrow at me from one of his dead eyes. The whole dream shatters and falls around me like confetti.

I try to scream, but nothing comes out. I look around my room. The sun's shining. The picture of me and Iggy sits on my dresser. We're both holding fishing poles, smiling. In that picture I am boobless and topless, just like in my dream.

I can smell bacon, salty and heavy with grease, and Momma's famous cheese eggs sizzling on the griddle. I yank on some jeans, leaving my bed unmade, like always. I haven't straightened my sheets since my birthday party, and they're nothing more than a wad of fabric at the foot of the bed. Momma used to try to make me clean my room. Then she gave up. She just closes the door to my room if company's coming over, which is almost never, because Daddy doesn't like to have people in the house.

Today is Saturday, which means Iggy and me can go fishing. We've spent our entire lives trying to catch Paul Bunyan, a seven-pound trout that haunts the river, eating all the biggest lures and giving Barnaby's best fishermen the slip. Lately we've been using corn for bait. I read in one of Daddy's hunting magazines that's what fish are eating these days, though I can't figure for the life of me how they got a hankering for corn down under the water. If it was stuck on the end of somebody's hook, you'd think they'd stay as far away from corn as they could get. But if corn's what they want, then corn's what I'll give them.

When I get to the table, Momma greets me with a smile that's only now starting to show signs of age. The blue of her eyes is fading, like someone dumped bleach in them, but Iggy tells her she's still pretty when she cries about getting old.

"Made you breakfast," she says, setting a plate loaded with billows of soggy eggs and bacon in front of me. Daddy's already gone, maybe off to buy fertilizer for the fields.

"Thanks," I say.

Momma scoots out a chair and plops down next to me. Resting her chin on her fist, she watches me eat. Every forkful I shove down seems to feed her. I can almost see her belly getting fatter. She smiles and nods at me, like we are carrying on a conversation, instead of me slobbering over a platter of eggs.

"Quit looking at me like that!" I want to say. But I'm

afraid that will send Momma into one of her crying jags, so what I really say is, "Why don't you have some too?"

"Oh, no," she says. "I'm watching my weight."

I study her as I chew, trying to work out the puzzle that's my momma. She hasn't eaten since I was twelve, as far as I can tell. I don't know how she's still alive. Some days she has more energy than a whole troop of acrobats. She dances around the house, singing like Ethel Merman, who I think is her personal hero. Those days, if she's not dancing, she's working, scrubbing down this or that, or whipping up some dinner she thinks will turn out like the picture in her Betty Crocker cookbook, but usually ends up looking more like something a puppy might leave on the floor. But then she has her sick days. Those days, she barely moves. Those days, she's as quiet as the universe before light. Inside my head I hear Reverend Winchell say, "Without form and void, when darkness was on the face of the deep." Thinking of Reverend Winchell makes me remember my dream, which reminds me that I am an abomination, which makes my chest hurt.

"You like your breakfast?" Momma asks.

I nod.

"Good," Momma says. "You should have seen your brother go after that bacon. He ate more than your daddy, even."

"Imagine that," I mutter.

I take another bite of eggs, while Momma watches me. She lives through us, my momma. We're her chance to make up for the life she lost when she got married. People say that you only live once, but that's not quite true. You can live two, three, or even four times, depending on how many kids you have. It irritates me suddenly, like a mosquito buzzing my brain, the way my momma's trying to steal my life away.

"Iggy's probably got an appetite since Daddy's gone to town and he can't try to kill him today," I say through a mouthful of eggs.

It's mean-spirited, and I know it. She winces, and the color fades from her cheeks. Slowly, she pushes away from the table, wanders over to the sink, sagging like a deflated balloon. Sharp guilt stabs at my belly.

"Good eggs," I mutter, trying to make up for what I said about Iggy. She turns around again, wearing her beauty-queen smile. But her lips are trembling.

"I tried, Mara," she says. I'm not sure what she means by that. If she's talking about the eggs, well, they *are* pretty good. If she's talking about Daddy beating Iggy, I guess maybe she has tried. Daddy hurts her, too, when he's mad. I bet she's scared as a stinkbug in a hen house.

Just as I'm shoving the last bite of eggs into my mouth, Daddy's boots pound up the front steps.

"Morning, Rosebud," he says as he bursts through the door, all covered in sweat. He kisses me on the cheek.

He's carrying two rifles, the one he gave to Iggy in one hand, his own in the other. When Iggy comes down the stairs, Daddy tells him to dust off his hunting boots, they're gonna go killing. I see the red fear flare behind Iggy's freckles, but Daddy's too busy shining up his barrel to notice. Not that he'd care if he did.

I glance over at me and Iggy's fishing rods propped up by the door, waiting for us to reel in the fattest, oldest trout anyone in this town has ever seen.

Iggy's hands tremble a bit. He shoves them into his pockets. "All right, Daddy," Iggy says finally. "I'll come."

I almost fall out of my chair. "I wanna go." I gulp down my last bit of milk. Iggy won't live through this without me.

I suppose my chicken chopping is why Daddy doesn't question me wanting to tag along. Instead he shakes his head mournfully, like it's a shame the only son he's been given has a full-grown set of boobs and nothing between her legs.

"Well, put on some long sleeves then," he says finally. "You sure can't go scrambling through the woods like that."

I race up to my room and slip into one of Iggy's torn flannel shirts, thinking that if God needed someone to protect Iggy, he sure should've sent an angel tougher than me. I hate chopping the chickens, and I imagine I'll hate putting a bullet in some poor flea-bitten jackrabbit even more. But it's go along or let Daddy kick the crap out of Iggy again, which is a boatload worse than killing rabbits.

"Hurry up," I tell Iggy when I reach the front door.

He's squatting on Momma's lilac rug, lacing up his boots slower than a toothless old maid eats walnuts. "Coming," he mutters.

After what feels like a million years, he finishes with his boots, and we head down the winding driveway and into the hills by the river. The air is cool and clean, stuck somewhere between winter and spring, all the snow melting away, all the trees threatening to push out new buds. Even the frogs seem to be getting into the spirit of things, croaking away. I feel bad for them because I know this isn't real spring. This is fake spring. New Mexico does that sometimes. Heats up so you start to believe winter is over, and then, *bam*, it hits you with another blizzard.

While we tromp through the mud, Daddy's expression is far away and hopeful, the kind of expression people wear when they know they're about to win the lottery. The kind of expression people wear when spring's on the way, and all of the animals are coming out of hiding just in time to be shot.

Iggy isn't so happy. His brow is wrinkled, and his nostrils

are wide and searching, sniffing, I suppose, for a secret path that will lead him away from this torture. I try to forget about fishing and enjoy the scenery, enjoy the smell of the earth giving birth, which smells a whole lot better than a pig giving birth. I know from personal experience.

Daddy's rifle is slung over his shoulder, the butt sticking straight up behind him like a dog's tail, and his hair is standing up on the sides like two ears. I yank on Iggy's sleeve and slow him down a little, whispering, "He looks like a bird dog."

The fear bleeds out of Iggy's eyes for a minute. I forget all about being mad about having to protect him after that. That's the way things go when you share a secret with someone. You forget everything else between you except that sweet, golden, honey of a secret. Me and Iggy are thinking about Daddy looking like a dog and trying hard not to laugh about it when a rabbit shoots out in front of us.

"Hot damn!" Daddy shouts, pounding along behind the rabbit. He's losing the footrace miserably, but he still has the advantage, being that he's carrying a metal cylinder loaded with enough lead to make soup of that little rabbit's brains, even from a long, long distance. The rabbit disappears into a cluster of bushes, and Daddy drops down on one knee and raises his rifle.

"Get down, boys," he hisses, forgetting in his excitement that I'm one organ short of a boy.

We do.

Daddy cocks his head to the side, sniffs the air. His hands are steady. He waits. The bushes move. The rabbit's trembling. Iggy and me feel sorry for it. We want to cuddle it and take it home for a pet, but Daddy wants to kill it, and whatever Daddy wants is the thing that's gonna happen. So we watch the bushes and the barrel of Daddy's rifle and wait for his finger to move. We pray that the rabbit won't suffer too much, that the bullet will hit him in the head or the heart, not the leg. The bushes move again. The rabbit makes a break for it.

Daddy's finger moves. My ears are swallowed by echoing waves of black thunder. *Boom, boom, boom!*

We wait for the rabbit to fall. He doesn't. Daddy's running again, and we're running after him, still deaf from the gunshots, waiting for the rabbit to die, praying that it will be quick. Praying that he is really a he, not a she with a nest full of orphan bunnies, waiting with aching bellies for a mother who will never come, searching the air for the smell of her. We think and pray and run, but the rabbit never falls.

When Daddy stops, we gasp, partly because it feels like our chests have been stuffed with exploding grenades, partly because we're shocked that Daddy didn't get what he wanted. The rabbit disappears into the thickest part of the woods. Iggy and me smile at each other, not with our lips, but with our eyes, so Daddy won't know we're happy.

"Well, boys," he grunts. "We tried. Can't say we didn't give it our all, now can we?"

We both say that no, it's such a shame, but we'll sleep better knowing we gave it our all, now how about we go home and have Momma make us a tuna fish sandwich, because all this disappointment has got us aching for some kind of nourishment. Daddy thinks a tuna fish sandwich doesn't sound nearly as tasty as a nice thick flank of fried rabbit, and he tells us so, plodding deeper into the woods.

The joke's old now, and me and Iggy don't laugh about him looking like a dog anymore. We just watch our feet and try to avoid tripping on rotted logs. We pray even braver prayers, our confidence bolstered by Daddy's failure. We pray that Daddy will miss all the rabbits, and that we'll go home empty-handed.

The logs keep tripping me, and by the by I forget to pray. I forget to watch for rabbits. I even forget that I'm hungry. The earth around me sucks me up. I'm swallowed by the sounds of the churning river and the mournful whisper of the breeze.

"You kids doing okay back there?" Daddy asks, and his concern touches me.

"We're fine, Daddy," I say, studying him. He's tall and paunchy around the middle, and his shoulders are stooped a bit, like he's tired from carrying his gun. But his steps are quick and smooth, made young by his excitement. I remember how he was when I was little, how he would whisk me up in his arms and spin me around and around in circles. I remember the blue skirt of my dress flaring out behind me. I remember screaming, "I'm flying, Daddy!" I remember his eyes, how they danced, bright with fireworks and stars. I remember how I felt, dizzy and so full of happiness, when he set me on the tile. All I could do was fall to the floor and laugh.

Even though I promised myself I'd never forget what he did to Iggy, I do. I forget I hate him for a while. Right now I want to be his little girl. I catch up with Daddy, and say, "Hey." Slowly I slip my hand into his, a little bit shy. He jerks some when I do, like he's surprised, but he doesn't pull away. His face flushes. He's happy, my daddy. I made him happy.

Me and Daddy walk together like that, hand in hand, with Iggy traipsing along behind us. The clouds whisper over us, making pictures of daddies dancing with their little girls. We're so happy with the warmth coursing back and forth between our fingers, we forget all about rabbits until one runs right in front of us, practically steps on Daddy's toes.

Iggy grabs his rifle before I know what he's doing. He shoves out in front of me and Daddy, hot on the trail of the rabbit.

"I'll get him, Daddy!" he shouts.

Daddy gets so excited to see his boy acting like a man, he drops my hand and runs after Iggy. "That's it, son. Get him!"

He's never called Iggy "son" before, and it's like Iggy grows a whole foot. His footsteps get faster. He's running so quick and smooth, I feel like I'm watching one of those athletes from ancient Greece instead of my very own brother. The rabbit freezes in the middle of an open field, and I want to shout at him how dumb he's being, why in God's name didn't he find a bush before stopping dead in his tracks?

Iggy drops to one knee, and I can't believe what I am seeing. He raises his rifle and closes one eye, the way he does when he's shooting soup cans. I can see the rabbit watching him, quivering, praying not to die, even though Reverend Winchell says animals can't pray. Maybe the rabbit's not praying to God. Maybe he's praying to Iggy, begging not to be killed, like the chickens always do.

But if the rabbit's praying, Iggy's not listening. He can't hear anything over "son" booming in his brain.

The rabbit lifts his ears, twitches his nose. He can smell his death on the breeze, the smell of his orphaned babies dying alone in their nest.

Iggy moves his finger.

Funny how Daddy's gun was so loud and now all I hear is quiet. Half the rabbit's head disappears in a cloud of red, and Daddy's saying something, though I can't hear what it is for the life of me. I can see his lips moving, his big, brown teeth showing when he smiles, dust devils rising from his pant leg as he slaps his knee with delight. Iggy grins at Daddy.

This is like the part in the Bible when the prodigal son finds his father. And I'm happy. Even though rabbit brains are sprayed over the tender dead grass, thick joy is rushing through my veins, warming my cheeks and hands. Daddy loves Iggy. Everything's all right. It's all been a bad dream.

Iggy walks toward the rabbit, as if to take it by one foot and hold it in the air. His first kill. I think that maybe the three of us will walk home hand in hand, that tonight we'll toast with our glasses of milk in Iggy's honor, and Daddy will tell Momma to bake Iggy a special cake, just like on his birthday, and write *Congratulations, Iggy!!!!* on the top with red icing.

But as Iggy gets closer to the rabbit, his steps slow, until he's stumbling more than walking. He falls on his knees by the twitching body. My heart bangs against my windpipe. I wait for him to lift his kill. Even though I can see his shoulders sagging, I'm waiting.

He doesn't touch the rabbit.

Daddy watches him, the fire in his eyes melting to ice. We're both hoping against hope that Iggy will lift that rabbit and whoop and holler the way a boy should when he draws his first blood.

"Go on, Iggy," I say. "Show us."

Iggy doesn't move.

Daddy walks toward him, his steps measured and slow.

I break into a run. I'll lift the rabbit myself. I'll wave its body in the air and kick Iggy until he whoops and hollers so Daddy will still love him. I reach him before Daddy, but Iggy's face stops me short. His eyes are wide and empty. Tears spill over his freckles, and he sobs, slobber dripping from the corners of his lips.

"God, no," he chokes, staring down at the mangled rabbit. "I'm sorry."

The rabbit jerks, as if in answer to Iggy's apology. Hot blood spurts onto the ground.

It's never until something dies that you see how truly beautiful it was. That's the way it is for me and Iggy, staring down at that dead rabbit. We see two billion little hairs, tawny brown, tipped with white, blowing gently in the breeze. We see the exquisite pads on the bottom of its twitching feet, like pink rubber, and the perfect circle of its eye, already turning a milky white. We see its ear that isn't shot off, the tiny hairs around the edges, the soft red insides. We see the small nose, no bigger than the tip of a child's thumb. We say to ourselves, this is the greatest work of art ever made. This is better than a Michelangelo or Botticelli or Rembrandt. This is God's best masterpiece, and we just blew its brains all over the grass.

We try to tell ourselves that it was quick and painless, but it doesn't help. We saw the way he smelled his death on the breeze, the way he thought of his babies and prayed to Iggy to let him live. We saw him die, and a quick death is still a death, no matter what the hunting books say.

Daddy's with us now. He's not thinking of art. He's looking at Iggy the way he looked at the mouse our cat threw up on the doorstep. His eyes are bulging with rage, his jaw tight and pulsing. He's ugly again, and I don't know how I ever thought I loved him, even for a minute.

"You make me sick," he tells Iggy, and kicks him lightly in the gut, as if his disgust is so heavy, he can barely lift his foot off the ground.

Iggy falls over. He catches himself with his hands, and

his fingers slide in the rabbit's blood. His sobs aren't muffled now. He's screaming and blubbering like a first grader, rubbing his eyes with his fists, smearing blood and tears and snot everywhere.

Slowly Daddy picks the rabbit up by a perfect foot and turns to go.

"Daddy!" Iggy screams at his back, his broken voice shattering like shards of a windowpane.

Blue jays squawk in a nearby tree. Yellow-orange sun dips behind dancing clouds. Rabbit's blood clots on the yellow grass. Daddy heads into the darkness of the woods.

"I'll never be like you," screams Iggy. "Never!"

"And you'll never be my fucking son!" Daddy yells back. I guess he keeps on walking.

CHAPTER 11

WE LIE ON OUR BELLIES BY THE RIVER, Iggy and me, watching brassy ants dance. It's cool out, but above us the sun hangs heavy. Our shoulders grow pink, then red. The sting of sunburn travels into our muscles. Still, we don't move. Here in this place of moss and cattails, we pack sweet-smelling mud around our broken hearts and heal them, the way Indians used to heal their broken bones.

Though we've washed our hands a hundred times, the rabbit's blood is still hot on our fingertips. Last night we fell asleep to the memory of his pleading eyes and were wakened by his squealing in our dreams. Daddy's gone hunting again and will not be home until tomorrow morning, so we've told Momma we're staying by the river today. We whisper about never going home again, but our ham sandwiches have been gone for hours, and soon hunger will drive us home, whether we like it or not. The rabbit's dead. Not much we can do about that. And Daddy's meaner than Satan himself. Not much we can do about that, either.

Iggy turns over on his back, still as a lump of clay, staring up at the sky. I listen to the sound of his breathing, heavy and slow. Since the rabbit, Iggy's eyes are hazy and dark. I can't sit by and watch him die slowly on the inside. I've brought him something.

Carefully I pull her from my pocket, feeling the smooth wood of her face. She's my masterpiece. I love her so much, I almost don't want to let her go. I thought about Xylia when I made her. Maybe Xylia is the reason she's so beautiful. She has lips and cheekbones and ears, this angel. She has fingers and toes with dainty nails. She's the color of sand in travel brochures and smells sweet and sharp like freshly hewn pine. She's perfect.

"Iggy." He doesn't move. "I got something for you."

He sits up slowly, as if the effort's killing him. He looks old. I press the angel into his hands. He stares at her, turns her over in his muddy fingers. I notice the scabs on the backs of his knuckles. I want to kiss them, the way Momma used to kiss our broken places, but I don't. Just when I think he's not going to say anything, he breathes, long and low.

"She looks for real." He runs his thumbs over the wrinkles in her gown, the tiny dip in her throat, the individual feathers that make up her wings. He keeps rolling the angel over and over, studying her.

"I made her because I wanted you to know," I say.

He looks up, his face all wrinkled with questions.

"I wanted you to know that I love you, Iggy."

Iggy stares at the angel, then at the ground. A fish jumps in the river in front of us. When Iggy looks up, he has water on his face. At first I think the fish splashed him. Then I see he's crying. Wiping at the tears with the back of one hand, he pulls me to him with the other. I bury my face in his chest, breathe in scents of sweat and river mud and the ham sandwiches we ate for lunch.

"She's the prettiest thing I ever seen," he says.

I smile into his shoulder blade.

"She reminds me of God."

I pull away.

He stares into the water with this dreamy look in his eyes. The river rushes along, and crows laugh somewhere far away. "Pretty like God." He says it like he means it.

I'm almost sure he's not playing games with me, but I still giggle. "How would you know?"

Those see-clear-through-you eyes of his connect with mine. "I saw God."

"What? Like in a book? Those pictures on the walls in Sunday school?"

"No, for real. I never told anyone, but remember the day when we were hiding from Daddy under the porch?"

"Yeah," I say slowly. A chill ripples along my skin that has nothing to do with the time of year. I want Iggy to unlock the secrets of the world for me, tell me things I've always wondered about, answer all my questions about God and life and love, leave me stunned, but I'm pretty sure he's finally lost it for good and is going to be taken off to a hospital in a padded wagon.

He goes on talking, staring into the water, seeing the way things were that day, with the sun and the gold dust and Daddy's angry eyes. "Daddy was mad. So I said, 'God, help.' Daddy hit me with that big board. I saw you standing there crying. Then I was somewhere else. There was light everywhere. I wasn't scared anymore. I was all quiet inside."

Iggy stops there, as if I can wait for what he's about to say, as if I'm not dying to know what God himself said to my brother. And he picks his nose. Right in the middle of all of this, my brother picks his nose.

"Oh for mercy's sake, Iggy!" I say, "Knock that off."

"I can't help it," he says. "It's stuffed up."

"Use a tissue then."

"I don't have one." Iggy wipes his finger on his jeans and stares into the water for a long time. "I came back, Mara," he says. He looks at the angel in his hand. "I was scared I'd miss you."

My throat gets tight. I want to believe that my brother has seen God, who is a warm light and not a lightning bolt ready to strike. I weigh Iggy's words against my good sense. I glance over into the water. My face and Iggy's stare back at me. I'm surprised, because after all of this God talk, I figure we should be glowing and perfect, like the pictures of heavenly hosts on Christmas cards, but we're still two grubby teenagers. Iggy's hair is sticking up on one side, and his face is red and swollen from the crying. His freckles are faded, the way they always are after they've been washed with tears. My hair dances around my scalp in a tangled jumble of short, choppy curls, and my lips are bigger than usual, which means they're practically watermelon slices. My cheeks are smeared with river mud. Daddy says I'm near as pretty as a poster-calendar girl, but looking at my shabby reflection, I don't know where he comes up with that crap.

It seems like I should say something important, but I'm not quite sure what it is. "You hungry?"

Iggy nods.

"Guess we should be getting home."

"Guess so," Iggy says, but neither one of us moves. The light around us turns to gray. The fishes' feeding frenzy slows to an occasional plop. The river runs smooth and quiet, its only sound the tinkle of water over stone. The bushes behind us flutter in the breeze. It's all perfect, the way the world should be, like Eden. We don't say a word. We're afraid that if we move, the spell will be broken. We're Cinderella at midnight. Maybe we'll never go home after all. But then we hear footsteps behind us, the bushes swishing apart as someone moves through them.

Iggy jumps up, afraid that Daddy's back from his hunting trip and has come to box his ears. Grabbing his hand, I remind him with a squeeze that Daddy doesn't know about this place. It's ours, always has been. Still, my heart beats a little faster as I wait for what's about to come through those trees. We watch. The rustling gets louder, and a soft, white face attached to a scrawny body bursts from the bushes. Xylia's eyes are wide when she sees us. She seems to know she's interrupting something important. Xylia always knows things. I'd told her about this spot, about the way the light falls through the trees just perfect, the way the rocks around it stand like walls, making it feel secret and sacred, but I never in a million years thought she'd care enough about me to find it.

"Sorry," she says. "I didn't know anyone was here. I didn't hear anyone."

My heart pounds the way it always does when she's around. "You're not interrupting anything." Trying to sound casual, I wipe at the mud on my face with the backs of my hands.

Iggy's watching Xylia like she's one of the seven wonders of the ancient world. His mouth's even hanging open a little, wearing a big, dopey grin.

"Look, Sis. It's your angel," he says.

"Shut up," I snap.

"It is!" He pushes the angel into my face. "See?"

My cheeks burn. "Please, Iggy," I whisper, pushing his hand down. "Put it away."

His face falls, and so does his hand. Watching the angel descend, I can't help but think about Christmas, "Lo, unto you a child is born," and all that.

I glance at Xylia. "You can come sit with us."

"All right," she says. "I have a while before dinner. If you're sure I'm not interrupting."

"You're not," Iggy and I say unison.

She walks toward us, so graceful it seems she must be gliding. Carefully she winds her way around rocks and sticks, protecting her sandaled feet. She sits on a log next to Iggy. When she has adjusted her bottom, she pulls her knees up to her chest and wraps her slender arms around them.

Iggy watches Xylia, not saying a word. I try to talk, but my mouth is dry. We all sit there with our mouths shut. The quiet isn't beautiful anymore. It feels like a slab of concrete sitting on our heads. Xylia shuffles her feet, and Iggy plays with his angel.

"You make that?" Xylia asks.

"Nah," says Iggy. He looks at me, not sure if he's allowed to tell her.

A trout jumps just in front of us.

"Yeah." I shrug. "I made it." I thrust my hands into my pockets.

Xylia reaches for the angel's wing, caressing it with her long, elegant fingers. "She's incredible." She sighs, bending her face toward the angel and inhaling the fragrance of the wood. "She's way better than the ones in your room. I mean, those are good, but I think this is a bazillion times better. You blow my mind."

"Thanks." I don't know what else to say. Words aren't big

enough. Every time Xylia compliments me, the air around me gets quiet, like the moment is holy. I know that I will remember what she said forever.

"Can I hold her?" she asks.

"Yeah, sure." I yank the angel away from Iggy and thrust it into Xylia's hands.

She lifts the angel and studies it in the fading day. "My dad's an artist too," she says. "Like you. I mean the mediums are different, but the spirit is the same. Words. Wood. Same difference."

"Your dad sounds nice." I toss a rock into the river.

"He was," she says. "Is, I mean. I don't see him much. Not since the divorce. It's expensive to get back to San Francisco."

I don't know what to say. I want to feel sorry for her, but I'm jealous instead. I wish I never had to see my daddy.

"That's why me and my mom moved here. To get a fresh start. Plus, she could buy a house for cheap." I don't know why she's telling me this now. Maybe to make us even, since I told her my secret about Momma and Daddy being drunks? Or maybe because she can tell how sad Iggy and me are. Maybe she wants us to know we aren't the only ones.

I want to say exactly the right thing, but I don't know what that is, so I slap an imaginary mosquito on my knee.

"Yeah," says Xylia. "Dad's a writer. Did I tell you that?"

She did, but I don't want to make her feel bad for repeating herself, so I ask, "What kind of stuff does he write?"

"Everything. Novels. Poems. There's nothing he can't write."

"Oh," I say. "I love poems. I memorized 'The Highwayman' in sixth grade just for fun."

"That's a great one," she says. She's the only other person I've ever met who loves "The Highwayman."

That's when Iggy decides to go for a swim. He doesn't take off his clothes, just jumps right in, shrieking, splashing everything within a mile. The water is like ice.

"Iggy!" I leap up. "You got us all wet."

Xylia stands, starting to laugh. She puts a hand on my arm. "He didn't mean any harm."

"Wanna swim?" Iggy calls.

She looks at me. "Wanna?"

I get all tingly. "Sure. But it's freezing."

"So?" Xylia says. Before I can say anything else, the angel is on the bank, and Xylia is in the water, shrieking about how cold it is and laughing with Iggy.

"Wait for me," I yell, and in I go, with my best cannonball ever. The icy water makes me stop breathing for a second, but I won't get out, can't get out of the river, because this is where Xylia is. I go under, squinting to watch Xylia's legs in slow motion under the green water.

Gasping, I think crazy things about Persephone and Hades. Maybe Persephone went to hell every winter because she had to be with him no matter how much it hurt. I think about other great love stories too, and then I realize that I'm writing my own. This is a chapter in my love story with Xylia. I don't know how it ends, and I can't even begin to imagine it, because nobody writes love stories about people like me. Still, Xylia, Iggy, and me write our own story, swimming there until we can't take the cold anymore. We drag ourselves, dripping and shivering, from the river. A slice of moon starts to show, and the eye of the night's first star blinks open. Xylia says she should be going. "Shall we sit and dry off?" I ask, not wanting this day to end. I point to a rock where I tossed my sweatshirt this morning.

Xylia smiles. "I wish. Mom'll kill me if I stay out past dark." When I say nothing, she adds, "My mom worries."

"Our mom too," Iggy says. "Our mom worries too, huh, Mara?"

"Yeah, Iggy." I watch Xylia wringing the water out of her hair, looking even more perfect in the twilight than she did earlier. Her clothes are plastered to her body, and I can see the outline of her shape, the dent of her collarbones, the soft swell of her belly. She's shivering. I get my sweatshirt, wrap it around Xylia's shoulders.

"Thank you," she says. She seems suddenly shy.

"Our mom worries too," Iggy says again.

By my foot, nestled in the river mud, is a quarter-size frog, so shiny green his skin sparkles in the dying sunlight.

"Look," I whisper.

Xylia and Iggy look where I'm pointing, and without speaking, we agree to make a game of catching the frog. Iggy tiptoes around behind it while Xylia and me crouch in the mud, forming cups with our fingers, waiting like baseball catchers for the frog to come our way.

Iggy brings his hands slowly down, but before they close over the small, shiny body, the frog hops. I barely have to move. He leaps into the air, and with a small shift of my hands, I'm holding his slick body.

"Hiya, little fella."

He chirps his frantic reply.

Clustering together, the three of us study him, his tiny webbed feet, his bulging eyes, his lumpy hide, his tight line of a mouth.

"He looks like a balloon someone blew up too big." Xylia giggles.

"I think he's beautiful," I say.

"We should probably let him go, though, right?" Xylia says. "I mean, it seems like he'll be happier here than in some jar."

"Yeah," I say, and I put my hands to the ground. The frog hops away.

"You look pretty," I tell Xylia, blushing.

She grins. "Thanks. You too."

My legs feel weak. I'm afraid if I try to stand, I'll fall.

"Our momma worries too," Iggy says.

Xylia and me look at one another and laugh.

We wander home together, our wet feet slap-slapping against the road. For a moment, Xylia and I clasp hands. I never want her to let go.

It's not until bedtime that Iggy remembers we left my angel by the water. The next day we try to find her, but the river's swallowed her.

CHAPTER 12

AS PREDICTED, A BLIZZARD BLANKETS Barnaby in white just when we're all starting to believe spring has sprung. Some of the trees have been fooled into blossoming, and now, their buds will die. They'll bear no fruit this year. The good news is we get a snow day.

I still get up early, when it's dark. My alarm clock didn't get the memo about the day off. Iggy's must have because I can hear him snoring through his bedroom door. I bet he'll sleep most of the day, the way he always does on snow days. I wander into the living room. Momma's wrapped in a quilt, reading from the Bible, which I have never seen her do outside of church. She closes it when I enter. "Just trying to make sense of things," she says, embarrassed.

I sit down beside her, tracing the gold lettering on the cover. "Did it help?" I ask.

She stares out the window. "The parts where it said, 'God is love,' made me feel better."

Muffled by the snowfall, the world outside is so quiet that her breathing is all there is for me. I can feel her sadness. Her desperation. I want to fix it, but how the hell do you fix a mess like that? "I think maybe those are the parts we're supposed to believe," I say. I lean my head on her shoulder. The sharpness of her shoulder blade cuts into my cheek.

"You think?" She drapes an arm around me.

"I do," I say.

"I hope you're right."

We stare out the window together, watching the snow flurry and fall. "Where's Daddy?" I ask.

"Out plowing," she answers. Sometimes when it snows, Daddy makes extra cash by clearing people's driveways, which means he will be gone all day. When he's out with the plow, he doesn't come home until long after dark. My heart leaps.

"Momma, would it be okay if I invited a friend over?"

She shrugs. "Well, I suppose. As long as they leave before Daddy gets home."

I bolt from the couch and toward the kitchen, where our only phone is. Daddy doesn't believe in cell phones because they're expensive and might cause cancer. At least that's what he says. I think he just wants to make sure he can control who we talk to.

"It's a little early to be making phone calls," Momma says.

I stop. "You're right." I look at the clock and sigh. It's not even seven. I can't call Xylia until at least eight. "You want me to make you some coffee?" I ask Momma.

"I'd like that." Her eyes are far away. I love her so much, as screwed up as she is. I think about God being love. Whether God is a man or a woman or a ball of light, God has to be love, because if a little girl like me can love a broken woman like Momma, shouldn't a great big God be able to love her even more?

I go to the kitchen and get out the Folgers, the filters, and the flavored creamer Momma likes best. While I make the coffee, I try to fill it with peace. It's weird, I know, but why not? "Can't hurt. Might help." That's what Grandma used to say before she moved to Albuquerque. It's weird that I even remember her saying that, because I was in kindergarten when she left, and Daddy never lets us visit her. When she asks to visit us, he always makes excuses. He tells Momma that Grandma is a shrew, but I don't remember her that way.

"Can't hurt. Might help," she'd say as she pressed a cool ice cube to mosquito bites on my knee that were driving me crazy.

The coffee finishes brewing, and I pour some into Momma's favorite mug, the one that says, *Expect a miracle*. I wonder if that's what's kept her going all these years, thinking a miracle might be hiding just around the next corner. I put in lots of creamer, the way she likes it, and take it to her. The Bible is sitting closed on the coffee table, and she's back to reading *Cosmopolitan* magazine, like always.

"What do you think of this hairstyle?" she asks.

The model has shaggy bangs, lots of layers. "Looks like it would be a ton of work to keep up," I say.

She sighs, as if this news has deflated her completely. "I suppose you're right," she says, closing the magazine.

"But I bet you could pull it off," I add quickly. "Everyone says you look like you should be in a magazine."

She smiles. "Did I ever tell you I was Miss Teenage New Mexico?"

"Really?" I say, genuinely impressed. She's never told me that, and I can't imagine why. She picks up the Bible and opens it, pulls out a stack of photographs, and shuffles through them. Placing one carefully in my hand, she says, "See?" Her voice is tinged with wonder, as if she can't believe she was this girl in the photo, this beaming, glorious creature wearing a shimmering tiara and a sash that proves her boast true. *Miss Teenage New Mexico.* She's holding a huge bouquet of roses, and the beauty queens who didn't win stand around her in a semicircle trying to look happy for her.

"You were gorgeous," I say, stunned not just by her beauty, but by the hope that radiates from her eyes.

She smiles. "We had to do this dance, all of us, to open the pageant. We danced to Ethel Merman."

"The circus song?" I suddenly understand why Momma is always listening to that CD.

"Yes," she says. "The circus song. I wore a sequined bodysuit, like a tightrope walker, for that number."

"I bet you were amazing. You're a great dancer."

She beams.

"Why didn't you ever tell me?"

She takes the picture away and tucks it back into the Bible. "What's the point talking about dead dreams?" She slams the book shut. "Go call that girlfriend of yours."

My heartbeat quickens. Does she know how I feel about Xylia? No. She always refers to her friends as girlfriends. "When I was in high school, my girlfriend Sasha was the captain of the cheerleading squad," she'll say.

I start toward the kitchen, but she stops me.

"Mara," Momma calls.

I turn.

"If ever, ever you have a chance at happiness, take it, no matter what. Don't end up like me." She looks like she might cry.

I can't tell her that the thought of ending up like her scares me more than anything in the world, so instead I say, "Why wouldn't I wanna end up like you? You're beautiful, Momma."

"Go call your girlfriend," she says.

The phone rings three times, and then Xylia's voice mail picks up. A rock song plays in the background, and she says, "Hey, it's Xylia. Odds are good that I'm busy falling in love with something. Leave me a message, and if I like you, I'll call you back." I've heard the message several times now, but every time it makes my pulse pound. "Odds are good that I'm busy falling in love with something." *Let it be me. Let it be me.*

I leave a message. "Hey, Xylia. I, um, just thought it might be fun if you came over, since we have the day off. We could build a snow fort or something. Oh, this is Mara. Bye."

I hang up, wanting to smack myself in the face with the phone. Has a dumber voice mail ever been left in the history of voice mails? I meant the part about the snow fort as a joke, but she probably won't get that, and then she'll think

I'm some juvenile from the time warp that took her away from San Francisco.

I pour myself a cup of coffee, lots of creamer, just like Momma, and sit down by the phone, willing it to ring. I have gone through three cups of coffee by the time it does.

My heart goes crazy. I'm not sure what causes it—the caffeine or the fact that it might be Xylia.

"Hello," I answer, my voice sounding shakier than I mean it to.

"Hello, Mara." My heart stops beating altogether. It's not Xylia.

"This is Henry. My father says that since we're having a snow day, I should try to get out and make some friends. I thought seeing you might be ideal since we're already friends."

I'm silent. I want him to come over if Xylia can't, but what if he comes, and then she calls?

"Mara?" Henry's voice sounds tinny and far away. "If it's an inconvenience, I won't come, of course."

How can I tell Henry he's an inconvenience? "No, no," I say. "Sorry. I just got distracted for a second. Why don't you come over here?" I suspect I should recommend an activity, so I say what's at the forefront of my mind. "We'll build a snow fort."

Henry laughs. "A snow fort it is!"

I set the phone in its cradle. "Oh, shit." I plop my forehead on the table. Henry's great and everything, but he's no Xylia.

When the phone rings again, I almost jump out of my skin. I answer.

"A fucking snow fort? Are you kidding me? I've always wanted to make a snow fort!" Xylia doesn't bother to say hello. "Should I bring anything? I mean, like, do you use nails or what? I have no fucking clue."

I smile so big, I think my face might break. I didn't know she'd actually *want* to build a snow fort. "Just bring yourself, and maybe some warm clothes. No nails. All you need is snow. That's why they call it a snow fort."

Xylia laughs. "We don't build too many snow forts in San Francisco."

After we hang up, I run to my room and rip apart my drawers, trying to find the perfect outfit. Sexy without looking like I'm trying to be sexy. Hip but casual. What I settle on is a pair of faded jeans and a *Teenage Mutant Ninja Turtles* sweatshirt, which doesn't sound sexy at all, except it kinda hugs my curves and brings out the color of my eyes. I comb my hair and even put on a little lip gloss, which is new for me.

Of course Henry shows up first. This seems to be the way the universe mocks me, making anyone but Xylia show up when I'm expecting her. Henry's wearing a weird, striped scarf that was clearly knitted by hand. The brightly colored lines are all crooked and lumpy.

"Cool scarf," I say, needing to comment on it, but feeling like it might be rude to call it ugly.

"Thanks," he says. "My mother made it for my father before she died. He gave it to me."

So it's true then. His momma did die. I don't know how to respond. "Well, it's awesome," I say, thinking "awesome" is a generous word for a scarf that resembles unicorn vomit.

"Thanks." Henry pushes his glasses up with one finger. "Wanna start on the fort?"

"Not until Xylia gets here," I say too quickly.

He looks crestfallen, as if he has figured out the fort building is all about Xylia, not him.

"Maybe we could build a snowman while we wait," I suggest.

He perks right back up. "Would you believe that I have never built a snowman?"

"No way," I say.

"Yes way," he answers.

"Momma," I call, feeling like I'm twelve again, "we're gonna build a snowman. Do you have any old clothes we can use?"

"Look in the Goodwill boxes in my closet," Momma calls back.

We pound up the stairs, all excited. "We should make it look like someone," I tell Henry.

"Like who?" he asks as we step into Momma's room.

"I don't know. Marilyn Monroe. Elvis. Someone." I open Momma's closet. "Let's see what's in here." We rifle through the treasure trove, tossing faded dresses and ripped jeans aside. At the bottom of the box we find this ugly, striped suit jacket, which I'm sure Daddy has never worn, along with a faded red button-up shirt and a weird silk hat.

Inspiration strikes us both at exactly the same time. Grinning, we say in unison, "Reverend Winchell!"

In no time flat we're almost knee deep in snow, rolling the orbs that will make up reverend Winchell's body. We laugh as we stack them, and Henry tells me secrets. I don't know why. Maybe I'm the first friend he's ever had.

"My name isn't really Henry," he tells me out of the blue.

"What is it then?" I ask, thinking it will be some longer version of Henry, though I can't think what that might be.

"Charles," he says.

"Charles?" I ask, confused. "How'd they get Henry from Charles?"

Henry shrugs. "My father started calling me that after my brother died."

I stare, still confused.

"My brother's name was Henry," he explains. "Some days, I think my father really believes I *am* Henry, that he's forgotten everything." He pauses. "My brother died, drowned in a bathtub, when he was three years old. That was eleven years ago. Father keeps his obituary in a frame over the bathtub."

Poor Henry. "That's gotta be depressing," I say, thinking maybe my family isn't so strange after all.

"Not really," says Henry. "I'm used to it. I read it sometimes, lying in the water, all of me submerged but my face. When I'm done reading, I let my arms and legs float, like a dead boy's."

This is really getting macabre. I feel like I'm unwittingly starring in a horror film. I'm pretty sure Henry's dead brother is going to possess the snowman and ax us to death or something. Seemingly unaware of my discomfort, Henry presses on. "He must have been tiny when he drowned, but he was still strong enough to take our whole world down with him."

When he says that, I forget about horror movies. I think about how my whole world went down too, on the day Daddy broke Iggy's brain. I feel sad for Henry, who isn't even really Henry. I put a mittened hand on his shoulder. "That's gotta suck."

Henry takes off his glasses, which have gotten foggy, and

cleans them on his scarf. He turns back to the snowman and keeps packing snow. "My mother left the year he died, though I can't remember much of her, either. She'd say 'yum, yum' when she fed me with a spoon. I remember that much."

"I thought you said she died."

Henry looks confused for a second. "Well, *I* know she died. No one else does."

"How do you know?" I ask.

"Because I see it in my dreams," Henry whispers. "In my dreams, I see things most people don't see."

Whoa. So Henry is either crazy or psychic. Both are weird.

"I'm sorry," Henry says. "I shouldn't have told you all that."

"No, no," I say. "It's cool. I mean, I've never known a psychic before, so it's kind of scary, but it's cool, too."

"I don't think I'm psychic," Henry says.

"Xylia says you are."

"What do I say?" I turn, and Xylia has crept up behind us.

I squeal and throw my arms around her. "Xylia! We were waiting to start the fort until you got here."

"We're making a Reverend Winchell snowman," Henry pipes in.

"Oh my God. That is hilarious," Xylia says, looking at the

striped jacket sitting on the porch. "I can't stand that guy."

Henry laughs. "Me either."

"I'd rather wipe my butt with sandpaper than listen to one of his sermons," I say, and everyone laughs.

So we give the Reverend Winchell snowman a face wearing an ugly pebble frown. We put Henry's glasses on him, just for now, and we dress him up in the hideous shirt and suit jacket and hat. Then we get really industrious and build pews from snow. Xylia and I sit on them, and Henry goes behind the snowman and does his best Reverend Winchell imitation.

"What is that godless heathen doing in our town?" he shouts. "It is an abomination for a man to have long hair."

"Fuck you!" Xylia shouts back. "Jesus had long hair!"

"Yeah," I say, jumping in, but feeling scared that someone will hear. "The Man himself had long hair. Was he an abomination?" Xylia grabs my hand, bolstering my confidence. "You go on and on about abominations," I say, "but what about you? What about the way you go around hating and judging? That's an abomination, if you ask me."

"That's an abomination if you ask Jesus," Xylia says. "Judge not, or you will be judged!"

I look at her, surprised she can quote the Bible.

She shrugs. "My daddy thinks Jesus's teachings are cool.

Not so much the religion that grew from them, but the teachings."

"Awesome," I say.

"Women burning for women!" Henry shouts in his Reverend Winchell voice.

"Fuck you!" I yell, and I can't believe I'm saying it, and I can believe even less what I do next.

I jump up and start to kick the crap out of the Reverend Winchell snowman. Pretty soon, Xylia and Henry join me. After placing Henry's glasses carefully on the porch railing, we punch Reverend Winchell's fat face until it explodes in a flurry of snow and pebbles. Xylia puts the hat on her head sideways, and on her it looks sexy. Henry slips on the striped jacket, and it sets off his ugly scarf just right. I wear the only snowman clothing left, the faded button-up shirt, and then we push the snowman's body over.

"*Sayonara*, motherfucker!" Xylia yells.

Henry and me laugh.

"We gotta get a picture," Xylia says, taking out her cell phone.

We all stand in front of the decimated snowman, smiling, our arms around one another, wearing our Goodwill clothes. Xylia reaches her arm out far in front of us, the flash goes off, and there it is: our blasphemy saved forever.

"I'll e-mail it to you guys," Xylia says. She takes off the hat and sets it on the porch railing next to Henry's glasses. She puts her phone inside. Then she falls into the snow and starts making a snow angel. "I've seen this on TV, but I've never done it before," she giggles. "It's wondrous!"

Wondrous. She used my word for her. I fall down and make an angel of my own. Henry joins us too.

When our legs and arms are too tired to move anymore, we lie there in the freshly fallen snow, three blasphemous angels, laughing and gasping and catching snowflakes on our tongues. I think, *I am tasting God*, and even though it's the wrongest thing I've ever thought, I feel closer to heaven than I ever once have in church. Closing my eyes, I grab Xylia's hand. Her warmth seeping through my glove feels like the Virgin of Guadalupe's smile.

CHAPTER 13

THE SNOW MELTS QUICKLY, AND TRUE SPRING finally comes. I have detention again, this time for calling Elijah an asswipe loudly enough for Mr. Farley to hear. In my defense, he deserved it. He was acting like a crazed ape, shrieking over the picture of Michelangelo's *David* in our textbook. Never mind that the editors covered David's private parts with a little black square. The very suggestion of genitalia sent Elijah into a frenzy.

I've industriously scrubbed the blackboards and the coffee cups in the teachers' lounge, as Mr. Farley instructed, and emptied all the trash cans.

Finally Mr. Farley says I can go. The bus is long gone, and it's a couple of miles home. It's not so cold. I enjoy the feeling of the fresh air rushing in and out of my lungs and the sounds of the world going on around me. Bees buzzing and cows mooing and the wind gently whooshing between trees.

I've almost started to look forward to detention because it gives way to these lone walks. Mostly I spend the time thinking about Xylia, about all the funny things she says, or the smart comments she makes about God and life. I love listening to her talk. She's like a preacher, only a nice one that says "fuck."

Best of all, when I walk home, I don't have to see Elijah Winchell. On the bus he always makes sure to get behind me and say things about my butt, which makes me want to smack him.

Today, however, as I am cutting across the woods toward our farm, I hear voices yell and stones roll, as if feet are scrambling over them. I stop to listen.

"You might as well quit running, Ringworm!" It's Hannah from school.

"Yeah, you might as well quit," Keisha echoes.

Henry's in trouble.

"I'm gonna make you pay for ruining my shoes!" That voice can belong to no one but Elijah.

"We only want to make sure you're a boy," Hannah taunts.

"Yeah, we won't hurt you. We just wanna look." That's Keisha.

More rocks clatter, and I imagine Henry stumbling down the hill up ahead, trying to get away from those evil people. I break into a run, heading toward the sounds of their voices.

"We only want to take your picture!" Hannah shouts.

I burst through a stand of trees and see them. Henry's foot catches on a mossy stone. Down he goes. He tries to get back up, but they're on him. Elijah squats above his head, pinning his arms to the earth, and Keisha kneels on his legs, giggling. Hannah crouches beside him, fumbling with his belt buckle. When he kicks, Keisha stays on like a bull rider, holding tight with her knees.

"Hey!" I scream, running faster. Either they don't hear me, or they don't care that I'm there. Keisha tosses his belt to the side.

"No!" Henry's voice comes out shrill and weak, like a little girl's. "No," he says again. "Please."

Hot adrenaline surges through me, and I have all sorts of terrible thoughts. I think of smashing in their skulls with stones, but what I actually do, when I reach them, is swing my backpack as hard as I can, slamming it into the side of Elijah's ugly face. "Get the hell away from him!"

Elijah falls to the ground. "You bitch!" he wails, swiping

at the blood trickling from his nostril. When he sees red on his fingers, he looks like he might start to cry.

"You ain't seen nothin' yet!" I'm itching for a fight.

Hannah gets in my face as Henry scoots away from us, trying to button his pants.

"Bitch!" she screams.

"Bring it, fatty! You think your rapist ass can handle me?"

She must decide she can't, because she and her stupid little sidekick scamper off into the woods, shouting ugly words.

"Keep running!" I yell, watching them go, and then I pick up a rock and toss it at their retreating forms for good measure.

"You want some more?" I say to Elijah, who is still sitting on the ground, looking stunned that he can bleed. I swing my backpack at him again. "Get the hell out of here before I break your head open with this thing."

Elijah's eyes go dead, just like my daddy's do. "You're gonna pay for this." He reminds me so much of my daddy that, for the first time in my life, I'm scared of Elijah. But I have the good sense not to show it.

"You might wanna bring a bigger posse to our next fight, then," I say. "You sit there one minute longer, and I swear to God, I will bash your pimply head in."

He stands and dusts off his jeans. "Just wait."

I hold my backpack poised to strike again as I watch him stumble away through the woods.

When I'm sure he's gone, I look to Henry. He's sitting, his face buried between his knees.

"You okay, Henry?"

He doesn't answer, so I sink down beside him and put my arm around him. I wish I could think of the right words, but I can't, so I don't say anything.

When Henry finally looks up, his glasses are foggy. "I hate them," he says simply.

"Me too. They make me sick."

"It was like this at the reservation, too," Henry tells me. "All the kids hated me. Why does everyone hate me?"

"I don't hate you," I say. "I think you're pretty cool."

Henry takes off his glasses and cleans them on the edge of his shirt. He puts them back on and stares off into the distance. "Would you like to come over for dinner?"

"Well," I say, "I'll have to call my momma when I get there, make sure it's okay, but sure."

Henry picks up a dead beetle and looks at it. It shimmers in the sunlight. "I should warn you, my father's a little strange."

"I should warn you, my father's a freaking psycho," I reply, and we laugh together.

"Is that where you learned to fight?" he asks.

"Something like that," I say, helping him up.

"Will you teach me?"

I think for a second. "Not sure how to teach rage."

We walk through the woods. Some of the junipers have little purple berries on them.

Henry says, "Sometimes I imagine eating them by the handful."

I laugh. "You'd better not. They're poison."

"Oh, I know," he says, smiling. "It's only a pipe dream."

I raise my eyebrows.

"That's what Father calls things that can never be. I did taste a juniper berry once, just one tiny nibble."

"What was it like?"

"It was bitter. Disgusting, actually. But there are other berries you can eat that won't poison you. Also *piñon* nuts when the time is right. And even ants."

"Ants?" I'm completely grossed out.

"They're surprisingly sweet."

"I'll take your word for it," I say. "Why would you eat ants?"

Henry looks at me, screwing up his face a little, like he's trying to figure out if he can trust me. He must decide he can. "Sometimes my father forgets to buy groceries. He's not bad. He just gets sad sometimes. About my mom and my brother."

My stomach hurts when he says this. "I'm sorry." I put my arm around Henry's shoulder again. We walk like that for a while, then Henry pipes in with, "Some of the things you can eat are as purple as the juniper berries. Cactus fruit, for example, is also purple."

Henry is nuts, but I like him. "I tried eating cactus fruit once," I tell him. "I got a mouth full of stickers."

Henry laughs. "Rub the spines off on your jeans next time."

"Will do."

The shadows fall low and cool now, slanting down through the branches and making stripes on Henry's speckled jeans. The sun's going away. In school they said that stars burn brightest before they burn out. That's the way it is with the sun. It blazes orange and then disappears behind the hill.

Soon I smell something thick and sick-sweet. It makes my throat close tight. As we walk, it gets stronger. Before long I can see what's making the smell. A dead coyote is lying in a lump by a fence not far away, its downy, brown fur swaying in the breeze. Its mangled paw is clamped in the steel jaws of a trap. There's a dark brown, crusty spot on its side. Henry and I walk closer. Its eyes are sunk into its head.

Flies buzz around its ears. Some farmer probably caught it and shot it for eating chickens.

"Someone was sick of this old coyote lurking around," Henry says sadly. He sinks down on his knees, and even though the smell is strong, he reaches out and touches its snout with trembling fingers. "There, there," he says. "There, there."

I stand silently beside him, taking in its brown fur and clotted blood. Its black-purple tongue lolling to the side.

"Mean kids tried to take pictures of me, coyote," Henry whispers. A fly buzzes up from the coyote's face and lands on his hand. He doesn't brush it away.

Henry is *really* weird, but watching him talk to the dead coyote, I realize that I like him just about more than anyone in the world, besides Xylia and my brother. He gets it. He gets how sad it is when things die, how beautiful life is.

We sit there like this for a while, me, Henry, the coyote, and the fly, and we think about life. We think about why things have to be the way they are. The light in the sky starts to fade.

"Henry, we should get going," I whisper.

"Thank you very much for listening," Henry says to the coyote. He stands. We are silent during the rest of our walk. When we open Henry's front door, he calls, "Father, I have a guest."

"Oh, good," his father calls back. "I told you you would make friends here."

There are no decorations anywhere. The walls are plain white. Everything is perfectly clean. The books on the shelf are arranged in alphabetical order.

I follow Henry to the kitchen. His father stands at the stove, stirring something, his back to us. I can see the bumps of his spine through his T-shirt. His jeans sag around his backside. He has braids like Henry.

"Hello, Henry," he says, turning to smile at us. His teeth are big and white. "Soup's on."

"Father, this is Mara."

"Hello, Mara," Henry's father says. He wipes his hand on a dishtowel and picks up a spray bottle from the counter. He walks to Henry and me and squirts us both. The air smells like bleach.

"We're going to go to my room now," Henry says.

"All right," says his father. "Dinner is in an hour."

"Sorry about the bleach," Henry whispers to me as we walk to his room. "Father is afraid of germs."

"I remember you told me that," I say. Henry's father's as weird as he is, but I like him just as much. There's something about both of them. Something that makes you wanna squeeze them and tell them everything's going to be all right. "What kind of soup is he making?"

"Oh, it's not really soup. I don't think Father has ever made soup. 'Soup's on' is just how he says he's making dinner."

After I call Momma and make sure it's okay that I stay for dinner, Henry and I play chess in his room. I can barely remember the rules, but Henry's a pro. He checkmates me twice in forty-five minutes. Then we get bored and lie down on his bed.

"Henry, can I ask you something?" I gaze out the window at the stars that are just starting to twinkle in the sky.

"Sure," Henry replies, his hands woven together behind his head.

"Those kids. You know they pick on you because they think you're gay, right?"

"Right," Henry says. He keeps staring at the ceiling.

"I know you told me you weren't gay, but do you think there's anything wrong with it?"

"What could be wrong with it? In my tribe, gays are honored."

"Really?"

"Of course," says Henry. "We aren't as crazy as you guys."

I smile. "So, like, if you found out someone was gay, you would still be their friend, right?"

"What a silly question," Henry says.

"Still, could you answer it?" I pick at a hangnail.

"Yes," Henry says. "I would still be their friend. Of course I would."

"Well, Henry, I need to tell you something," I say. When I was little, I used to roll down steep hills with Iggy. When I'd stand up, the world would be spinning around me. That's how I feel now, about to tell my secret for the first time to someone who's awake and listening.

"What?" Henry says. "That you're in love with Xylia?"

I look at him, stunned.

He laughs. "It's rather obvious."

"It is?" I panic. If Henry knows, then everyone must know.

"Well, it's obvious to me," he clarifies. "I pay attention more than most people. You know what else is obvious to me?"

"What?" I am almost afraid to hear his answer. How many of my secrets does Henry know?

"That Xylia's in love with you, too."

CHAPTER 14

AFTER HENRY TELLS ME THAT XYLIA LOVES me, I'm too excited to eat anything for about a week. He's a psychic, after all. If he says Xylia loves me, she loves me. I imagine all the different ways we might say "I love you." Maybe we'll write it in letters. Maybe we'll say it over pizza, watching some movie from the sixties about giant, people-eating ants. Maybe we'll be . . . Oh, who knows? The point is, any minute now she may tell me she loves me, and that keeps me too occupied to eat anything.

Of course there may be other reasons for my lack of appetite. Science class, for one. Mr. Farley titled this month's science section "The Timeless Beauty of Dissection." He gets a thrill out of cutting up dead things with his sharp silver knife. Frogs. Birds. Sheep. As far as he's concerned, slicing and dicing are the ultimate peek holes into the mind of God. And Mr. Farley is a man of science. Anyone can see that by looking at his glasses thick as ice on a February pond.

"I wish we could afford for everyone to have their own crawdad," he apologized on Monday. "But I'm afraid our school just doesn't have that kind of budget." Then he dissected a crawdad in front of the class and had us all stand in line to take a look inside.

"I almost threw up," I told Xylia as we were walking home from school that day. I didn't have detention. I could've taken the bus, but Xylia and me decided we'd rather walk.

"Maybe you're less scientifically inclined than the average person," she told me, grabbing my hand. "Artists often are. Next time, try thinking of something pretty."

So on Tuesday, when Mr. Farley cut up a frog in front of the class, I looked out the window and thought about the pretty blue wildflowers growing down by the river. On Thursday, when he cut up a cat, I thought about the little tadpoles about to lose their tails. And the next Monday, when he cut up a sheep, I almost felt like I was there by the water, wiggling my toes in the gooshy, sweet-smelling mud. Still, the smell of formaldehyde in the classroom was so strong, I could never escape completely.

Today though, as I enter the classroom, I don't smell formaldehyde. A little puff of relief escapes my lips until Mr. Farley says, "Take your seats. We're going to have a slide show."

I slump into my desk. Mr. Farley has a gift for digging up the most disgusting slide shows known to man. Last month we saw a slide show about diseases of the foot. I had no idea how many funguses and molds could grow underneath a person's toenails. But today it's even worse. Mr. Farley turns on the projector, and there's a picture of a naked dead guy sprawled on a metal table. He's so white, it looks like he's made out of porcelain. My throat tightens.

I'm so busy thinking about the fact that he's dead that I don't worry about the fact that he's naked until Elijah whispers, "We're watching a porno."

"If that turns you on, you're even sicker than I thought," I whisper back.

The rest of the class laughs, and Elijah gets mad. I look back at the screen.

Months ago Mr. Farley promised us all a trip to the medical school to look at the cadavers. Unfortunately, we ruined our chances of that when we sang "Ninety-Nine Bottles of Beer on the Wall" on the bus during our field trip to the bread factory.

"If you think you will get to visit the cadavers after your disgusting behavior today," said Mr. Farley, "you've got another thing coming." No one seemed very disappointed. I think today's slide show is Mr. Farley's happy medium. We don't get to see cadavers in person, but we still get to see some dead-guy slides. Lucky us.

"This John Doe was found by a freeway," says Mr. Farley. "In life, he was a bum, but in death, he made his first real contribution to his fellow man. He donated his body to science."

I know I'll puke again if I look at the slide too long, so instead I stare at the blue jays hopping on the benches outside. I let my thoughts wander. The way John Doe was found by a freeway reminds me of "The Highwayman." It's about a handsome robber who falls in love with Bess, the landlord's black-eyed, red-lipped daughter. So strong is their devotion that they die beautiful, bloody deaths for each other. The poem's words whirr over and over through my mind as the blue jays peck at bread crusts under the benches.

> *Bloodred were his spurs in the golden noon;*
> *wine-red was his velvet coat,*
> *When they shot him down on the highway,*

Down like a dog on the highway,
And he lay in his blood on the highway
with the bunch of lace at his throat.

I can see him there on the dusty road, Bess's fallen Highwayman, his hair matted around his white face. The buzzards begin to circle. I want to cry for the Highwayman, dying all alone like that, becoming a snack for the birds. I want to kiss his lacy throat and tell him that death isn't forever, at least not according to my brother. I want to tell him that he'll see his Bess again someday.

Something soggy bounces off my forehead, making me forget all about the Highwayman. I look up just in time to see Elijah aiming another spit wad at me.

"Do that again, and I'll take out your spleen with a chain saw."

He glares, but he puts the spit wad down. I lean back in my chair. The plastic edge of my seat digs into my back. My knees keep knocking against the bottom of my desk. I can't concentrate. You can tell we had onions on our hamburgers at lunch because the whole school smells like them now.

Mr. Farley clears his throat. "And now, ladies and gentlemen, we move on to the workings of the circulatory system." He says it with so much gusto, you'd think he was introducing Oprah Winfrey. He seems disappointed when nobody claps, then points his yardstick at a place inside Mr. Doe's cut-open chest. "This is the heart."

I can't help but look up at the slide. A purple lump of veiny muscle rests in a nest of bloody ribs. *So that's where love comes from*, I think, sickened by the discovery. Seems to me, a heart should be soft and round and pink, like a ball of cotton candy. But here I see it, this nasty mess of blood and meat. No wonder people are so rotten to each other. After seeing the human heart up close, I can't help but wonder if anything good, let alone true love, could come from that thing. If that's what Xylia has in her chest, she'll never love me back, no matter what Henry says. It's just too much. I race to the trash can and throw up.

Mr. Farley spins toward me. "Mara Stonebrook." He says my name like a death sentence.

"Sorry," I say, mopping my mouth with the back of my hand.

He gets all red around his neck. "I think it's time you went to see Mr. Harris."

"Seriously?" I ask. "You're sending me to the office for puking?"

"I have had more than enough of your antics."

Five minutes later I'm standing in front of Mr. Harris's

desk. He's wearing that gray suit he always wears, his bald spot shining in the light that falls through his venetian blinds. He scribbles furiously on a yellow notepad. At the sound of my footsteps he looks up.

"Mara Stonebrook." He's not surprised to see me. He puts down his pencil and folds his fingers together. "To what do I owe this pleasure?"

"Apparently Mr. Farley viewed my spewing in the middle of biology as a deliberate act of rebellion." I slump into the chair across from him, studying the poster on the wall behind him. *Dare to dream.* Above the white letters some guy is climbing a mountain.

"Why did you, er, 'spew' in biology?"

I continue to study the mountain climber. I wouldn't mind having an ice ax like his, to gouge out Mr. Farley's squinty pig eyes. I shrug. "I was sick. I couldn't help it."

"Couldn't help it?" Mr. Harris is incredulous. "Ms. Stonebrook, this is not a public school. I hope you know that we have standards here. One of those standards, may I remind you, is that young ladies are expected to act like young ladies."

That mountain climber has cool sunglasses.

"Ms. Stonebrook, are you listening?"

I nod.

"I hope you will take care to behave like a young lady. That means—in addition to vomiting in the toilet—dressing like a young lady. Would it be too much to ask you to purchase women's clothing? And perhaps to comb your hair?"

I want to ask him if wearing boots like his mountain climber would be a good compromise, but it seems like a bad idea. Instead I shrug and say, "Sure."

Lucky for me, Mr. Harris feels it's unethical to expel a girl for getting sick and tells me to call my mother for a fresh shirt. The one I'm wearing is decorated with little blobs of half-digested hamburger. I figure if Mr. Farley had seen the pepperoni, he would have considered my presence in his class that day a gift from the good Lord and given the students a lesson on the wonders of the digestive system. But Mr. Farley's glasses are too thick to see much of anything.

"School's almost over anyway," I say.

"You're right." Mr. Harris nods. "Just go back to class."

As I get up to go, Mr. Harris adds, "Mara, let's not see you back here anytime soon, you hear?" as if he, too, believes I deliberately barfed to make trouble.

I slouch out of Mr. Harris's office, still queasy. The bell rings. Thank God. I almost stop to wait for Xylia. Then I remember that she's in Taos with her mother for two weeks.

She invited me to go along, but Daddy said no way was I going to miss two weeks of school to, and I quote, "run around a bunch of fairy museums and look at artsy-fartsy crap."

I head toward the exit. I think about going to ride the bus with Iggy. I've been so busy with Xylia and Henry, I haven't had much time for him lately. But my belly is still rumbling, and I think I could use some cool ice cream to settle it. I have ten dollars in my pocket. It's half the money me and Iggy got helping Mrs. Walden with her laundry after she had her twins. Iggy didn't do anything but laugh and throw baby blankets over my head, which drove me nuts, but I gave him his share anyway. He spent it the same day on candy. He got a stomachache and moaned all night.

I wander down the dirt road to town. The sun's warm on my back and head, heating up my hair until I feel like a little furnace is burning on top of my scalp.

"Mara!" I hear Henry's voice behind me. "Wait up!"

I stop and turn. "Hey, Henry."

"Where're you going?" He runs to catch up to me, his backpack thumping. He looks kinda like the Hunchback of Notre Dame with a movable hump.

"To Dairy Queen. I'll buy you an ice cream too if you want one."

"Sure!" Henry seems excited, like he just won a trip to New York. "I love ice cream!"

"Me too." Around us the air is damp and alive with the clean scent of oncoming rain, but there aren't any clouds in the sky.

"Smell that?" I ask.

"What?"

"Rain," I say. "It's gonna storm before nightfall."

"Good." Henry nods. "A good rain is more cleansing than any bath could be."

"Yep," I say. "Sometimes I think it's God crying on my head."

"That's depressing," Henry says.

"Nah. I like to think of God crying all over me. It makes me feel close to him somehow. Or her. Xylia says God's a girl."

"God is everything," Henry says confidently. A crow squawks at us from its place on a branch. "That crow. That crow's a piece of God. How do you think it walks around? How do you think it exists? Everything is a miracle. Everything is God."

"Even me?" I ask.

"Even you. You are a piece of God."

I beam and kiss Henry's cheek. "You're okay, kid," I tell him. A car drives by, leaving us choking in a cloud of dust.

"Slow down, asswipe!" I call, just like Daddy would. Then I start to laugh. "Some piece of God I am."

Henry laughs too.

"Hey, you wanna know something else we have in common?" I ask.

"What?" Henry takes off his glasses and fogs them with his breath, then wipes them on his shirt.

"Barfing in public," I say. "I threw up in the trash can during biology."

"What happened?"

"Mr. Farley was showing us slides of this dead guy."

Henry seems horrified.

I say, "Yeah. A cadaver. He showed us his guts, and I just couldn't take it."

"Is he crazy? Who shows a dead guy to high schoolers?"

"I know, right? There goes my hard-won popularity. Right down the toilet."

"I guess you can kiss your bid for homecoming queen good-bye."

I blow a kiss. "*Sayonara*, motherfucker." I liked it when Xylia said it to the snowman, so I try it out. It feels good to say it.

When we get to town, I carefully make my way over the sidewalk.

"Why are you walking so slow?"

"Step on a crack, break your mother's back. You ever hear that?"

"No."

"When we were kids, Iggy and me used to do it. We thought that if we didn't step on any cracks, our momma would stay safe. I guess old habits die hard."

At the Dairy Queen a woman I don't know is buying a small cone for her crying, half-naked toddler, who's so dirty I wonder if he's been washed since Christmas. He reaches for his mother's skirt with a pudgy hand every few seconds, trying to get her to pick him up. She's too busy talking to the counter girl, Alisa Perkins, to notice much of anything though.

We wander to the cooler. It's hard to see inside. The glass doors need cleaning.

The phone rings, and Alisa answers it with a formal, "Dairy Queen, how can I help you?" But then her voice gets all relaxed. She kinda grunts at what the person on the other end is saying. I figure it's probably her husband, Sheriff Perkins.

"I think I'm gonna have a Dilly Bar," I tell Henry. "What about you?"

"You know what I really like? Those butterscotch dip cones. I haven't had one in years, but I can still taste it."

"Well, then let's get you one." I pull a Dilly Bar from the

freezer and hide it behind my back. "Guess which flavor is my favorite," I say.

"Chocolate?"

I show him. "Butterscotch."

"No way."

"Another thing we have in common," I say.

We walk to the counter. Alisa hangs up the phone. I think she's going to wait on us, but instead she starts talking to the lady with the baby. Alisa's shrill voice drones on and on, and I wish to God she would shut up and sell me my ice cream.

I look at Henry and roll my eyes. He smiles, like he is embarrassed to be rude to Alisa, even though she's being rude to *us*. I consider cracking open the Dilly Bar before paying, but with my luck I'd get hauled into the slammer. A Mr. Harris look-alike will be there to lecture me on which ice cream novelties are proper for young ladies.

I don't pay much attention to anything Alisa says until I hear, "Yep, said the woman's jaw was broken right in two." My ears perk up. It must be my meaty, black heart that makes me so interested in violence.

"He didn't know who it was?" the lady asks.

"He hadn't gotten any names yet. Just got a call about what happened from one of the deputies."

"Was it really an accident?" the woman asks, picking up

her toddler, who has managed to smear ice cream all over his shirt.

Alisa shrugs. "Who knows? He said something about her husband finding a letter. Maybe she was whoring around or something? I'll call you tonight as soon as I find out for sure."

My hands clamp onto the edge of the counter, and my mouth gets dry. My brain starts buzzing like someone's blowing a hair dryer inside my head. Alisa keeps talking, but my feet are talking louder than she is, telling me to run. So I do.

"Mara!" I hear Henry calling. "Mara, where are you going?"

The bell jingles as I shove open the door. I want to tell Henry where I'm going, but I can't. My feet won't let me. Feet can be very persuasive. When they want to get somewhere, they have ways of making you not care that you're stepping on every crack in the sidewalk. They make you not care that your mother's back is now broken in a hundred places. They make you forget your manners and your "excuse me"s, make you forget to say you're sorry when you shove little kids into the dirt.

"Mara!" I hear Henry shout again. "Wait up!" But he can't keep up with me. My feet are fast.

They take me to the river where Reverend Winchell does his baptizing. Then I cross it. Then I'm home.

There aren't any red lights like I expected. Only the house, looking quiet and cool. Gasping, I climb the front steps.

"Momma," I call as I step inside. I'm crying, but I don't care if she sees me. I hear footsteps. "Momma?"

Daddy comes around the corner. His face is red, the way it gets when he's sorry. "Momma had to go to the hospital," he says, throwing his arms around me. "She fell, Rosebud. Fell right off the ladder while she was cleaning the windows." He points to the ladder that's leaned up outside the kitchen. "Broke her face right open. Don't worry. She's not alone. Iggy rode to the hospital with her in the ambulance. I was waiting for you."

A bite of the hamburger I ate for lunch jumps back up into my mouth. My feet tell me to back away from my daddy. I try to argue, but they are not to be argued with. So I take a step, trying to keep from throwing up the rest of my lunch.

"I'm sorry, Rosebud," Daddy says, and I believe that he is. His face is scrunched up like a washrag, and his fists are clenched tight, so tight I almost don't notice the pink paper in one of them. But I do. I know it's Momma's stationery, and even though I can't read any of the writing, I know what it says.

I turn and run. Out the door. Back through the fields to the river. I fall on my knees in the cattails and claw the ground, looking for something to hold on to as the world spins like a Ferris wheel.

Inside my head I'm saying things like, "Oh, God, Momma's in the hospital." Logical things: "My daddy did this." But also: "I did this." I did this by throwing that letter into the plant. I did this by not burning it when I had the chance. A water bug skips over the surface of the river. I watch his progress. He moves in slow motion. Jump. Jump. Jump. His little insect knees fold and expand with every hop.

"That bug's knees are a piece of God," I imagine Henry saying. I think about my knees and the rocks that are digging into them. I want to get up, but my legs feel like they're made of rubber. I shriek inside my head. The noise echoes over and over in my brain as I crawl to a nearby tree and rest my back against its scratchy bark.

This bark is scratchy, I think. That's the kind of thing you think when you're going crazy.

Your hands still look the way they always have—dirty under the fingernails. The birds still sing. The river still roars. Nothing changes, and it bothers you, all the sameness going on around you. And it makes you insane. You want to scream, but you can't. Something inside you tells you to keep your wits about you. Something tells you that man back there is pure evil, and that it's only a matter of time before he kills someone: your momma or Iggy or maybe even you, if he finds out what you really are.

You sit with your back against the tree for what seems like hours. You stare up at the sky, at the swirling gray clouds painting pictures overhead. You can't believe this is real. A wet spot appears on your cheek, just a drip, so small you wonder if you're imagining it. Then another comes, and another.

The sky begins to weep, and at last you let out that scream that has been ricocheting around in your head. It echoes off the bank of the river where Reverend Winchell does his baptizing as God's teardrops christen you.

You bury your face in your hands and start to shout for God to help you. A raindrop falls in your mouth, like magic. *I am tasting God*, you think.

You feel close to her now, closer than you ever have before, because she's crying with you over your batshit-crazy daddy and your momma's pretty, broken face.

CHAPTER 15

DINNERS ARE QUIET WITH MOMMA GONE. She'll be in the hospital for two weeks, maybe more. With her jaw wired shut the way it is, she sucks her dinners through a straw.

Some afternoons I visit her with gifts. Peanut butter shakes. Pureed vegetables. Even baby food. Daddy brings flowers. Iggy brings shiny rocks. When we give them to her, Momma tries to smile at us, but she can't.

Still, she looks better than she did. At first she was so ugly, so broken and bloody and blue, I could barely look. Now her face is more normal, except for the wire and the fading bruises.

When she was well enough, I asked her what happened.

She looked away and said, "I fell off a ladder." She could talk, but it was hard to understand her.

"I heard Alisa Perkins on the phone," I whispered. "I heard her say Daddy found a letter."

Momma's eyes were wet. "I must have told the police that after I fell. I hit my head pretty hard. I wasn't in my right mind."

I squeezed her hand. "It's okay to tell me, Momma."

In the hallway some old lady walked by wheeling an IV behind her. "I fell off a ladder," Momma said again, sounding like a bad actor in a school play. "Now give me some of that shake." She nodded at the Dairy Queen shake sitting on the table beside her. I grabbed it and put the straw up to her broken mouth. I could tell it was hard for her to suck on the straw. I felt sick for Momma, lying in that bed all shriveled, unable even to eat.

Honestly, our dinners at home aren't real dinners either. The first few days people from church brought over casseroles. When people asked what happened to Momma, Daddy told them about the ladder and no one batted an eye. It seems to me someone in this town should start to wonder how Momma and Iggy get in so many scrapes, but no one ever does.

After a couple of days the casseroles stopped coming. I'm

the only girl around, so it's my job to make dinner, but I'm not very good at it. Momma never taught me to cook, so we eat microwaved hot dogs and peanut butter sandwiches and frozen pizzas, always on paper plates, always on the couch, always in front of the TV. Never at the table. Daddy picks the shows we watch, so I know more about the weather and crime and politics than I ever wanted to.

The first night I cooked I set the table, even though I was just making corn dogs and frozen fries. Iggy was already sitting, his napkin in his lap, ready to eat, but Daddy walked in and said, "Fuck this shit." I was worried he'd be mad about how bad my cooking was, but he didn't say anything. He just yanked a paper plate from the pantry, plopped a corn dog and fries on it, pulled a beer from the fridge, and strode into the living room.

The TV came on. Iggy looked at me, confused.

"I guess we're eating out there, sport," I said. I made him a plate and poured him a glass of milk and shoved him out of the kitchen. "Don't sit next to Daddy," I whispered as he walked away, worried that if he did, he'd chew too loud, and Daddy would kill him.

When I sat down between them, Daddy said, "Well, this is the life, isn't it, kids? Just the three of us, living like bachelors."

I didn't remind him that bachelors are boys, nor did I break Momma's favorite vase over his head, like I wanted to, because how dare he act like Momma being in the hospital was some kind of vacation?

It's been a week and a half. We're pretty used to the paper plate routine now. Daddy keeps acting like we're on vacation, and he never says anything bad about my cooking. We're all slouched on our couch, which used to be white, but is now brown. Our plates are mostly empty, except for gnawed bits of crust and pepperoni shreds. Iggy's making a tower with the lump of shriveled bell pepper chunks that he carefully picked from his pizza before eating it. It's more interesting than the news, so I'm watching his building project.

In my peripheral vision I see Daddy bouncing his plate up and down on his knee. His eyes are angry slits. I think Iggy's tower is the problem until I hear the newscaster on TV say "gay rights." I feel myself blushing when she says it, and I stare straight at the TV, afraid that if I look at Daddy, he'll see my shame. When I finally get the nerve to look at him, he's glaring at the television, muttering swear words.

The newscaster is speaking with a pretty woman who says that in some states gays have the right to be married. She says it won't be long before gays everywhere will have the rights that should be available to every American citizen. She smiles when she talks about it, and I can't believe that there are people out there who are happy about gays getting rights. I have never met someone who thinks that being gay is okay, besides Xylia and Henry. I try to imagine what it might be like, two gays getting married. Two girls, for instance. Me, maybe. And Xylia. In our two dresses we wouldn't look like a regular wedding, of course. Those little figures they put on top of wedding cakes have one person in a white dress, and one in a tux. Wait. If I wore a tux, we would match. I imagine Xylia, blushing in white, wearing red flowers in her hair, dancing with me in my tux. My heart jumps.

A man comes to talk to the newscaster now, a man with slick hair and a puffy face. He smiles too when he talks, but it's a tight smile, more like a snarl. He reminds me of a weasel. Or maybe Elijah Winchell. They're pretty much the same thing. He says that gays are undermining the American social structure. He says that of course gays are people—they *are*—but marriage is not a human right. It is, has always been, a sacred covenant between a man and a woman. He says that the institution of marriage is being threatened by these gay marriages.

Daddy says a bunch of words I won't repeat, then

elaborates on what the guy on TV said. He says if God had his way (and he will), all the fags and dykes would be stoned to death in the streets, just like in the Bible.

I hate my daddy. Staring at the TV, thinking about my momma in a hospital with her jaw wired shut, I wonder why everyone's so worried about marriage being undermined.

The man keeps talking. His lips move, two worms writhing on the gray sidewalk of his face. I hold my breath and wait, listening. He says it. "Abomination." I imagine Reverend Winchell's pissed-off God, and I get dizzy.

"Wanna go have some Otter Pops?" I ask Iggy, standing.

"Yeah!" He jumps up, knocking his plate to the floor and sending bell pepper chunks all over the rug.

"Oh, for God's sake!" Daddy thunders.

"Don't worry, Daddy. I'll get it," I say, my heart banging. Quickly I bend and gather the chunks into my waiting palm. As I pick up the plate, Daddy mutters and turns back to the television. "Let me take your plate too, Daddy," I offer. His silence sounds like permission. I carry all three plates and the pepper chunks to the kitchen and drop them in the trash. The place by the stove where Momma always stands looks empty and cold.

"Sis!" Iggy yells from the porch. "I want grape!"

"Okay, Iggy." I turn away from the stove and pull two

Otter Pops from the freezer, purple for Iggy, red for me.

"Here, Iggy," I say as I walk onto the porch.

He's sitting on the step, watching fireflies cartwheel through the air. They're not lit up yet, or if they are, it's not dark enough to tell. I sit next to him. Iggy and me gnaw open our ice pops, waiting for the fireflies to do their stuff. As Iggy eats his Otter Pop, his lips turn purple. He looks dead. My lips must be red, the way Xylia's always are.

Inside, the newscaster drones on and on, talking about who knows what. We hear Daddy grunt once in a while, shifting his weight on the couch so it creaks. I try not to think about Momma's messed-up face, but trying to talk a wrecked heart out of hurting is like trying to talk a ripped skin out of bleeding. You tell yourself that the wound's not there. But it keeps bleeding, and if you ignore it for too long, it gets infected.

I've been walking around with a festering hole in my heart for almost two weeks. Sometimes I'll be sitting in class, reading about Joan of Arc being cooked, and that hole will start to ache and throb. The pain bleeds through my chest, and I want to scream in the middle of history class. I want to run to my momma and kiss her broken face. I want to go home and curl up in my closet, cry all the water out of my body until I shrivel up like a raisin and die. But I can't die. I don't have the guts to pierce my rib cage with a dagger or put a poison asp to my breast or burn myself on a pyre. And even if I did, what would Iggy do without me? Who would protect him then?

"Look, they're lighting up," Iggy says, pointing.

I stare at the tiny fireflies flitting and floating on the evening air. Iggy squeezes his eyes shut and grunts.

"What are you doing?" I ask Iggy, concerned that he may have forgotten the proper place for a bowel movement.

"I'm lighting up," Iggy says.

"You can't light up, Iggy. You're a person, not a bug."

"Can too," Iggy says. Iggy grunts again.

I shake my head. "My brother, the lightning bug." Iggy's hand slides into mine. He squeezes my fingers and grunts some more.

"Did you hear what that lady on the news said?" I ask, ignoring his attempts at becoming a human firefly.

Iggy grunts.

"Gays can get married. What do you think about that?"

Iggy grunts so hard, he farts.

"Iggy!" I yank my hand away.

He opens his eyes. They're see-clear-through-you.

"I think everyone should have a shot at love," he says.

Then he closes his eyes and starts to grunt again. "It's the best thing about life."

My belly grows warm. I slip my hand back into Iggy's and listen to him trying to light up. "You did it, Iggy," I want to say. "You lit up." But I don't.

Still, that night, after Iggy and I have climbed the stairs to our bedrooms, I dream ugly dreams again. The landscape is cold and blue, and Elijah Winchell is there, calling me an abomination. Someone is laughing across mountains made of steel. I wake up sweating. I think about God and hell, my thoughts going round and round until they feel like a tornado inside my skull.

"I'm sorry, God. I'm sorry, God," I whisper.

He doesn't answer. I slip from beneath my comforter and tiptoe to the bathroom. In the mirror, I say it over and over. "Abomination. Abomination. Abomination."

Being mindful of the squeaky hinges, I open the medicine cabinet and take one of my pink razors in my hand.

I run it up and down my arm, along the veins that branch like purple rivers just under my skin. I imagine what it would be like to cut, watching my life pour out and pool on the white bathroom tile. I would wear a bunch of lace at my throat like the Highwayman, and I would suck an Otter Pop first so my lips would be red.

Staring out the window at the stars and the hills, imagining the cows and their calves sleeping in the grass, I lie on the floor and feel the tile's coolness seep into my back. I ask Iggy's God to take me into his arms when I die. I beg him to hold me the way he held Iggy, to patch up that hole in my heart. "When it happens," I whisper, "let me meet you instead of Reverend Winchell's God."

Then I press the razor to my skin, imagining I'm cutting. I move slowly, because I think the sharp edge would feel soothing slicing into my white flesh, like scratching a deep down itch. Slowly I shave the word "ABOMINATION" in capital letters on my forearm. But when I hold my arm to the light, I can't see the word mown into the almost invisible blond hair.

I bring down the razor once more, press hard. This time it marks me. A miniature bullet of blood leaks out. It hurts more than I thought, but I like the good, fresh pain. I smile a little and wander back to my bed.

When I wake the next morning, the scrape has scabbed over. What I did last night seems like part of my bad dream. I comb my hair, not because Mr. Harris said so, but because Xylia might like it. She's supposed to be back from Taos today. I can't wait to see her again.

I do have to wait though, because when I get to school, Xylia is not there. At lunch I sit with Henry.

"How's your mother?" he asks as soon as I sit down.

"Good," I say, searching the cafeteria for signs of Xylia. "She's getting better." Henry asks about Momma every day. The day after she went to the hospital, I explained why I ran away, how I just knew my momma was the one that got hurt. He said that I was psychic too. I didn't tell him that I only knew because my daddy is a monster, and it's only a matter of time before he kills somebody. I repeated Momma's lie. "She fell off a ladder," I told him and everyone who asked. Most people didn't care.

"I'm glad she's better," Henry says. "I hope you don't think this is too forward of me, but I brought her a feather too." He unzips his backpack and gives me a hawk feather, just like the one hanging over my bed. "I blessed it to help her heal."

I almost start to cry. Henry is the only one besides Iggy who seems to care that Momma got hurt. "Thank you, Henry." I hug him. Over his shoulder, I see Xylia's teacher at the corner table, grading papers. I kiss Henry's cheek. "I'll be right back, okay?"

I go to Ms. Elibee.

"Excuse me," I say.

She looks up, smiling. "What's up, Mara?"

"Do you know where Xylia Brown is?"

"She's home sick," she says. "Just a bug, I think. She should be back tomorrow." She smiles again and turns back to her papers.

For the rest of the day I worry, imagining cancer and diabetes and leprosy. I can't think about anything but Xylia, wasting away in her bed. Mr. Farley gives us an assignment. We are to write two hundred words about the light spectrum. I pick up my pencil and screw up my face, trying to think of what to say. I mean to write about light, but instead I write about Xylia. It goes:

Mara Stonebrook
Science POEM

Xylia is a rainbow. ROY G. BIV—the colors
of the light spectrum.

She has red for her lips, which are the
prettiest I've ever seen.

And she is orange, because sometimes she's
so happy, she's as bright as the sun. She
sings and shouts, and part of you wants to
hide your eyes from her shining, but you

want to be close to her too, so you can soak
up some of that warmth.

Yellow is for butter on popcorn. At the
movies, she tells the guy behind the
counter "more butter please" until the
popcorn is shriveled and wet.

G is green, for the way she is a blade of
grass, so close to the earth. So fresh and
new. She reminds me of a baby deer
sometimes, all knobby and not much
knowing or caring what anybody thinks
about her. She smells flowers and tastes
honeysuckle blossoms and closes her eyes
to feel the sunshine.

And blue is for the way she cries when she
talks about her daddy, for that hole that got
carved inside her when she had to leave
him.

Indigo is because she cares when other
people cry.

Violet is last, and that's because purple is
the color of queens, and Xylia has a gentle
dignity, a violetness about her, the ways of
a princess.

Xylia has more colors than anyone I've
ever known, even Iggy. There aren't many
people who have that many colors inside
of them. Look at my daddy. He's not real
colorful inside. And me? I'm blue. Nothing
else. Just blue.

Since I met Xylia, the whole world has
leaped into high definition. It's like I
walked from a normal movie into a 3-D.
That's saying something, considering how
shitty everything else has been. I guess
you could say Xylia Brown has saved my
life. (I'd draw an illustration, but I left my
colored pencils at home, and you can't
draw a rainbow with just a gray pencil.)

When Mr. Farley asks us to turn in our papers, I wad mine
up and shove it in my pocket.

"Where's your paper, Mara?" he asks, his eyes squinting behind those thick glasses.

"I couldn't think of anything to write about."

He opens his grade book. "Ze-ro per-cent," he says as he writes.

When school lets out, there are army recruiters in our hallways, sitting behind folding tables and smiling. They have set up giant signs with pictures of uniform-wearing men and women staring at the camera and looking heroic. BE ALL YOU CAN BE, the signs say. Some kids are talking to the recruiters, leafing through brochures, and dreaming of being all they can be. I don't stop though. I don't care about being all I can be. I just care about being with Xylia. I shove past the dreamers and run all the way to Xylia's house. When I knock, Juliette answers.

"Mara, come on in." She swings the door wide before I can even ask if Xylia's home. Her hair is done up in crazy braids, and she isn't wearing a bra. Her boobs are still perky, though, poking out through the thin fabric of her turquoise T-shirt.

"Is Xylia okay?" I ask as I step through the doorway, surprised, as I always am, at all the colors in this house.

"She's fine," Xylia's mother says. "Just a flu."

"Can I see her?"

"Of course."

I run to Xylia's room. Xylia's a lump underneath a mountain of purple blankets. She sits up when I knock on her door frame. Her hair looks like mice have been using it to nest. Her skin is sick-white. She's lovely.

"Hi," I say, feeling shy all of the sudden, even though we've spent hours and hours together now, studying and sharing secrets. "I just wanted to see how you were."

She rolls her eyes. "Thank God you're here. I was about to die of boredom."

"Brought you something." I drop my backpack on the floor and pull out a stack of books. "Just some stuff I got from the library."

She takes them, reading the title on top. "*The Complete Works of Yeats*? Yes! Did I tell you my dad loves Yeats?" I nod. "'And what rough beast, its hour come round at last / Slouches towards Bethlehem to be born?'" she snarls, curving her fingers like claws. I smile. She sorts through the books. Auden. Pound. Sexton. She quotes a line from each one off the top of her head. I watch her lips move until she catches me staring.

"You're the smartest person I know," I say.

She laughs and waves a hand dismissively. "Whatever. I know poetry. Algebra, not so much. Xs were not born to become numbers."

"What were they born for?"

"To make words, silly. Beautiful words." She falls back on the bed, clutching Yeats to her breast. I sit cross-legged on the floor in the corner.

Beautiful words like "Xylia."

"What are you doing way over there?" she asks, even though I'm only feet away. She pats the bed next to her. "Sit."

I do. Xylia leafs through the book, gasping a little when she gets to a page she really likes. Through the window I can hear a train chugging along the tracks by the river, whistling every once in a while to let little kids playing on the tracks know they're about to die.

"Hear that?" Xylia asks.

I nod.

"That's the song my heart sings." Coming from anyone else, this would sound like a bad Valentine's Day card. From her, it sounds like church bells.

"You want to ride the train?" I ask.

"I want to wander," she tells me. "Hit the tracks like the old-time hobos."

"Where?" I ask, not liking this wandering talk. I bite my lip. I can't imagine this place without Xylia. Not now. Not ever.

"Anywhere." She grins, and the tiny wrinkles around her

eyes come out for a second. It's like I'm getting a peek at what she will look like when she's old. "Everywhere." She reaches for my hand and grasps it. I might be melting. Her fingers are warm and a little sweaty. "You should come with me."

"Where?" I ask again, feeling stupid as soon as I say it.

"Everywhere!" She waves her hand in a sweeping arc. "The whole wide world. Wanna go?"

"Okay," I say. I can feel my meaty heart smiling.

Xylia's eyes are wide. "Have you ever seen the ocean?"

"No."

"You'll love it. It makes you feel so small, but in a good way." Xylia stares out the window.

"I thought you wanted to leave without me," I confess.

"No way, José. When we leave this place, we're leaving together. Maybe I'll be the train conductor, and you can sleep in one of those rich-people cars. First class. I'll make sure you have clean sheets."

My head feels light at the thought of leaving this town. For a second I think about Iggy, how he'll feel if I leave him behind, but I push it out of my head. Him and Momma were ready to leave me, after all, even if it wasn't exactly Iggy's fault. "And we'll stop to live where there's an ocean nearby. Maybe California. I'll fish every morning, make us fillets for breakfast, lunch, and dinner."

"I might get sick of seafood," Xylia warns.

"Not the way I make it, you won't. You should taste my pan-fried trout."

Xylia's whole face gets pink. "I'll wear flowers. Wreaths and wreaths of them. And when we get tired of the ocean, we'll hop another train and keep on going, all the way to Mexico."

"We'll cut open cactuses and drink the water from them. You can learn to do that fancy Mexico dancing with wild-colored dresses, and I'll buy a sombrero."

She points at my hair. "I don't think a sombrero would fit over that mess."

I feel close to Xylia, our hearts pounding out the same train-whistle song. I feel like I can tell her anything.

"You ever wanna die?" As soon as I say it, the pictures of Mexico evaporate.

Xylia breathes deep, and the train whistle blows again, far away now. I imagine myself jumping onto the tracks just before the sharp wheels cut me in half.

"Yeah," she says finally, squeezing my hand. "Sometimes I do."

"Me too."

When you strip your heart naked in front of someone, it's the same as wading to the middle of the river and getting caught in a strong current. You can't go back, so you keep on going forward. "I'm scared," I whisper. "I thought my momma was gonna die." I lean my head on her shoulder.

"I'm scared too," she says, pressing her head against mine. "Life can be hard."

"It was harder before I met you." I stare at the lines of purple throbbing beneath my skin, my own little rivers of life. The train is gone now, and it is quiet. Somewhere a crow caws.

"Henry says crows are pieces of God," I say.

"Of course they are."

The heat of her skin leaks into mine. I start to feel like I'm on fire. I never want this moment to end, and I'm afraid if I don't say something soon, it will, so I ask, "What kind of house will we have in Mexico?"

"A mansion!" she says. "Duh."

We talk about running away some more and decide that we should have purple carpet, and one of those big couches with only one arm, so we can lie down on it and eat grapes. We also decide to have a pool inside, so we can swim even when it's raining and not worry about being hit by lightning. Xylia wants a glass shower, but we disagree on that subject. I'd rather have a shower with some privacy, just in case someone walks in. She says we will have a lock on the door, but that's not much of a consolation. What if the pool cleaner is coming by but I'm in a hurry to shower, so I forget to lock the door, and what if he needs to talk to me, because there's dog hair stuck in the pool drain, and he thinks the neighbor's golden retriever may have found a way to sneak in to take a swim, and he bursts in on me? I wouldn't be able to handle that. We need a private shower.

When I say that last part, Xylia does something I will never forget. She leans right over and kisses me. Soft. On the lips. Her lips taste like strawberry lip gloss. I almost faint. Then I kiss her back. I've never felt anything like what I feel when I'm kissing Xylia. I feel perfect. Whole. I feel like I could die, and it would be okay. I feel hot everywhere. Her hands travel to my face, holding it gently as she continues to kiss me. Then all the sudden she stops and pulls away.

"Sorry," she whispers.

"No need to be sorry." I take her hand. We don't say anything for a minute, but the memory of our kiss hangs in the air, hot and thick. "My daddy would kill me if he knew I just did that."

"I'm sorry," she says again.

"No." I squeeze her hand. "I liked it. A lot." We lie there feeling all warm, like someone has spilled hot cocoa right inside us. I want to say, "I've loved you since the first time I saw you," but I don't. Still, I think she knows. Love is zinging all around us. How could she not know?

That night I dream I'm on a train with Xylia. The whistle is calling our names. We have hay in our hair, and Daddy's running behind the train, trying to catch us, his face all wrinkled and mad. But we only laugh, because he could never run that fast. We hop off in a place that has cactuses and colors and showers made of glass.

We never go home again.

CHAPTER 16

MOMMA COMES HOME FROM THE HOSPItal, and everything is like a Hallmark movie for a while. Daddy picks her flowers and even buys her a pretty necklace that must have cost tons of money, because it has a little heart-shaped diamond pendant. When Momma sees it, she smiles and says, "Oh, Russ." And I might forget all about what Daddy did if it wasn't for the fact that her smile is crooked now.

Daddy can only keep up the nice-guy routine for so long, and soon he's drinking and yelling and calling Momma names again. Momma doesn't even cry when he does it anymore. She just stares, the way Iggy did that morning after Daddy broke his brain. I imagine she's remembering that day she won Miss Teenage New Mexico. I bet she's picturing herself all covered in sequins and dancing. Or maybe she is thinking of Willy. Maybe he was handsome. Who knows? Probably was, to get someone as pretty as Momma to fall in love with him.

Daddy was handsome too, believe it or not. I see it when I look at old pictures. But now it's like all the ugly in his soul has made its way to his face. He looks kinda apeish, and it doesn't help that he doesn't take care of his teeth. Half of the ones in back have been pulled, so when he smiles, you see the gap right away. Anyway, things have gotten so bad around our house, I'd way rather be at school, mostly because Xylia's there, but partly because anything is better than being near Daddy.

So even though Mr. Farley's droning on and on, I'd rather be here than home. He pronounces "mummified" funny, enunciating each syllable. We're discussing different cultural perspectives, examining the ways in which they fall short of God's commandments.

Elijah snorts when Mr. Farley talks about the Egyptians pulling a person's brains out through his nose and says, "Brain donors." Everyone laughs. Everyone but me.

If I spoke out of turn in class, I'd be in the principal's office in two seconds flat, but Mr. Farley keeps talking like nothing happened. He calls the Egyptians fools and begins to speak of all the lies, apostasies, and half truths that have sprung from that particular part of the world. He walks to his desk and melodramatically spins the globe as he says this, trying, I guess, to make an impression. No one seems particularly impressed. A fly buzzes behind the window blinds.

Mr. Farley's undaunted. He starts to talk about Islam. He reminds us of the World Trade Center and the way it crumbled. Then he says, "This, boys and girls, this is the goal of Islam. It is a belief system based on violence. Murder in the name of Allah." I think about Daddy talking about stoning the fags and dykes and wonder how murder in the name of Jesus is any different. Islam doesn't have a corner on violence.

When class is over, the students cluster and migrate toward the cafeteria. I meet up with Henry and Xylia, and we walk together. Xylia is wearing a purple paper flower in her hair, and I reach out and touch it, just so I can touch a part of her. "That's pretty."

She smiles, and her dark eyes flash. "Thank you," she says. "How was class?"

I groan.

"That bad, huh?"

"Yeah, Mr. Farley was doing his best Reverend Winchell impression. Talking about how pissed off God is at people."

"Awesome," she says. Even when she's rolling her eyes, she's pretty.

I never want to look away from her, but I have to because Henry starts talking. "God isn't pissed off at anyone," he says, speaking in that strange way of his. "I think God's all the mystery and beauty in the universe rolled up into one word." I think about what he's saying, wishing I could feel that way too. I want to believe in that kind of God, but Reverend Winchell's pissed-off one is always in the back of my head, wanting to kill me.

The cafeteria smells like grease and bleach and dirty kids. A lot of students are already sitting at the metal tables, eating mushy peas from trays or sandwiches from baggies. We walk to the back of the line that winds through the cafeteria like a snake.

"There were some interesting parts in class," I tell Xylia. "We talked about mummies and stuff." The clattering of silverware on the tables and the chattering of voices is so loud, I wonder if she'll hear me.

"Mummies are cool," she says. "The King Tut display came to the museum in San Francisco when I was a kid. It was amazing."

"Seems crazy to go through so much trouble for a corpse, though," I say. "Dead is dead."

"I wouldn't be so sure," Henry says.

"Why wouldn't you be?" I ask.

"Well, you never know until you get there, now do you?" Xylia says. She winks. Her eyelids are painted blue and sparkly. I want to touch them.

I shove my hands into my pockets and mull it over. "Well, no, you never do," I finally admit. "I'm not saying that people's souls don't go on living. I just think it's stupid to go through so much trouble trying to keep the body, well, human. I mean, dust to dust and all that. Someday we're all going to turn into dirt. Then we'll be something else. Trees. Worms. Whatever."

"You're smart, Mara," Henry says.

"She is," Xylia says, and she smiles at me.

I'm trying to think of the perfect words to say when Hannah and Keisha saunter over.

"How!" they say to Henry in unison, raising their hands in salute.

"Piss off," Xylia says.

Hannah and Keisha don't. "Do you do rain dances?" Hannah asks, like she thinks that's clever.

I'm about to say something in Henry's defense when he surprises us all by saying, "This is how I dance." Then he moonwalks halfway across the cafeteria. Xylia starts to clap, and I join her.

"Woo, Henry!" we chorus.

"Who knew Henry could fucking dance like that?" Xylia says, laughing.

Some of the other kids start clapping too, and Henry glows, like maybe this is the best day of his whole life.

"You go, boy!" Xylia shouts, and she snaps high in the air.

After Henry moonwalks back over to us, we grab our trays and head toward a table in the corner.

"That was so cool," Xylia tells Henry.

"Thanks."

"Cool as shit," I say. I've picked up on Xylia's cussing more and more. I like it. It makes me feel strong. I don't notice Elijah walking over until he's standing right there, looking at me. His eyes are ablaze with those hell flames he always talks about.

"Mara Stonebrook, swearing is a sin."

"Yeah?" I say. "I'm pretty sure I've heard you cuss before, preacher boy."

"Me too," Henry says.

"Me three," Xylia says, yawning like Elijah is the most boring thing she has ever seen.

"So, let me get this straight." I glare at Elijah. "I can't say 'shit,' but you can stand behind me on the bus and make comments about my ass?"

"I can pretty much do whatever I want to you," Elijah says. "You're a slut."

Xylia gets mad. "Are you fucking serious? You can do anything you want to her because she's a 'slut'? What century is this anyway?"

"You're going to hell. All three of you," Elijah says.

Before I can think of an answer, Henry says, "I don't think God burns us, but if he did, I think we would be the last people he would burn."

"Sure as shit," Xylia says. "Did you see the way Henry moonwalked? You think God's gonna destroy someone who can dance like that?"

Elijah turns his angry eyes on Henry. "God doesn't base his judgments on whether or not people can *moonwalk*."

"How do you know?" I ask. "Does it specifically reference moonwalking in the Bible?"

Elijah snorts, turning his attention back to me. "I'd watch my mouth if I were you. God isn't real partial to women. I doubt he's going to cut you any breaks." He stares at me with milky-blue eyes, letting his words go one at a time like arrows.

I stand up and look straight into his ugly eyes. "How would you know?"

"My daddy says. And even if he didn't, I can read. It says

right there in the Bible, woman was taken from man and is good for nothing more than being his helpmeet."

My fingers ball themselves into fists, but I hold back. Instead of punching him, I say, "Preacher boy, I've read that book you keep talking about from cover to cover. As far as I can tell, Jesus didn't have much use for hypocrites. You're a hypocrite if I ever saw one. I'm pretty sure Jesus and me would get along just fine. Let he who is without sin cast the first stone. Remember that part?"

Elijah gets all red around his mouth. He says something about me being of the devil and idle hands being the devil's workshop. I'm really confused, trying to follow his logic, until it occurs to me that he's crazy. Like, certifiably insane, which makes a lot of sense to me. Before I can tell him so, he stomps away.

I sink back onto the bench. "I hate him. I hate his guts."

"Who gives a fuck what he thinks?" Xylia says. "Do you really believe someone so full of hate knows anything about God?"

"No," I say, but I'm not sure.

Maybe Elijah does know about God. If he's right, I'm bound for hell, and that scares the living shit out of me.

I think about it all day, so much that by the time I get home, I'm not in the mood to talk to anyone. The house is dead quiet, which means Daddy's not home yet, and Momma's sleeping. She always naps these days.

"Want a snack?" I ask Iggy.

He roars in response. He's wearing a lion mask he made from a paper plate in art class. His eyes show through two lopsided holes.

"Is that a yes?"

Iggy roars again. I'm not amused. "Whatever." I grab an apple from the fridge. "Here. Eat this."

Iggy growls and then tries to figure out how to eat his snack without moving the mask. He realizes it's impossible and lifts the plate. The sight of his freckles makes me feel guilty. I've been so busy with my new friends, I haven't had much time for him. It used to be just me and my brother. Now it's my brother and no one. "How've you been?" I ask.

Iggy takes a bite of the apple. "We made masks."

"I saw that. It's awesome."

"Mine's a lion." He plays with a piece of orange yarn, part of the lion's markedly sparse mane.

"I could tell." Iggy was always a loud chewer, but since Daddy broke him, it's ten times as bad. I fight the urge to scold him.

"What was your mask?" he asks me.

"I didn't make one, Iggy."

He scrunches up his face. It's like he almost remembers what school used to be like. "In your class, you listen to stories, right?" he asks.

"Yeah. Something like that." I'm exhausted. I want to go to my room and shut the door behind me, but Iggy practically oozes loneliness. "Hey, you wanna listen to some music?" I offer, even though the last thing I feel like doing is hanging out with my brother.

Iggy beams like I invited him to Paris. "Yes! And you know what else?"

"What?"

"We could make masks." He points to the pantry. "The plates are in there."

"All right, sport." I retrieve a stack of plates.

"We're going to make lots of masks?" Iggy asks.

"Maybe. I don't know," I say. "We'll see where the muses lead us."

"What are muses?"

"People who inspire you," I tell him. "People who make you so happy, you just have to make art to express it."

"Muses are coming over?"

I think about Xylia being my muse and mutter, "I wish."

"What?" Iggy asks.

"Nothing."

As Iggy follows me upstairs, he roars repeatedly. I try not to complain, but after roar five, it gets to me. "Iggy, quit. You're giving me a headache."

He roars again.

"Iggy!" I warn, turning to glare at him.

He brings his face close to mine and roars, sonic-boom loud this time.

"Damn it, Iggy!" I shout. The second I say it, I wish I could take it back. Behind the mask, his eyes get wet. "I'm sorry, Iggy. I just had the day from hell, you know?"

"I'm gonna go to my room." He pushes past me.

"Iggy!"

His door slams.

Staring down at the plates in my hands, I curse myself. "Mara, you bitch," I whisper. I go to Iggy's door and knock. "Iggy?" I press my ear against the door.

"Leave me alone," he sobs.

"Iggy, I'm sorry. Would you please help me with my mask?"

"No."

"Iggy, I need you. I don't even know how."

"You cut eyeholes."

"I don't know where they go."

Iggy rustles around in his room, and then the door swings

open. His mask is perched on top of his head, and his face is red. "In the middle," he says, pointing to the plate. "So you can see."

"Can you come show me?"

"This is ridiculous," he snorts.

I almost laugh. Momma says that sometimes when she's frustrated.

"You're right," I say. "Still, I could use your help. Will you?"

"One minute," Iggy sighs. He goes into his room and returns carrying a giant box of crayons. "You need these."

A few minutes later we're lying together on my rug coloring plates, and Iggy has completely forgotten about me yelling. As Xylia's Dylan CD plays, Iggy tells me about lions, his mask pulled over his face again. "They live in families called prides."

"That's cool." I give my plate red lips.

"Lions don't have lipstick," Iggy says.

"Mine's not a lion."

He scoots closer to get a better look. "What is it?"

"My muse."

"Muses have lipstick?"

"Mine does."

"That's cool," Iggy says. He tosses the lion he has been

working on aside and grabs a new plate. "I'm making a muse too." He draws a pair of crimson lips.

"Your muse looks just like mine," I tell him.

"Nah," he says, scribbling brown, curly hair onto his plate. "Yours is the color of rainbows."

I stare at my mask. "No, she's not. She has black hair and red lips."

"In you. She looks like a rainbow in your heart."

"What do you mean?" Stunned, I remember the poem I wrote about Xylia.

Iggy's see-clear-through-you eyes study me from the holes in the plate. "I don't know. I just saw colors in your heart for a minute. It was pretty." He goes back to decorating his mask. "Did you know what lion families are called?"

I grab his hand. "Iggy, stop for a second. When you saw the rainbow, did you see my muse?"

"The rainbow *was* your muse. Do you know what lion families are called?"

"What do you mean the rainbow was my muse?"

Iggy has either gone deaf or isn't interested in talking about muses anymore. "Do you know what lion families are called?" he asks again.

Giving up on getting any more information about Iggy's apparent ESP, I sigh. "Prides."

"Do you know why?" he asks.

"No, why?"

"I don't know. I asked you."

I stare at my brother, watching the sunlight falling over him, thinking there is an angel sitting beside me in a paper mask. How does he know all my secrets? "Maybe they call them that because they are proud to be related to each other."

Carefully Iggy presses his crayon into the box and chooses another. "Maybe," he agrees.

That night I lie in my bed, staring up at nothing, remembering the day. I try to decide whether Iggy really saw into my heart, or if he was just thinking about crayons. I hear Elijah's ugly words, and then I hear my own: "Damn it, Iggy!"

I toss and turn all night, feeling guilty for making my brother cry. Like he doesn't have enough problems without me making it worse. Maybe Elijah is right. Maybe I will burn in hell.

CHAPTER 17

O N THE LAST DAY OF SCHOOL WE LEARNED
that the same old water has been rushing along
our earth ever since time began. The rain that
falls from the clouds isn't God's tears after all. It's just someone's pee or old chicken soup that got sucked up into the
sky, cleaned, and dropped back down again. I'm sad to know
that heaven has never washed me, but I get a little thrill
from thinking that when I go for a swim in the river, I might
be bathing in Michelangelo's tears, the very ones he cried
when the pope locked him in the Sistine Chapel and made
him paint the story of God.

There's something about my skin that loves the feel of
water. Water is silky soft, and in one little spot of water there

could be up to twenty-thousand-billion-jillion little creatures slithering around. That's what Mr. Farley said, more or less. And he proved his point by letting me look through a microscope. I gasped out loud when I saw them—dozens of little squiggly animals sliding around and dancing. Not pretty animals, mind you. Not cats or dogs or baby deer. But ugly little things with two hundred legs and no eyes. They looked the way space creatures might look if they happened to visit our planet.

It was a good way to end the school year. It made me think that our existence is bigger than I ever even imagined. I mean, if there are worlds in drops of water, imagine what else is out there. Our earth is a tiny speck in a giant universe, just the way that water drop is a tiny speck on our earth. And how can we pretend we have everything all figured out when we're so very small, compared to all that is?

I think all this as I start to walk home from school. I could have ridden the bus, but I walk when I can these days. It's relaxing, and I don't have to worry about Elijah. Iggy does fine getting himself home.

Pretty soon, like always, I'm thinking about Xylia. I worry that I won't be able to see her every day anymore. Her momma has all sorts of summer trips planned, and Daddy says I can't join her for any of them because he needs my help around the farm. Also, she will be visiting her dad for a while.

For the first time ever I'm sad that summer vacation is here. I already feel the loss of her. She and her momma left this afternoon to go to Albuquerque and see a production of *Angels in America*, which is apparently a play about a gay man dying of AIDS. It sounds depressing, but Xylia saw it once. She told me I would like it and I should really, really, really ask my parents if I could come. "There's this part where an angel comes down from the ceiling!" she said. "It's crazy beautiful." I told her I couldn't because Iggy was graduating. I didn't tell her the part about my daddy maybe killing me if I asked to go see a play about gay people.

"Mara!"

I hear Henry's voice behind me. I stop and wait, watching a tiny finch hop from branch to branch overhead.

"I just wanted to say good-bye," Henry says out of breath when he catches up with me.

"I thought you were gone," I say. He's going to stay on the reservation with his aunt for the summer.

"Not yet."

"You're lucky you get a fun vacation." I kick at a pebble, jealous that everyone but me is going somewhere.

"You've obviously never been to the res."

"Does it suck?"

Henry thinks about my question before he answers. Henry always thinks before he speaks. I like that about him. "No. It's slow paced, but at least I won't get bleached there. Maybe I can get some clothes without freckles." He smiles.

"You wouldn't be you without freckled clothes," I say, laughing. "When are you leaving?"

"Not for a couple of weeks," he says. "But I wanted to say good-bye just in case I didn't see you again."

"Well, good-bye," I say. "I hope you have the best summer ever."

"Frankly, that wouldn't take much. Summers haven't always been kind to me."

I think back to last summer, to Iggy's broken brain. "Me either," I say.

I hug Henry good-bye, but he doesn't leave. Instead he walks me all the way home. We don't say much. That's one thing I like about me and Henry. We can be quiet, and it doesn't feel weird. It's like we both know what the other one is thinking without saying anything. When we get to my doorstep, I get nervous because I wonder if he's going to ask to come inside. I can't say yes. No way will Daddy be okay with a heathen being in the house. I mean, my birthday was one thing, but this is quite another. Thankfully, Henry doesn't ask.

"Well, catch you on the flip side, Mara," he says.

I wonder where he heard that. "Adios, amigo."

Henry wanders off down the road, getting tinier and tinier. I sit on the porch and watch until he's gone, making sure he's not coming back to piss Daddy off.

When I finally go inside, Iggy's skipping around the kitchen, wearing Daddy's best suit, singing, "No more school, no more books, no more teacher's dirty looks." Seeing him in Daddy's clothes makes me realize how big he's gotten. The polyester pants are too short, and his arms stick out from under the jacket sleeves. Still, he looks good. His hair's gelled back, and his eyes are shining, the way they do when he's happy.

"I'm gonna be a graduate, Momma," he says. He pronounces "graduate" wrong, like a verb instead of a noun. Grad-u-eight.

Momma's looking at her reflection in a window, patting her hair. "That's right, Iggy." She says this funny, out of the side of her mouth. Since she got home from the hospital, she says everything out of the side of her mouth. She's still pretty though, when she isn't talking.

Daddy shakes his head and flaps the newspaper he's holding. I wonder why he's still sitting at the table, not gussied up and ready to go like Momma and Iggy, but I don't ask.

"Don't these kids have to pass some tests or something before they can graduate?" he laments.

Momma turns away from her reflection and walks to Daddy's side. "He was special ed, honey," she whispers, as if Iggy doesn't know already that he was special ed.

"Special ed," Iggy repeats. "I was special ed, Daddy."

Daddy glares and goes back to his paper. "These goddamn terrorists blew up another bus full of goddamn innocent children."

"Goddamn terrorists," Iggy repeats.

"Don't swear, Iggy," Momma says, reaching down to adjust her sandal strap.

"He can goddamn swear about the goddamn terrorists if he wants to goddamn swear about the goddamn terrorists." Daddy pounds the table with his palm for emphasis.

"I know, honey," Momma says. She keeps playing with her sandals, showing that she isn't listening at all. The hairs on the back of my neck prickle, and I wait for Daddy to do something awful. He doesn't, though.

"Mara, go get dressed," Momma tells me. "We have to leave in twenty minutes." I do. I'm not excited about wearing a dress, but I'll do it for Iggy. I pick the yellow one I wore on my birthday because it reminds of me of Xylia. I run my fingers through my hair and put on some lip gloss. I look pretty. I wish Xylia would be there to see me, but she'll be off watching angels come down from ceilings.

As I walk into the kitchen, Momma click-clacks to the fridge and pulls out the pie she made for the post-graduation potluck. It's cherry with little hearts carved into the crust. She sniffs the pie and smiles.

"I want some pie, Momma," Iggy whines.

"It's for the graduation, sport."

"I'm ready, Momma," I say.

"Good." She closes the fridge and stands there, staring pointedly at Daddy. When he doesn't look up, she says, "Honey, we should be going."

"What are you talking about?" He acts like this is the first time he's heard about Iggy's graduation, even though we sent out invitations to everyone from church months ago. Inside each monogrammed envelope was a smiling picture of slick-haired Iggy, his chin resting awkwardly on his fist. A big version of that picture hangs on the living room wall. There's no way Daddy could've forgotten.

"Iggy's graduation," Momma says. "We have to be there an hour early so he can get ready."

"Oh," Daddy says. He seems irritated. He flips to the sports section. "Go ahead without me. I'll catch up."

Momma opens her mouth to argue. The stiffness in her

jaw must remind her that she shouldn't talk back, because she closes it again. When we walk out the door, Daddy's still reading his paper.

Iggy and me pile into the back of Momma's green car, which still smells new because she almost never drives it. Iggy reaches toward the pie on the seat beside him. "I want pie, Momma."

Momma slaps at his hand. "I said not now. Later." She uses the rearview mirror to apply a fresh coat of candy-apple lipstick. After a minute she must feel bad for being snippy because she smiles and says, "Doesn't anyone want to ride up front with me?" She snaps the cap on the lipstick and drops it in her purse.

"I do!" Iggy says. Instead of getting out and going around the car, he flails his way over the front seat, kicking me in the head.

"Ow," I yell.

"Oh, Mara, stop being dramatic." Momma blots her lipstick with a tissue, then reaches over and pats Iggy on the knee. "You're the handsomest graduate I ever saw."

I look at him. She's right. All slicked up like he is, Iggy does look kind of handsome. If he'd keep his mouth shut, he might pass for normal. I rub my head and glare into the rearview mirror. No one notices. As Momma starts the car and pulls down the driveway, Iggy keeps singing about no more teacher's dirty looks.

"That's enough Iggy," Momma finally says. Bits of gravel knock against the bottom of the car.

"Sorry." Iggy looks down.

"Oh, honey, *I'm* sorry," Momma says, rumpling his hair. "You sing all you want. It's your graduation day, for God's sake."

Iggy grins. "NO MORE TEACHER'S DIRTY LOOKS!" he shouts.

Momma winces, but she doesn't say anything.

When we get to the gym, everyone from school is there, looking all shiny and new. There's a stage where a basketball hoop usually stands, right in front of the painting of our mascot, the mighty fighting rattlesnake, who has crooked eyes and a tongue that looks too big for his head. Rows of chairs are set in front for the parents of the graduates.

Momma presses Iggy's cap and gown into his hands. "Go make me proud," she says.

"No more teacher's dirty looks!" Iggy sings as he runs off to his classroom to get ready.

As Momma leads me to a place up front, I crane my neck, looking for Daddy. He's nowhere. Momma's watching too. Staring at the door, she drops her purse on a folding chair next to her. Her knee jostles up and down, up and down.

"He'll be here soon enough, Momma," I tell her, even

though I'm not sure that's true. I wonder if Daddy could be bad enough to miss Iggy's graduation. Who knows?

It looks like he can be that bad, because when Principal Harris comes to the lectern to say an opening prayer, the chair beside Momma is still empty. She blinks a lot, but her eyes get red and teary anyway. I reach out and grab her hand.

"Maybe his truck wouldn't start," I whisper.

She nods and manages a weak little smile. The high school band starts playing *Pomp and Circumstance*, and the graduates file in, one by one. There are eleven of them. Iggy's near the end. Stonebrooks are always at the end. Still, he marches proudly down the aisle, wearing his cap and gown, beaming.

"Woo, Iggy!" I shriek as he passes. He looks over, grinning until he sees the empty chair by Momma. Then his face goes flat like a deflated tire.

"Woo, Iggy!" Momma echoes, raising her fist like she's at a political rally. "Iggy is the best boy ever!" Someone behind us snickers.

I've never been to a graduation before, but I figure out right away that I never want to go to another one again. Principal Harris drones on and on about the future and dreams and sunrises and crap like that. Then the valedictorian does the same thing. Then the valedictorian runner-up starts in about his family and God. Then we get the mayor, who's the keynote speaker and is only interesting when he starts to choke on a gob of spit. He recovers quickly though, and sets in again about hope. Finally, Principal Harris introduces the graduates. He tells us something about every one of them. Kitty Addison, for instance, is interested in becoming an ER nurse. Dave Bass really does like to fish. Bass. Fish. Ha! Isn't that funny? No, it's not. A million years later, Mr. Harris gets to Iggy.

"Iggy Stonebrook," he calls, and Iggy shuffles to the stage, stopping at the edge of the steps to look around, like he's not sure if he's really allowed to go up or not. "Come on, son," Principal Harris calls, and everyone laughs. Iggy laughs too and ascends the stairs. "Iggy," Principal Harris calls, "may end up being one of our heroes."

I'm surprised to hear this. I didn't know our principal thought of him so highly. "Iggy," he says, clapping Iggy on the shoulder, "has been speaking to recruiters about serving in our armed forces."

The whole place erupts into applause. I feel like somebody punched me in the gut. I glance over at Momma, and she looks like she feels the same way. Her face is pale.

"What?" I whisper.

Momma shakes her head. "I don't know. There must be some mistake." Her fingers are clamped around her purse strap. Her knuckles are white.

Iggy saunters to his seat with his paper, and Principal Harris babbles on. I don't hear anything else though. I keep thinking about what Principal Harris said. I keep remembering those recruiting tables set up in the hallways. I keep wondering who Iggy talked to those days I was too busy to walk him to the bus.

When the graduation is over, Iggy comes clomping over, laughing out loud. "I'm a graduate, Momma," he says. He says "graduate" wrong again. Momma hugs him close.

"Iggy," she says. "Baby, what did they mean about you maybe volunteering to serve in the armed forces?"

"I'm gonna be all I can be," Iggy says, still smiling.

"You most certainly are not," she whispers, pulling away from Iggy and grabbing his shoulders. She shakes him. "You have no idea what you're talking about." People stare.

I don't know why, but my ears start to ring, and I feel dizzy. I grab the back of a chair. "It's okay, Momma," I say. "They can't make Iggy go, no matter what he signs. They can't make someone like him go to a war."

Iggy's face gets mad. "I can too go," he says. "I can be all I can be." His eyes are squinty, like he might cry too.

"Don't worry." I put my hand on Momma's and squeeze. "They can't make him go."

Iggy's lip quivers.

Momma looks at the ground. "At least he'd be safe if he went."

I think she must be losing her mind. Does she know people get shot in wars? The dizziness goes away, and I let go of the chair. "They can't make him go." I say it louder this time.

Momma's eyes are still teary, but she smiles her poster-girl smile. "Let's go get some pie, graduate," she lilts, rumpling Iggy's hair.

At the mention of pie, Iggy forgets all about being all he can be.

We wait in line for refreshments. Looking at the rows and rows of pies and cakes and platters of cookies, Iggy grins. The whole room smells like sugar. I fill my plate high. So does Iggy. Momma skips the food and goes right for the punch. When we sit at a table, she reaches into her purse and pulls out a silver flask.

That dizzy feeling comes back. "Momma, no," I whisper.

She smiles. "Just a smidge," she says, holding her cup under the table. I watch as clear liquid sloshes from her flask into her punch. She takes a big gulp. I can already smell the sour, drunk smell coming from the cup. Soon it will be all over Momma, oozing from her pores.

Iggy wolfs down his goodies, but I can't touch mine. My

stomach starts to hurt, and when Momma goes back to the line to refill her glass, I almost start to cry. I think about stealing the flask from her purse, but it won't do any good. She'll know I took it and take it back.

Iggy goes for seconds. "Hurry up and finish," I tell him as he sits down with more pie.

"I'm hungry," he says.

"Hurry up!"

He doesn't hurry, and Momma fills her cup twice more.

"Can we go?" I keep asking.

"Not until Iggy is full," Momma says.

Finally he shoves the last bit of cookie into his mouth.

"Now?" I ask.

"I suppose," Momma says, slurring. I wonder if she should drive, but how else will we get home before she makes an ass of herself in front of God and everyone? She wobbles on her way to the car, but she drives better than I thought she would. She only swerves twice, and by the time she starts to cry, we're almost home anyway.

"It's okay, Momma," I say, patting her arm.

"Nothing is fucking okay," she spits back. "You think those army men won't take whatever they can get? You don't think they'll take my baby from me? Don't you see, Mara? He's dead."

Momma's words hang heavy in the air, like napalm. We're all poisoned. Next to me, Iggy starts to cry. "I'm gonna be all I can be," he says, rocking.

When we walk into the living room, Daddy's slumped on the couch watching sitcom reruns, wearing the same thing as when we left. Momma trips into the living room, crying big, gulping sobs. Daddy ignores them though, doesn't even look at her. He just keeps shoveling ice cream into his mouth and staring at the television. I expect Momma to admit defeat and retreat to the bedroom. Instead she stumbles over to Daddy and plants herself between him and the TV. He moves his head so he can see around her.

"Where the hell were you?" Momma screams. "Where the hell have you been?"

I almost pee, I'm so scared. I stare at Daddy, waiting for him to explode. He doesn't.

"Iggy volunteered to join the goddamn army!" she shouts.

Daddy snorts. "That moron? He can't even shoot a fucking rabbit without blubbering. No United States Army is gonna want his sorry ass."

The sitcom family jokes about the ozone layer. Momma's mouth hangs a little, like Daddy punched her in the face again. Iggy runs upstairs.

CHAPTER 18

WHEN I WAS LITTLE, I LIVED FOR summer vacation. Now I'd give my right leg for it to be over. It's so hot in the house, I'm constantly damp with sweat. When I go outside, gnats eat me alive. Cicadas buzz angrily all day, and it gives me a headache. Mostly I mope around missing Xylia, wishing it was September.

Iggy isn't any happier. It turns out Daddy was right. Iggy isn't going to be all he can be. Not even close. His test results render him unfit for military service, and when Momma tells him what the letter he gets in the mail means, he starts to cry. For a few weeks he silently does chores around the farm, his shoulders stooped, but finally he goes to Momma and says, "I wanna get a job, Momma."

Me and Momma are sitting at the kitchen table scrapbooking old photos when he says it. Momma likes to scrapbook our memories. I don't like it so much, but I have some pictures of Xylia and me and Henry, so I'm decorating them with hearts.

"Did you hear me, Momma?" Iggy asks. He's wearing his old overalls, and his hands are buried deep in the pockets. "I want a job."

Momma's eyebrows go up. "A job?" she says, like he has suggested he wants a pet alien. She sets down the page she's scrapbooking, a montage of me and Iggy when we were little. Sitting on the porch eating ice pops, swinging on a tire swing, holding puppies.

"Yeah," Iggy says. "I saw a sign on the door at the grocery store. They need baggers. I wanna be a bagger."

His shoulders are stooped when he says it. I think about how tall he looked when he said he was gonna be all he could be. He went from that to wanting to be a bagger. For a minute I feel kinda bad about him not being able to join the army, but then I think about the way people die when they go to war, and I decide bagging groceries is better than dying.

Iggy has to beg, but Momma finally gives in and takes him to the store, which leaves me alone with my photos. I carry them to my room, press them into my favorite book, the one that has "The Highwayman," and then head down to the river. I don't grab my pole. I don't want to fish today. I just gotta move. Do something. Anything.

As I walk, the sky drips with buttery sunlight. Red birds sing like they don't have a care in the world. When I reach the river, willows are dipping their shimmering green fingers in the water. Everything is shiny and bright.

I sit on the riverbank, watching a tiny finch twitter around. I think about Xylia kissing me, and for some reason I wanna cry—not in a bad way, in a good, I-don't-know-what-else-to-do way. Still, sometimes, people walk up on you when you're sitting by the river, and I sure don't want anyone to see me cry.

I try to keep the tears in my head. My trick is I find something round to stare at, like a plate or a clock or a quarter. I concentrate hard on the roundness, let my eyes wander around and around the edges of it. For reasons I can't explain, it makes the tears dry up. It doesn't work with squares or triangles, only circles. So I find a round nest in a tree, and the tears stay away.

After that I just lie by the river with my eyes closed, feeling the cool mud soak into my back, thinking about me and Xylia snuggling close on her bed, making plans to visit Mexico. Xylia's lips were bright red that day, begging to be kissed.

I glance up at the wispy clouds. In the movies men and ladies kiss and sail off into the clouds to live happily ever after. I wouldn't mind a happily-ever-after. I wouldn't mind slipping off with Xylia one bit.

I close my eyes again, deciding to practice my kissing so that next time Xylia kisses me, I'll be ready. I move my palm toward my face, slowly. I part my lips and press them against my hand.

This is *not* what kissing Xylia felt like. My hand tastes like dirt, and the calluses scratch my lips. There's no softness. It's more like smashing my nose and mouth against the truck window to make blowfish faces.

It occurs to me just how foolish I must look, lying here among the river grasses, making out with my own hand. I start up, look around. A turquoise butterfly hovers over my head. I'm so busy watching her that I am stunned when Xylia pops out of the bushes. My insides catch fire. I wonder if I summoned her with my thoughts.

"There you are," she says. I blush, wondering if she saw me kissing my hand.

"And there you are," I say back. "How was *Angels in America?*"

"Oh my God," she says, plopping down beside me. "I cried so fucking hard. I mean, I think my mom thought she was gonna have to take me to a mental hospital or something."

I laugh. "That makes me kinda glad I didn't go."

"No way." She slaps me on the arm playfully. "It would have been better if you were there. We could have had nervous breakdowns together."

"Sounds like fun," I say.

"Anything's fun with you."

"Yeah, well, I was a wreck without you. That's for sure," I say. She puts her hand over mine, and I get all nervous. "Was the angel pretty?" I ask, too fast.

"Pretty isn't even the word. I mean, she had really short hair, like a boy. Not what you'd expect an angel to look like, right?"

"Right."

"But, wow, she was gorgeous. She had this voice that just made your guts boil."

"Then I'm definitely glad I didn't go," I joke.

Xylia kisses me on the cheek. My skin burns. "I missed you," she says.

"I missed you too."

"I went to your house. Your mom said you must've gone fishing."

"Naw. Just wanted to look at the water." I don't know what else to say, and besides, my throat is so tight, I can't talk. I stare into the clear, cool water, watching long-legged water bugs dance on its surface.

Mara, you've got to do something about this. You can't love like this for too much longer without saying it, or your heart will explode.

"I'm glad you're here," I finally manage. Xylia squeezes my hand.

"Hello," a voice behind us says. It's Henry, with his hair combed slick and his freckled shirt tucked in.

Xylia takes her hand away. So much for gladness.

"Henry," I say. I've never been more disappointed to see anyone. "I thought you were at the reservation."

"Not until next week." He grins. "How's the fishing?"

I shrug my shoulders. "I'm not fishing."

"My mom wants me to learn to fish," Xylia announces. "Fish oils are good for your heart." She stands.

"You have a pole?" Henry asks.

"No." Xylia yawns and arches her back, stretching like a cat.

"You can use mine," Henry offers.

I hate Henry.

Before I can even wipe the mud off my butt, Henry has

Xylia all set up with his pole. She's giggling her head off because she doesn't know how to hold the stupid thing. Henry's laughing too.

"Just one hand in front of the other," he says, and he slips around behind her. What's he doing? He knows Xylia and me are in love.

"Here," he says, placing her hands on the pole, "just like that." I can see Xylia's white skin peeking out under his brown. "Now put your finger on the line, and jerk back over your shoulder." Henry yanks the pole. It looks like he's teaching Xylia to dance, they move so smooth together, two sets of arms and legs working like they're all part of the same creature. The line flies over Henry's head. Xylia's hook lands in a tree.

"Oh, for God's sake," I shout. I jump up and march over to the tree, swearing all the way. "I suppose I'll have to scrape myself up climbing this stupid tree because the two of you are too gooey eyed to even cast straight."

I'm a gifted tree climber. When I was little, I came up with excuses to conquer the branches and find myself look- ing down on the itty-bitty world, like I was an angel in heaven or even God himself. So it won't be much trouble for me to shinny up this trunk and rescue Xylia's hook. But it's the principle of the thing.

I wrap my arms and knees around the trunk and scoot myself toward the sky, keeping my head turned to glare at Xylia and Henry, who are standing on the ground looking bewildered.

"You okay?" Xylia calls out. She takes a step away from Henry. "I didn't mean to cast it up there."

She's so wide-eyed and worried, I can't stay mad. "It's cool," I say, which loosens them up. I crawl out to the limb where the hook is stuck and yank it free from the leaves. "Bombs away!" I shout, dropping the hook.

"Well, Mara," Henry says when I climb down, "we wouldn't do much fishing today were it not for you." He gives me a one-armed hug.

Xylia grins, showing me all her perfect teeth. "Thank you," she says. "I would've killed myself trying to climb that tree. How'd you do that?"

I feel like I'm Tiger Woods being interviewed after a big tournament. I answer the way I think he might answer. A modest bowing of the head, but with my shoulders straight to let people see I know how great I am, only I'm too modest to say so.

"It's nothing," I say. "It comes easy to me."

Xylia laughs that sweet, musical, belly laugh.

We're all quiet for a minute. Finally, figuring someone has

to break the silence, I nod at the water and say, "I'm guessing Paul Bunyan's out there today."

"Paul Bunyan?" Xylia asks. "With the blue ox?"

"Paul Bunyan's a fish." I put my hand on her elbow instructively. "Every once and a while, someone gets a glimpse of him. He's as huge as a whale, and he eats the bait right off of people's hooks without them ever even knowing he was there. He's that smart. Iggy and me have been trying to catch him since we learned to walk."

"Maybe Xylia will have beginner's luck and catch him," Henry says, and I consider slapping him. Why's he even here? Why'd he go through all the trouble of saying good-bye to me on the last day of school if he was just going to stalk me at the river?

After taking off our shoes, we sit on a log—Henry, then Xylia, then me. The bark scratches our behinds, but the mud feels cool and gooshy between our toes.

Henry fishes first. It's not long before he gets a nibble. He whoops, and me and Xylia jump up and start floundering about, shouting advice.

"Get the net!" I say.

"Hang on to him! He seems big!" Xylia hollers.

"Jerk it hard!" I yell. "Make sure the hook is set!"

"He's a fighter!" Henry calls over his shoulder, his arms

taut with the effort of wrestling the fish. Xylia dances from one foot to the other, clapping her hands earnestly, with that look fathers of football players wear when their sons are about to make a touchdown.

"Do you think it's Paul Bunyan?" she cries.

"No," I snap.

Henry reels in the last of his line. His prize flops on the end of the hook, just beneath the surface of the water.

"He's a whopper all right!" I shout, raising the net over my head. Henry's face goes from frenzied to flat.

"Awww," he says, letting his air out slowly.

"It's a toilet seat," Xylia squeals, doubling over.

Pretty soon we're all on our backs on the bank, roaring about how that toilet seat put up a good struggle all right.

Xylia sits up, gasping. "He's a fighter!" she cries, doing her best Henry imitation.

We all collapse again. I point at Xylia. "You were hopping around like a first grader locked out of the bathroom!"

"Yeah, well you practically broke your neck trying to get your hands on that net!" Xylia laughs so hard she snorts. Me and Henry snort back at her, poking fun a bit, and that's when things get ugly. Suddenly Xylia is on top of us.

"Watch it," Henry roars, "you'll mess up your pretty hair."

"I don't care about my fucking hair," Xylia cries, feigning fury.

"She doesn't care about her fucking hair," I echo, grinning and slapping Henry on the back, but no one notices me. I'm no longer a part of this wrestling match. After a few more feeble attacks, I sit up and watch.

It hurts to see Xylia and Henry tumbling over each other in the mud, laughing hard, trying to one up each other's best moves. Nobody wins. They both just slow down, then stop, like those wind-up dancing monkeys in old movies. They lie there panting, staring at the changing clouds. I lie beside them. Xylia is close enough that I can reach out and touch her hand, but I don't. She might as well be on another continent. I find a cloud that's round and try not to cry.

"Shall we go in for a swim?" Henry finally says.

I'm in. Anything is better than lying around watching Henry and Xylia get cozy. "What are we supposed to do?" I ask. "Go swimming in our clothes? These pants are so heavy, I'll drown if the current catches them."

"We swam in our clothes before," Xylia says.

"Yeah, well, I wasn't wearing these pants."

"How about you and I go behind those trees and strip down?" Xylia suggests. "Henry can close his eyes while we jump in. Then we'll turn our backs when he comes in."

My belly gets hot, and I think maybe I won't be able to speak, but I manage to say, "It sounds like a good idea to me."

Henry scrunches his eyes shut, and me and Xylia pick our way into the bushes. She's tough. She doesn't try to stop to slide on her shoes, which makes me admire her.

"You must have good calluses," I say.

"Yeah, dancers have tough feet."

"I do too, but not from dancing. I just like to go barefoot."

Xylia grabs my hand. "That's why I love you."

The word "love" echoes in my head. Is she trying to tell me she's *in* love with me? I want to say the perfect thing back, but instead, I blurt out, "Nice shirt." My face gets warm. I feel like an idiot. She talked about feelings. I talked about clothes. She's wearing a silky getup covered with wild splotches in every color of the rainbow.

Xylia doesn't seem to think I'm dumb. "Thanks. My dad gave it to me. He's always buying things for me."

"It's pretty," I say.

She shrugs. "Used to be. It's old. I still like it though. It reminds me of him."

I think about how much I hate the presents my daddy buys me. Xylia unbuttons the top button on her blouse.

"He used to cook, too. Did I tell you that?" she says.

Shaking my head, I pull my T-shirt off, suddenly

embarrassed of my dingy, gray bra. Xylia doesn't seem to notice. She unbuttons more, and I see a bit of red lace. I catch my breath.

"You know what I did once?" she says, slipping out of her blouse and draping it over a branch. She's wearing only a bra and her jeans and her skin, and my heart starts to bang inside me. I look away and I tell her of course I don't know what she did, since she hasn't told me the story.

"My dad was trying to teach me to cook, right? So I decided to surprise him by making corn bread, but I misread the recipe. I put in a cup of baking soda instead of a teaspoon. It was the prettiest corn bread I'd ever seen, all swollen and beautiful." When she says that, I can't help but look at the gentle swell of her belly. She unbuttons her jeans. "When dinner came, my dad kept saying over and over how delicious it looked, and then he bit into it. You should've seen his face. His eyes got huge. I could actually see his throat jerk like he was going to puke. But instead of spitting it out, he put on this big smile and swallowed it, composing some god-awful poem about heaven's fruit. I almost believed him, until I tried it myself. The corn bread was disgusting." Laughing, she wiggles out of her jeans. Her panties match her bra.

I'm composing god-awful poems about heaven's fruit too. "Your dad sounds so awesome," I say. I slide my jeans down around my feet. My blue cotton underwear doesn't match my bra, and looking at Xylia's lean legs, I feel suddenly chunky. I cross my arms in front of me. A bird says something. Xylia and me are quiet for so long, my stomach starts to hurt. Xylia breaks the silence.

"Holy shit, you have big knockers!"

I cover my boobs, which are popping out over the top of my bra.

"I'm sorry," she says. "That came out wrong. I mean, they're pretty. I wouldn't be ashamed of them if I were you." She puts her arms out to the sides like she's about to fly away. "Look at my chest," she says. "I look like a boy. The guys at home called me the pirate's dream."

"The pirate's dream?" I ask, staring at the pink of her nipples showing through the flimsy lace of her bra.

"Yeah, a sunken chest," she says.

We both laugh, standing side by side and sticking out our boobs.

"I guess no matter what you have in the boobs department, you'll always wish for something different," I say.

Xylia nods. "I guess so."

"Sometimes it stinks being a girl," I say.

"Oh, I don't know," says Xylia, and she starts toward the swimming hole. "Being a girl has its good points."

"Like what?" I ask, following.

"Well," she says, "you get to have babies for one thing."

"That's a good thing? I've seen animals have babies, and it didn't seem like too much fun if you ask me."

Xylia is quiet for a minute after that. "Yeah, but can you imagine having a little person grow inside you?" she says. "My cousin had a baby, and she said she never felt so close to anyone. She named her Sarah."

"Pretty name," I say.

"Yep," Xylia says. "I'm going to name my baby something different though."

"Like what?"

"Oh, I don't know. A name no one else has, like mine. Maybe Rapunzel. Delilah. Clementine." She starts to sing "Oh My Darlin' Clementine." She has a voice so pretty, it cuts into your soul. When she says "you are lost and gone forever," I almost break down right there, thinking about that poor old miner forty-niner finding his daughter blowing bubbles soft and fine.

At the edge of the swimming hole, Xylia pulls out her hairpins, letting her hair fall around her shoulders like a shiny black cape. She's the prettiest thing I've ever seen with the sunlight on her skin and her sleek curves showing through the red lace. I'm afraid she'll see me staring, so I scream, "Watch out, rainbow trout! Here we come!" I make a mad dash for the jumping rock where me and Iggy always dive in.

The cool water stings my skin as I plunge under, rushing up my nose. But I like the feeling. I can squint my eyes and see the rocks in the riverbed and the green, slimy plants swaying back and forth in the current. I'm almost sure I see a fish swim by. Xylia plunges in beside me. Together, we kick to the surface for air.

"Henry!" Xylia yells. "Come on in. The water's fine!" Me and Xylia turn away from the jumping rock, squeezing our eyes shut and licking the water from our lips, waiting to hear the sound of Henry's feet slapping toward us. We don't wait long.

Before we have time to dive for cover, Henry comes bounding over the edge of the rock. I open my eyes just in time to see him career over my head, flapping his arms and legs, wearing a look of terror. He lands feet first and sinks like a frying pan in dish water.

"Henry?" Xylia calls out, staring at the ripples he left on the surface. "Can he swim?" she asks me after a minute.

"Like a guppy," I say, even though I don't know if he can swim or not.

"What's taking him so long then?"

I shrug. "Who knows? He's probably petting a turtle under there or something."

"A turtle?" she repeats.

I flip over on my back and bob around a little, paddling my feet just enough to stay afloat.

"Sure," I say. "That's the way he is. Haven't you heard him go on about animals?"

Xylia swims toward the place where Henry disappeared and sticks her head under the water. I can see bubbles popping out behind her head, and I start thinking about Darlin' Clementine. Bubbles are a sign of life, not death. Maybe the songwriters made a mistake. Maybe Clementine survived after all. Maybe her miner forty-niner father saw the bubbles and pulled her out and gave her mouth-to-mouth resuscitation. For a moment, when the songwriter passed by, she might've looked dead, but after he walked away, she could've coughed and sputtered out a mouthful of water. She could've been alive. Her daddy would've hugged her and made her up a pan of corn bread and beans to celebrate, and that would've been that. They all learned a lesson from her almost drowning, and from then on they fed the ducklings together, with life preservers nearby, just in case. I like my ending better.

Xylia comes up for air. "Hasn't he been under there too long?"

I'm a little concerned, but I'm not quite ready to say it. "Would you stop your worrying? You sound like my momma. He'll come up when he's ready."

Which turns out to be right about then. Henry's head breaks the surface of the water just in front of Xylia. She jumps at the shock, but then relief washes over her face.

"I thought you drowned," she scolds.

"Hoped so anyway," I mutter.

"What?" asks Henry, clearing out his ears with his finger.

"Nothing," I say.

We swim and swim. When there's only one drop of energy left in us, we use it to scramble up the riverbank and stare at the setting sun. We don't have what it takes to worry about our modesty anymore. Xylia quotes poetry, something about a sunset and a style and a dominee, as the sun sinks into the horizon.

"What in the hell is a dominee?" I ask.

She says she doesn't know, but her dad used to always quote that verse to say good-bye to the day.

"Speaking of fathers, I should go," Henry says, and he stands. "My father expects me home before nightfall."

My father expects me home before nightfall too, but I don't say anything. Soon Henry is gone, and it's just me and Xylia lying by the river in our undies. I do something then, the bravest thing I have ever done. I reach out and grab her hand.

"Xylia," I say. The red in the sunset seems to get redder at the sound of her name.

"Yeah?" she asks, squeezing my hand.

"I gotta tell you something."

"What?" Xylia turns her head to look at me. I stare into her eyes, thinking I understand how much the Highwayman loved the landlord's black-eyed daughter. I'd get shot to avenge Xylia any day of the week.

"Xylia, I think I love you," I whisper.

She smiles. "Me too," she whispers back. She kisses me again. Gently. Her lips taste like the river.

It's not like when I practiced kissing with my hand. I know just what to do. I know because my body tells me. My hands know how to run themselves through Xylia's hair, thinking its wetness is the most beautiful thing in the world. My lips know how to pull away from her mouth and move along her neck, tasting the sweet softness of her skin. My eyes know when to close, so I can feel the cool sensation of her hands sweeping along my back, and when to open, so I can see her eyes burning with the same fire that is inside me. I know when to roll on top of her and look down, loving her more than I ever knew I could love anything. She gazes back up at me. Her lips are opened a little, as if they're asking a question. "Do you really love me?" she seems to be saying, and I answer with a kiss, a kiss that is hard and full of all the longing I've felt since the first time I saw her. I break away and say it out loud again. "Xylia, I love you."

"Mara, I love you too."

I'm the luckiest girl alive. It makes me want to cry. It makes me want to melt into Xylia and become one person. I want to spend the rest of my life touching her, tasting her, smelling her.

We kiss and kiss, so long and hard that we don't hear the bushes rustling. We don't notice Elijah Winchell, his eyes burning with that ugly fire, until a light flashes in our faces.

I open my eyes, and Elijah is standing over us with his cell phone. A bomb goes off inside my head. I cover my boobs and roll away from Xylia. He turns the phone so I can see the picture he took of me and Xylia, half naked, making out.

It's like Elijah reads my mind. "Fucking abominations."

"Don't tell. Elijah, please," I say, wanting to cry, imagining what my daddy will do if he finds out.

"You fucking slutty dykes," he says. Panic takes hold of me.

I sit up and grab for his legs. He jumps back.

"Give me the phone!" I scream. I remember the day

Daddy broke Iggy's brain. I remember Momma's shattered jaw. I imagine my face being on the receiving end of a two-by-four. "Please, Elijah!"

Elijah laughs. I jump to my feet and lunge for the phone, but he holds it over his head, just out of my grasp.

"What will you give me?"

"What?" I ask.

"In exchange for the phone, what will you give me?"

"I don't know." I start to cry. "What do you want? I don't have any money."

"Mara," Xylia says behind me, "let him go. Who cares what he thinks?"

"My daddy," I yell. "My daddy cares. My daddy will kill me, Xylia. For real. You don't understand."

"Show me your tits," Elijah says.

I look at him, astonished, thinking he must be joking. He's not joking. "Take off your bra," he orders.

Suddenly Xylia is beside me. "Screw that, you fucking piece of shit. Tell whoever you want. Mara Stonebrook and I love each other. Who cares?"

"Oh, I'll tell," Elijah promises. "I'll tell the whole fucking world."

He turns and walks into the woods.

"Elijah, wait!" I scramble after him.

Xylia grabs my arm. "Let him go, baby," she whispers. *Baby*. She called me baby. She pulls me to her and wraps her arms around me. "I've got you."

Elijah trips away through the woods. Burying my face in her cool hair, I cry and cry and cry.

CHAPTER 19

FOR WEEKS AFTER ELIJAH TAKES THE PICTURE, I
can't sleep. I wait up all night, expecting that any
minute Daddy will walk through my door and kill me
for being an abomination. But Elijah must not have kept his
promise, because nothing happens. No one even looks at me
funny in church.

I go to Xylia's one day, and we lie in her bed with our
arms around one another, talking about the picture, wondering why we have not yet been murdered. Her room
smells the way it always does. Like her. Like flowers. Also,
there's something else. The smell of her momma baking
the hippie bread she eats. It has raisins in it, but it still
tastes like shit.

"Elijah's probably using the picture to masturbate," Xylia says angrily.

"Sick," I say.

"Sick is right," she says. "He's a sick, twisted, little bastard. Someday that kid's gonna hurt someone."

It's weird for me to hear that someone else thinks of Elijah Winchell that way. "I get so confused," I tell Xylia, touching the freckle under her eye, the one that I love. "People say you and me are evil, but what I feel for you is . . ."

"Holy?" she asks, breathing deeply. She always tells me she loves the way I smell. She says I smell like sunshine.

"Yeah, that," I say. "Our love is like the purest thing I've ever known."

"Me too," she says, and she kisses me soft.

When she pulls away, I say, "People like my momma say Elijah is holy, but he's so full of hate. So mean. He hurts people all the time, but he quotes the Bible, so it's okay?"

Xylia closes her eyes, the way she does when she's thinking hard. "My dad always told me the only people I have to be afraid of in this world are people who think they're right. Not blacks. Not whites. Not Muslims. Not Christians. Just people who think they have it all figured out, and everyone who thinks differently than they do is wrong. My dad says there's a fine line between zealotry and murder."

I think about this, wishing I had a daddy like Xylia's. "My daddy says people like us should be stoned in the streets." My voice shakes a little when I say it.

Xylia pulls me closer. "Anyone touches you, I'll kill 'em," she says. We lie there like that for a long time. I try to memorize the moment, the sound of the ceiling fan buzzing overhead, the sunlight glinting off Xylia's hair, the smell of her momma's awful bread. I'm so busy memorizing, I don't notice Juliette come into the room.

She clears her throat. "Sorry to interrupt."

I sit up, my heart pounding, but Xylia doesn't move.

"I just wanted to know if you'd like some cider and cheese." Juliette looks embarrassed, but not mad.

"You want some?" Xylia asks me.

"Um, sure," I say, still stunned that Juliette found us holding each other and did nothing but offer us a snack.

When Juliette leaves the room, Xylia reaches up to touch my face. "You're the prettiest thing I've ever seen. You know that, right?"

"Holy shit! Your mom scared me."

"Why?" she asks.

"Because if my mom found us like this, she'd tell my dad, and then—"

Xylia laughs.

"No, Xylia," I say. "He really might kill us. You don't know what I've seen him do. He hates gay people, and he tries to kill people he hates."

"Well, then, we'll just have to run away to Mexico sooner than we thought."

I ponder really and truly leaving this town behind, leaving Iggy behind. He's got his job now, and even a couple of people from the store who he calls friends. He helps pay Momma and Daddy for groceries, and sometimes he buys me things. Little things. Dolls. Stuffed animals. Lollipops. Things I'm way too old for. But I love them. They're pieces of his heart.

Now that Iggy's not in the house so much, Daddy doesn't get mad at him as often as he used to, but still, Iggy wouldn't last a week without me. There's no way I can leave him here. I'm about to tell Xylia this when she pulls me down onto the bed beside her. "Come back here." She kisses me hard on the mouth.

When she pulls away, she takes the Virgin of Guadalupe ring from her finger and slides it onto mine. "I want you to have it."

"Are you serious?" I ask. "It's your favorite."

"You're my favorite."

Warmth floods me. I feel more loved than ever before.

Precious. Tenderly I touch the Virgin, who smiles softly at me. "Thank you. No one has ever given me anything this beautiful." The ring could be a painting of Xylia. They are both lovely and holy. "I wish I could give you something back, but I don't wear jewelry."

"You've already given me more than anyone ever has."

Xylia's momma returns carrying two glasses of cider. She pauses for a moment, as if she is trying to decide what to do. Then she presses the glasses into our hands and walks out of the room, looking worried.

Xylia doesn't seem to notice. She rumples my hair and says, "I love your crazy hair, kid. It's perfect."

"Kid?" I ask.

"Yep. Did you forget that your girlfriend is an older woman?"

My girlfriend. Xylia is *my girlfriend*. I'm so happy, I want to scream.

Later, long after I have gone home, Xylia calls me, crying. She says her momma asked her about our relationship.

I freak, glad we only have one phone so Daddy can't be listening on the other end. "You told her?"

"Half of her friends in San Francisco were lesbians. She doesn't think there's anything wrong with it, but she's worried."

"Why?" I ask. Dumbest question ever.

"She says this town is stuck in the Stone Age, and if they find out, they'll hurt us. She says if she needs to, she'll send me back to San Francisco to live with Dad."

My chest hurts. "Then we can never, ever let anyone find out," I say. "You can't leave me here alone."

If I believed in things like jinxing, I would believe that Xylia's momma jinxed us with her worrying. The next morning I wake up to the sound of Daddy screaming.

"Little fucker!"

I run downstairs in my pajamas. The front door is wide open. Daddy's outside staring at the wall. Someone's written "DYKE" on it in red spray paint. When I say someone, I mean Elijah. Who else would it be?

I'm terrified that Daddy might know the message is for me, but Daddy doesn't seem to realize the graffiti has any basis in reality. "I'm gonna find out who did this and make him clean it off with his tongue!" he shouts. He calls the police, and Sheriff Perkins shows up a half hour later. Daddy goes out to his car, and I run up to my room and open the window. Their conversation drifts up to me.

"Yours wasn't the only house that was hit," Sheriff Perkins says. "Those new folks. What were their names? The Browns. Someone tagged their house too."

"Little fuckers," Daddy says. "Do you think there's a gang in town?"

"Could be," Sheriff Perkins answers. "A lot of Mexicans have moved in recently."

"Fucking wetbacks," Daddy says.

I've never been so happy to hear a racist comment in my life. No one seems to suspect this might have anything to do with me and Xylia loving each other. As soon as Sheriff Perkins leaves, I throw on jeans and a T-shirt.

"Where you going?" Daddy asks as I walk to the door.

"To the river," I say. I'm not lying. Xylia and me planned to meet by the river today at ten o'clock. I'm supposed to bring a picnic, but under the circumstances, I'm not.

"All right," Daddy says. "Just be back before dark. Looks like there are some oxygen thieves running around." "Oxygen thieves" is Daddy's favorite term for people who don't deserve to live.

"Okay, Daddy," I say, slipping out the door. I force myself to walk until I am in the trees, and then I run the rest of the way to the river. When I get there, Xylia's already sitting on a log by the place where we first said "I love you."

"Xylia," I call.

She turns to look at me. She's crying. "Mara." She runs to me. Throwing her arms around me, she says, "Oh, God."

"You okay?" I ask.

She shakes her head. "I gotta tell you something," Xylia whispers. She leads me to the log, and we sit down together.

My skin goes cold. "What?" I ask her.

"Our door got tagged."

"Ours too," I say.

Xylia looks scared. "Well, my mom got all upset. She thought I told someone about us. So I told her about Elijah taking the picture."

I sit bolt upright. "You told her?" I can't believe Xylia told her mom. I'm dizzy. The very worst thing I could imagine is happening. The world is about to find out what I am.

"I kinda had to. Here's the thing."

She stops then. I sit beside her, clutching the log, waiting for "the thing." She doesn't spit it out, so finally I ask, "What, Xylia?"

"My mom thinks I'm not safe here. She says these backwoods hicks will hack me apart."

"Oh no," I whisper. I know what's coming. I want to plug my ears so I don't have to hear it.

"She's sending me back to San Francisco to live with my dad."

Two days later we sit by the river again. Xylia is leaving tomorrow. My heart is broken clean in half, and no amount of staring at round things can keep me from crying. We're sitting on our log together, holding tightly to one another, as if we're lost in an angry ocean, and this log is the only life raft we have.

"I thought I was a lesbian before," she tells me, pushing a curl away from my face. "I knew for sure the second I saw you."

"I think I always knew I was a lesbian," I say. "I just didn't admit it until I fell in love with you." It's the first time I've ever thought of myself as anything but an abomination. There is a word for the way I am. A pretty word. A word that used to be just a vocabulary word to me, but now represents everything that is beautiful in the world. It means loving Xylia. "Lesbian," I say again through my sobs.

Xylia squeezes my hand. "I brought you something." She opens her purse and takes out a stack of CDs. I look at them. Janis Joplin. Bob Dylan. All her favorites.

"Thank you," I whisper, wondering if I will be able to listen to them without crying.

We kiss a lot there by the river. When we aren't kissing, I'm resting my head against Xylia's chest, listening to the pounding of her heart. I hold on to her as long as I can, like maybe I can keep her from leaving.

I can't. The next day Xylia is gone. The emptiness she

leaves behind is too vast for words. I stay up all night, listening to her CDs with my headphones, imagining us dancing to them. Janis Joplin is my favorite. Her voice is like a sledgehammer in the face. *Wham!* When she sings "Piece of My Heart," I get exactly what she means.

Xylia has taken more than a little piece of my heart. She's taken every last bit of it.

A week after Xylia leaves town I'm still moping. I don't want to get out of bed. There doesn't seem to be a point. I miss Henry, too. What I wouldn't give to get bleached by his dad right now. I call Henry's cell phone, but his dad answers and says Henry forgot to take it with him to the reservation. He gives me Henry's aunt's phone number. When I call, a woman answers. "Can I talk to Henry?" I ask.

Henry gets on, breathing heavy. "Are you moving furniture?" I ask, trying for humor.

"No, I was playing with the dog," he says. "His name is Alex."

"That's an odd name for a dog."

"I suppose so," Henry says. It's awkward talking to him on the phone. Not like when we're together.

"So how's your summer going?" I ask.

"It's moving along nicely," he answers. "And yours?"

I quickly realize Henry is the world's worst telephone conversationalist. Most of the time when we're together, we're quiet. Silence doesn't translate well to the telephone. After a few minutes of forced small talk, I make an excuse to get off. I don't tell him about Xylia being gone. It doesn't feel like the right time.

Iggy works all the time, and when he's home, he's usually too tired to do much but sleep. Whenever I ask him to play checkers with me, fully intending to let him win, he says he can't. Even my retard brother is too busy for me.

Most days I just wander around the house, looking for something to do. I watch tons of bad TV. Judge Judy and me have become pretty close friends. But Judge Judy just gave some guy the what for, and now old cartoons are on. I don't want to watch Tom go around chasing Jerry. It stopped being funny when I was ten.

So I stare into the fridge, wishing that something in there looked good to eat, but nothing does. The grapes are wrinkled. The bread looks hard. There's some leftover chicken, but I don't want to heat it up. Finally, I go to the pantry, pull out the peanut butter, and dip my finger in. I'm just putting it in my mouth when Iggy walks through the door, home from work. He has lipstick on his cheek.

"Whoa, Iggy," I say. "Who did that?"

He laughs, blushing. "Rena kissed me when I bagged her bread."

"She kissed you?" Rena was Iggy's best friend in class, but I never thought she might have a romantic interest in him. Apparently I was wrong. I close the peanut butter and put it back in the pantry. "Does Rena work at the store?" I ask.

"No, but she visits me."

It never occurred to me that Iggy might get a girlfriend. I thought once his brain broke, that was it. But here he is. He has a job. He's making friends. And now girls are kissing him. My brother gets love, and all I get is shit. It doesn't seem fair.

Closing the pantry door, I turn toward Iggy, forcing a smile. "I guess she likes you, sport."

"She asked me to go over to her house on Friday and watch movies." Grinning, he takes off his blue apron and throws it on the counter. His name tag stares at me. HI, MY NAME IS IGGY, it says. HOW MAY I HELP YOU?

I want to say, "You could help me by bringing Xylia back." But I don't. Instead I say, "Cool, Iggy! What are you gonna watch?"

"Movies." He looks at me like I'm stupid.

That irritates me. I'm the stupid one? "*Which* movies?"

He shrugs. "Beats me." That's something Daddy always

does. It bothers me when he says things the way Daddy says them.

It's a good thing Momma comes into the kitchen then, 'cause I'm about to say something mean. "Iggy!" she says right away. "Who kissed you?"

"Rena kissed me when I bagged her bread," Iggy repeats. It's like he has a script or something.

"Oh, baby." Momma hugs him. "Rena's a real pretty girl." Iggy grins. "I know."

They're right. Rena *is* pretty. I don't know what's wrong with her, why she's in special ed. She looks normal. A lot like Iggy, I guess, except her hair is flaming red. She has a boatload of freckles on her nose.

They'd make a beautiful couple, as long as neither of them opens their mouths. It's a mean thing to think, but I can't help it. I've lost love, and Iggy is finding it.

"Well, at least one of my babies is settling down," Momma says.

"I'm sixteen," I say, truly pissed. "It's a little early for me to be settling down."

"You're certainly old enough to *date*," Momma says. "What about Elijah Winchell?"

The sound of his name makes me want to snap someone's neck.

"Elijah is the pimpliest, ugliest, meanest asshole I've ever met!" I can't believe I'm yelling. I've never yelled at Momma before. "I'd rather date retarded Rena!"

Momma's eyes go wide. "Mara! Don't even talk like that."

I think of all the ugly words I know. "Bitch." "Whore." "Slut." I want to call my momma all those things and more. It's like there's a hurricane in my brain. Instead I run to my room. When I slam my door, I hear Momma calling, "Mara! Mara Stonebrook!" Her footsteps pound on the stairs, and she knocks on my door. "Mara, please, talk to me. What's wrong?"

"Go away!" I scream. "Just get the fuck away from me!"

She does. It's the saddest thing in the world, hearing nothing now but the summer birds singing outside my window. I bury my face in my pillow and cry.

After that I leave the house early every morning, embarrassed that I yelled at Momma. I spend the rest of my summer days staring into the water, fiddling with Xylia's ring, which is a little loose, and writing her letters. I slip them into the blue mailbox by the post office, knowing I am risking my life to send them, not caring. My life is over anyway. I call her as often as I can, but it's long distance, and Daddy gets mad about that. And even when he's not home, there's always a chance he will come through the door, overhear our conversation, and kill me. When we do talk, she always begs, "Come see me, Mara." Like I could. How would I even get there?

By the end of summer it's like everyone but me forgot Xylia ever existed.

CHAPTER 20

TODAY IS THE FIRST DAY OF SCHOOL, AND MY new teacher, Ms. Elibee, is going on and on about new beginnings. I must have thought the same thing when I woke up, because I bothered to shave my legs and put on a skirt, which I never do. But now that I'm back at school, I think Ms. Elibee's full of shit. School's just like I remembered it. It even smells the same. Chalk dust, plain old dust, and kids who haven't figured out that they should be bathing once a day. The only thing that ever smelled good in this place was Xylia, and now she's gone. I miss her flowery smell. Hell, I miss everything about her. I've never felt more alone.

As I shuffle to my desk, people look at me with mean

eyes and whisper. No one talks to me. It was always like that, but I didn't used to care. I only care now because it makes me feel even more alone.

I write Xylia every day, but it's not the same as having her around. In my first letter I told her that if she wanted to write me back, she should send the letters to Henry's, because of Daddy. But I haven't seen Henry since the day at the river, so I don't know if she's written me back or not. I miss her so much that some days I want to die. Especially today.

"Okay, let's get started," Ms. Elibee says.

Ms. Elibee isn't like Mr. Farley. This is her second year teaching, and she's young and pretty. She talks with a twang that says she isn't from around here. She reads Yeats's "The Song of Wandering Aengus," one of Xylia's favorites. Her voice sounds like music, and you can tell by the way she weighs each word that she loves them. The last part of the poem pretty much sums up how I feel about Xylia. I stare down at my textbook, read the lines of the poem over and over again. Though I am old with wandering / Through hollow lands and hilly lands, / I will find out where she has gone, / And kiss her lips and take her hands. . . .

We discuss it for a while. Ms. Elibee tells us Yeats wrote it about a lady named Maud Gonne. He wrote most of his best poems about her. She was his muse, but she didn't love him back. This makes me so sad. It makes me even sadder that I have my muse, and she *does* love me back, but I still can't be with her.

Finally we get a break. I lock myself in a stall, sit on a toilet, and cry. I look at Xylia's ring. "I will find out where she has gone, and kiss her lips, and take her hands," I whisper. It is a promise. To me. To God. To everything and everyone. I wipe my eyes with some toilet paper and blow my nose. Then I leave the stall, ignoring the girls who stand at the mirrors, glossing their lips.

As I walk back down the hall, I glare at the stupid banners. WELCOME BACK SCINTILLATING SCHOLARS AND DANCE THE NIGHT AWAY AT THE HOMECOMING EXTRAVAGANZA. I know they were drawn by Martha Pinkerton, who prides herself on her ability to use words with more than five syllables and wants to be a news broadcaster, but she won't be without dental work, because she has tiger-striped teeth from a fever she had as a baby.

I pass Mr. Pauly, who has a scar on his chin that looks like a goat. He smiles while he empties the trash cans. I suspect he's pleased to have access to people's deepest, darkest secrets. I don't have the heart to tell him that this isn't the CIA. He's not going to find top-secret files, only plastic wrappers slimy with mayonnaise and maybe an apple core or two. All in all, except for my pretty teacher, high school is the same old everything, and I'm sorry I shaved my legs this morning.

At lunch, instead of going to the cafeteria, I wander to a grassy corner in the school yard, right by the tulip beds. I'd rather starve than deal with the kids staring at me. Plus I just can't stand to look at the table where me and Xylia used to sit, laughing and sharing secrets. Plopping myself down in the cool grass, I reach into my backpack for the orange I put there this morning.

"Hello, Mara Stonebrook." Elijah Winchell stares at me like the guy in *The Silence of the Lambs* looked at people he was about to eat.

"Fuck off," I say, peeling the orange.

"You have a good summer?"

"Yeah, I guess," I say. "I only killed twenty people though, which is kind of a step down from my usual summer crime sprees."

His mouth drops open, like he actually believes me. Hellfire flares in his eyes, and I can tell he's itching to tell me I'm bound for hell. An abomination and a murderess? Score!

"Mara Stonebrook, you're a devil." He storms away from me so quick, he smacks into Henry. Henry's glasses fall on the sidewalk. Elijah doesn't say he's sorry.

"You okay?" I jump up. Henry lifts his glasses and cradles them in his delicate hands. They're cracked.

"I'm fine, thank you." Squinting, Henry looks at me. "Oh, hello, Mara," he says. His eyes look small without his glasses. Small and sad. "I couldn't tell it was you."

"Wow, you really are blind," I say.

He smiles. "I am, in fact, nearly legally blind."

"I missed you, kid," I say, hugging him. "I'm sorry that asshole busted your glasses."

"I missed you too," Henry says. "And it's all right. I'm fairly certain my father's medical insurance will pay for new ones." He tucks the broken glasses into his pocket. "Mind if I join you?"

"Sure," I say.

We sit down.

"How was your summer?"

He shrugs. "Good, I suppose. I can't say I'm a huge fan of the res, but I love the ceremonies. They were fun."

"What are they like?"

Henry looks off into the distance, seeing, I imagine, nothing but blurs. "It's like hearing the heartbeat of the earth," he says finally.

I smile. Leave it to Henry to say something like that.

"Oh, I almost forgot." He pulls a stack of letters out of his backpack. As soon as I see the handwriting, I know who they're from. My heart catches in my throat. "These are for you."

"Thanks," I whisper. With trembling hands, I take them from him and set them in the grass beside me. I lift the first one from the stack and rip it open slowly, even though I'm dying to know what it says. I don't want to ruin Xylia's handwriting on the front. On the back she's drawn a million flowers, all different colors, with crayons.

Dear Mara,

I miss you every day, so much. I miss my mom, too. I wish both of you could have come back to San Francisco with me. The two of you are the only things I miss about Barnaby though. Okay, I lied. I miss Henry, too.

I stop reading to tell Henry that Xylia misses him. "I miss her as well."

I start reading again:

Today, I was sitting by the ocean thinking of you. A toddler was standing in the waves holding a purple balloon, and it was so perfect, so ethereal. I wanted to take a picture of the moment and send it to you, so I did. I thought if you could see this place, you'd fall in love with it, and you'd come running to me. So many people here are like us. They read poetry books. They wear flowers in their hair. And no one cares if you're a lesbian. It's almost perfect. The only thing missing is you. I told Dad all about you, and he said I should ask you to stay with us. He said you could stay as long as you wanted. Will you come? Please say yes. We can love each other all we want here. There are great colleges here too. Maybe we could get an apartment together when we graduate. Think about it, please?

XOXOOOOXXXXXOOOOOO,

Xylia

The picture she described is attached. She's right. San Francisco looks like heaven. I stare at the outline of a toddler standing under an endless, misty sky. For a moment I thrill at the prospect of running away. Then I remember there's no way I can go off to San Francisco with Xylia. For one thing, my parents would never let me. For two things, if I left Iggy, he'd be dead.

I must look like I'm going to cry, because Henry hands me a handkerchief from his pocket.

I laugh right through my tears. "Who but you would carry a handkerchief?"

Henry laughs with me. "No one, I suppose."

Later, I'm walking home from school. I can almost feel the warmth from Xylia's letters seeping through the canvas of my backpack. I'm going to sit by the water and read every one, savoring every word. Beams of sunlight burst through the evergreen branches overhead. The grass smells extra sweet. As I pick my way through the bushes that line the river the water calls my name more clearly than it ever has before.

There's a shuffling in the bushes behind me. I spin, but I see only a raven flitting off through the branches. I laugh at myself for being so jumpy.

The river's warm this time of year. During fall and spring, it's so cold, your brain freezes if you stick your head in. But in late summer, it's just perfect. Humming a little tune my momma sometimes sings about a chameleon coming and going, I sit on the log where me and Xylia said good-bye. I take off my sandals and wet my feet. Then I reach into my backpack and pull out Xylia's letters. The bushes behind me rustle again.

"Hey, bird," I call over my shoulder, wiggling my toes deeper into the river mud.

"Hey, Mara."

I almost jump out of my skin. I whirl around just in time to see Elijah slide down the riverbank, flailing his arms and legs, obviously not used to being near the water. He lands at my feet like one of those dead lizards our barn cat sometimes leaves on the porch.

"What are you doing here?" I say. Elijah is probably number three on my list of people I'd rather not see, right under Hitler and Satan. I push the letters to the bottom of my backpack and zip it shut.

"Brought you something," he says, pointing back toward the reeds that line the riverbank. Stuck between two mossy rocks, a six-pack of the cheapest kind of beer is lodged. Well, it was a six-pack. Two of the little plastic holes are empty. Elijah smells like beer, so I guess he drank a couple of them. "A peace offering," he adds.

"What makes you think I'd want that cheap old beer?" I know it's not worth much because Daddy cussed and hollered when Momma bought it once.

Elijah pulls himself from the mud now, trying to wipe the mess from his knees and hands. When he's done, he shrugs, and his face gets so red, you can't tell where the pimples begin and the regular skin ends. "I thought a girl like you . . ."

I wait for him to finish. When he doesn't, I draw my own conclusions, conclusions that make a seed of rage sprout in my belly. "You thought a girl like me what? You thought I'd be a drunk?" The seed in my belly takes off like Jack's beanstalk, growing faster than lightning. I hate Elijah more now than I ever have. Calling me a whore or a Jezebel is one thing. Calling me a drunk like my daddy is quite another. "Get out of here," I say.

"Look, Mara . . ."

"Look what? Look, you think I'm some abomination? Look, you think I'm some old drunk? Look, you think I commit murders during summer vacation for kicks?" I glance at Elijah, trying not to cry. "You don't know a thing about me, Elijah Winchell."

Before I can close my mouth, Elijah starts talking nonstop, using big preacher words like "unpardonable sin" and "hermeneutics," which I think is some fat guy's name. He's trying to sound smart, yelling like he's a bad Shakespearean actor doing a monologue. This guy's train of thought must have gotten robbed. He sounds like no preacher I've ever heard, because usually by the end of most sermons, you have a good feeling about what the preacher was trying to say. You know, for instance, that you are bound for hell. But Elijah just goes on and on about nothing, using words the way they never were meant to be used, saying things like, "Don't you comprehend this, Mara Stonebrook. It's about the REVELATION!" I'm thinking, what *REVELATION*? You never mentioned any REVELATION before. Two seconds ago you were talking about hermeneutics. Elijah Winchell flunked first grade, and now I understand why.

Giving up on trying to understand what he's saying, I blurt out, "You're a nut job." I stand and grab my shoes, hating him so much, I want to spit. I yank my sandals on and turn to walk away.

"You sure you don't want a beer?" he calls. His voice sounds crazy, like the homeless guy who used to stand on the street corner talking to people who weren't there.

"Yep," I say, bending to pick up my backpack. He grabs my arm. Before I can think to stop it, my fist balls up and punches him. "Don't ever touch me again." Furiously, Elijah rubs the place on his arm where I punched him. I don't feel sorry for him. I lift my backpack and start to leave.

That's when something hits me in the back of the head. Stumbling, I drop my backpack. A beer clatters to the ground beside me. It gets my backpack wet. I think about Xylia's letters, getting ruined.

The world is rocking, but I'm still ready to punch Elijah's lights out.

"We're not even finished talking," he says. "Where are your manners, bitch?"

"I have nothing to say to you." My hands are balling up again. If he gets any closer, I'll clobber him.

"Yeah? Well, I got something to say to you." Elijah's eyes burn, the way they did that day he caught me kissing Xylia. "You're an abomination."

His eyes look so scary, instead of clobbering him, I back away.

Elijah comes at me.

I step back again and stumble. I catch myself and refocus on Elijah's face. I know that look. I saw it in Daddy's eyes before he tried to kill Iggy. I move to run, but my feet get tangled in my backpack straps, and I fall flat on my face.

Before I can say anything, Elijah has flipped me over like a pancake and is on top of me, grinding his lips so hard against mine, I taste blood. I scream. I can hear it even through the ringing in my ears.

You would never know it by looking at him, but Elijah is stronger than Hercules. He has both of my hands pinned with one of his. I fight with all my might, but I can't move an inch. He sits on top of my thighs, straddling me like a pony. Something hard in his pants grinds against me, and it scares me more than his eyes. I start to cry and beg and plead, which I have never once done in my life.

"Please, Elijah," I cry, tasting tears and snot and blood. "Stop!"

His cold hand slides up under my shirt. I howl no when he squeezes my boob, but he doesn't listen. I keep bucking, trying to get him off of me, but he stays on. I wonder if he's going to kill me. Sobbing and begging, I barely feel the jagged rocks cutting bloody designs into the flesh of my back.

"Please, Elijah!" It's like staring into the devil's eyes. Pure hatred. Undiluted insanity. Begging the devil isn't working, so I beg God. "Please, God!" My voice sounds like someone else's, and it is the scariest thing of all.

Elijah pulls something purple out of his pants. I know words for it. I've heard them before at school, but in my head, I call it what Momma called it. But Momma was wrong about the manhood. She said it was nothing to be afraid of. She said it would hurt a bit at first, but feel good, too. She lied. It's like a knife. It cuts me so bad, I leave my body, take the part of me that matters and get up and walk away. My mind sits down by the river and tries not to look as my body gets raped.

I stare into the water while Elijah rocks on top of me, grunting and sweating and calling me ugly words I didn't know had been invented yet. I look at the water gliding around the river stones, thinking about how they have been there since the beginning of time, thinking they will be here long after I die and go to heaven. I cry because I feel bad for hating Momma for not keeping her skirt down. Keeping your skirt down is harder than it looks.

When Elijah's done, he mutters that I'm the devil and struggles to his feet. As he zips up his pants, he says, "If you tell anyone about this, I'll show that picture of you and your slutty dyke to your daddy and everyone in this town." Then he stumbles away through the bushes. When I'm sure he's gone, my mind slips back into my body. It hurts in here. I don't like it anymore.

Don't ever let anyone tell you that life will get better. It won't. You stand up, it will strike you down. You might as well tie a rope around your neck and get it over with now if you're waiting for your luck to change. I imagine myself tying a noose, dying. I see me spread out on that table like John Doe, my belly cut open, my guts all twisted inside me. I remember that raven in the hospital parking lot, pulling strings from the dead thing. Do you know what I say when I think about that? This is funny. I say, "String's the thing."

Did you laugh like all get-out when I said that? I did.

It was all I could think to say.

CHAPTER 21

THERE ARE SONGS INSIDE OF YOU. DID YOU know that? I never knew either until now.

The ground is cold on my back, and the mud stings the places where I've been cut. My toes are numb. And I'm shaking like ice in a blender. Strangest of all, songs are sliding out between my lips, songs I never learned before. Fancy songs, songs that sound like "The Highwayman." Hear this:

"I will fly me to the ocean away, on wings of mother of pearl, there I will swallow the cold tears of time and swim me in God's roaring song."

I'll try to remember the words so Xylia can sing them for me some time in her nightingale voice. She sure can sing, that girl.

I can too, it turns out. When the time is right, songs bleed right out of me. I guess all those smart words from books have been stored in my brain and fit themselves together into songs if I don't think too hard. I can't think much right now. I wonder if my brain froze to death. Ha! Just froze like a grape Popsicle, bless its heart.

The clouds are coming for me. They are stalking across the sky like lions that are going to eat me. I would run if I thought being eaten by a cloud would be so bad. But worse things can happen to a person.

I'll tell you what the end of the world is though: somebody's manhood tearing you in half. That is the end of the world. I cry to think about it. Right now I wail like a baby, and don't you judge me for it. You would cry about the manhood. I know you would, so don't make jokes at my expense at a time like this. Crybaby. Crybaby. Just give it a rest.

Don't tell me clouds eating you are the end of the world either. That is what happens after the world is over. The rules aren't the same anymore. And clouds *can* eat people now. They can do anything they want. We all can. I could walk on water now if I so chose. The game is over.

I wait for God to pull open the clouds like curtains and say, "Gotcha! We've just been playing a prank on you. Come on back to heaven where you belong." I will be a good sport.

You know I will. I will say, "Good one, God. You sure got me. I thought all of that was real."

Milk and honey. That's what they eat where I'm going. I heard that in Sunday school.

Once I saw a baby mouse get eaten by a hawk. I wanted to save it, but of course I couldn't. You know how it is down here. No one can save anybody. So I just watched, whispering, "Think good thoughts. Think about your momma." And it did.

I take my own advice now. Think about my momma. She has soft hands, that woman. I never gave her proper credit for her hands. She knows how to soothe a fever just right, and you should see how she cries when she thinks you'll die in her arms. She cried like that when I was two and got bit in the face by the German shepherd. To this day I have a little scar above my lip from that bite, and I still remember Momma, carrying on like nobody's business and kissing my face. Blood ran down my chest like a crimson waterfall.

There's blood on my chest now, too. Did Elijah pop one of my boobs? I guess I should thank him if he did. Bye-bye boobies. I hate boobs. I think that's why he did this. He wanted to see my breasts.

It is getting dark. The clouds are gone from the sky. I hear crunching in the leaves behind me. Elijah. I try to stand up and run, but my legs don't work. It's like they're made of rubber.

It's not Elijah. It's Henry. His teeth look yellow in the twilight. I have to laugh at that. I tell him right off what has happened.

"I think he popped my boob," I say, and lift my shirt to show him the blood.

His eyes are so big, they take up most of his face.

It must be popped. What a bloody mess it must be.

Something is happening to Henry's face. It fades in and out. I can feel his arms underneath me, lifting me away from the rocky ground. We're moving. Xylia's ring lies on the ground, half buried in mud. "The ring," I say.

"It's going to be all right," Henry replies.

"He popped my boob," I repeat, but Henry only says, "It's going to be all right." He's crying, though. Can you imagine that? How can I believe that it's going to be all right when Henry's crying?

Henry's freckled T-shirt is soft and warm against my cheek. My blood is smeared across his face. Either that, or he's bleeding. Maybe we're all bleeding now that the game is over.

I look down to see if my boob is popped. I can't tell. Henry pulled my shirt back down to cover it. But there's plenty of blood on my shirt. I remember the way my momma carried on after the German shepherd's bite.

"Don't tell my momma," I say. I don't want her to cry again. It's one sad sight to see your momma go on and on like a child.

This is like a pony ride. Up and down. Bounce, bounce. I'm dizzy from the bouncing. I close my eyes. It feels good to do that. I'd forgotten about closing my eyes. I'd forgotten you don't always have to look.

Come to think of it, I'll never look again.

CHAPTER 22

HENRY PUT ME ON OUR PORCH. AFTER HE knocked on the door, he ran away. Someone was screaming—me, I guess—and that's when Daddy came. His arms picked me up, then carried me inside. "Cora!" he hollered. "Cora, get down here!"

His head floats above me. His mouth is moving. He's mad. I wonder if he's going to hit me. He's going to hit something. Noises are coming out of his face, but I can't make out the words. His head disappears from view, and I hear a bang. A gun? A firecracker? No, a door slamming.

I close my eyes. Colors come up behind my eyelids, red, white, swirling. I stay like that for a long time. When I open my eyes, the world is still swirling with red and white.

Daddy's face is there again. Red-white light flashes over his skin. Water leaks from his eyes. Why water? Wait. Daddy's crying. I laugh at this, the thought of my daddy crying.

A man stands next to him. A slick man in blue with a serious face and a shiny star on his chest. He's writing in a notebook. He keeps looking at me, saying things. He wants me to say something back, so I do.

"I will fly me to the ocean away on wings of mother of pearl," I say.

He shakes his head and writes it down. He says something again. The same words over and over. I squint, trying to watch his lips to know what the words mean.

"What happened? What happened?"

I flip the words over inside my head until they make sense. What *did* happen? I remember the river, but I don't want to talk about that. Something good. I will say something good.

"Clouds," I say, remembering how soft and cottony the clouds looked. That was such a good thing.

The man doesn't like that. "What happened?" he says again. "Who did this to you? Who raped you?" Those words come rushing at me like a train. Run me right over. I can't think of any more words of my own. I just scream, remembering the way it felt to be ripped in half.

"What happened?" the man asks again.

Words come to me now. "The manhood," I whisper. And then the screaming starts again. No. NO. I will not let my head go to that bad place.

I try to remember something else good. And then it comes to me, the warm smell of Henry's skin. I quiet down. Henry was good, good like the clouds.

"Henry," I say. "Henry. Good."

The man likes that. He writes it down.

CHAPTER 23

THAT DAY AT THE RIVER CAME AND WENT, BUT it changed everything. My life dissolved like sugar in coffee. My brain went with it. I was only in the hospital for one night, Momma told me, but I argued with her. "It was a hundred years," I said. She looked worried when I said that, but it was true.

They did horrible things to me there, things like what Elijah did, only there were bright lights and silver instruments, and lots of people in the room. They put my feet in stirrups. I screamed and cried, but it didn't do any good—just like it didn't do any good with Elijah. The worst part was Momma stood there while it happened, letting them do it.

"Shh," she kept saying. Like I could *shh*. How could I *shh* at a time like that? "It's a rape kit, honey," she said. "These people are here to help. We're going to prove Henry did this to you."

Henry. Henry. Henry. Everyone kept saying his name.

"Why did Henry do this?" people in white asked me again and again and again.

Why did Henry do what? I like Henry.

After the hospital, I didn't leave my bedroom. It was the only place that felt safe. I'd sit in my bed and stare and stare at the picture Xylia loved, the one of the mouse. I'd close my eyes and remember her saying, "It has beautiful lines." I'd sit there for hours like that, forgetting to eat, forgetting to sleep, forgetting to move.

I left me by the river. After Elijah attacked me, the best part of me walked away from my body and went on with my life. I think the real Mara is still down there by the water, staring at the stones and singing songs. This nightmare never happened to her.

My own voice screams at me from inside my brain. It's louder than usual, more wild. All day long it screams, *Run, run, run!* One time, it's so loud, I write *run, run, run* all over my arm, using my nail scissors. They're just little scratches, but Momma still cries when she sees it.

"My baby," she says, holding me against her boobs. They are soft.

"He popped my boob," I say, and Momma just cries harder.

I pull away from Momma, lift my shirt and look. My boob's still there. It has a long, jagged line on it. Purple. I pull my shirt back down.

"Henry's getting arraigned today," Momma says.

"What?" I ask.

"For what he did to you by the river."

The room starts spinning. I see Elijah's face, pimply and cruel, rising above me like a vision. I won't look. I close my eyes. I have never felt such terror. I'm falling off the edge of the world.

I watch the sun rise and fall outside my window a zillion times, like a basketball that's bouncing too slow. Sometimes Daddy comes into the room with Momma. They talk about me like I'm not there, which is okay, 'cause I'm mostly not.

"How's she going to catch up at school?" Daddy shakes his head. "She's missed almost two months."

Two months? Has it only been two months? They are wrong. Wrong. Wrong. Wrong. "It's been six million years," I say. Momma starts to cry. Why does that woman always cry?

Sometimes Iggy comes to visit. When he's there, I feel like maybe the world isn't spinning so much. I never want him to leave, but Momma says he has to go to work. So he goes to work and I wait for him to chase the ghosts away.

On Halloween he comes into my room looking scary. He's wearing a black cape. His teeth are sharp. He has blood on his face, like that day. "Hey, Sis," he says.

I start to scream.

Momma comes running. "Iggy, just go to work," she says. And he does. I look out the window, watching him walk down the driveway. "Iggy, come back," I say. His cape flutters in the wind. He doesn't turn around.

I keep looking out the window. All kinds of spiders and witches and vampires come to the door. One boy has an ax in his head. Something buried deep inside me whispers it's all pretend, but I don't believe it. It's not pretend. Bad things really do happen. I close my curtains and hide under my blankets, hoping the mean things won't find me. And then I remember they can't find me because I'm not real. I left the real me down by the river.

I know this because I'm not the same me. I used to be full of spring, and now I'm full of winter's rot. I like things neat now. My shoes are lined up in my closet just so, and when Momma saw the way I arranged the clothes in my dresser, she said, "My, Mara! You've turned over a new leaf."

"I liked my old leaf better," I told her.

For a long, long time, I lie in my bed. My chest hurts. Finally, the sky gets dark, and all that's left is the wind.

"Shh," I whisper to the wind, the way Momma did when I was in the hospital. "Shh." I put my hands over my ears, but the noise gets louder, like the sound of a train passing two feet in front of me. My heart begins to pound. *Bangbangbang!* Elijah's face is so close. I can see the red veins in his eyes and the blackheads buried deep inside his pores. He's looking through me, staring into the rocks that are shredding my back as he grinds, grinds, grinds inside me.

I can hear my voice, the way I sounded that day. "No, no, no." It is a whimper, the saddest sound I ever heard, like a dying puppy. He doesn't listen. To him, I'm not a person. I'm not even an animal. I'm nothing.

This memory closes in on me as thick, choking darkness closed in on Jesus when he died. At noonday it became as night. *My God, my God, why have you forsaken me?*

Run. Run. Run. I stumble toward my bedroom door, but I can't run far enough to get away from this. Because it's inside me. Wherever I go, it will follow me.

And then I come up with a plan.

Run. Run. Run. What is death if not running? It's the one way to get away from me. I'm ugly. I'm sin. I'm the devil. I deserve to die.

And so I stumble to the bathroom, fumble with the latch on the medicine cabinet. My hands shake. You wouldn't believe how ugly I've become. My face is skinny. My eyes are swollen. And my hair—what a sight. I try to smooth it back, but it won't stay. It's rebellious as me, my momma used to say. I wonder if they'll have one of those funerals with the dead person on display. I should at least try to look my best.

First I smear on a thick coat of Momma's lipstick. Candy-apple red. It makes me sad to see it spread across my swollen lips. I will miss that woman.

The lipstick's done now. But this hair! I grab the razor blade that gleams on the second shelf. It cuts right through the skin of my middle finger. It hurts, but it is a sweet pain, the kind of pain you want to hold on to. The kind that makes you forget to hurt inside. I lift the razor to my hairline, dripping blood over my tangled curls. *Slice.* The curls fall away.

It's hard to shave off your hair without also cutting your scalp. Hot pain sears over my head, and a tiny river of blood trickles along the bridge of my nose. I wince, but I don't let that stop me. Golden tangles fall to the tile by my feet, like so many sheaves of wheat. So much hair! I never knew how much hair I had until I saw it all lying on the floor.

I look into the mirror. What a relief. Those rebellious curls are gone. All that's left is a smattering of bristles protruding from my scalp. I look like a hedgehog. A hedgehog that got run over by a car maybe, judging from the way I'm bleeding. It stings. More than that, it hurts, deep down into my brain. I drop the razor blade and clutch my head in my hands and make the dying-puppy noise I made by the river.

The door creaks open, and it's Iggy, glowing in the moonlight. His see-clear-through-you eyes are shining. He kneels beside me, wrapping me in his strong arms.

I'm a baby again. I remember what it's like to be held and rocked in a warm set of hands you think were made just for you. I remember what it's like not to worry. I remember what it's like to bury my head in love and cry, cry, cry. God, how I cry against Iggy's chest. He's talking to me, but it might as well be chickens squawking.

The moonlight melts my brain. My thoughts blur away into a buzzing haze of sleep.

I wake up in my bed. I'm alive. Iggy is lying beside me, softly snoring. His arm is draped across my belly. I watch the sunlight fall over his face, thinking about the way I used to believe that I was his angel. Last night, he was mine. I bend to kiss his face, loving his freckles, his smell, everything about him.

My brain's back. I don't know why, but I can think straight

again. Maybe cutting my head made all the crazy leak out. All I know is that for the first time since the river, I can look around me and see things for what they are. My drawings are hung up all in a row. This is my quilt Grandma made me. And there's Iggy, my beautiful brother, sleeping beside me.

Last night comes rushing back to me, and I remember the way he held me. The way he saved me from myself. "Thank you, Iggy," I whisper. Then I holler, "Momma!"

She comes running. I must be a sight, because she just says, "Oh, baby," over and over.

She wraps her arms around me, and I hug her back. "It's okay, Momma," I tell her. "I'm back."

She pulls away from me and looks into my eyes. She must see what I'm saying is true because she says, "Thank God. Oh, thank you, sweet Jesus," and she wraps her arms around me again. She rocks me back and forth. I can feel her breath in my hair. "They'll make him pay, Mara," she tells me. "Don't worry. They'll make him pay for what he did to you."

"Who?"

She pulls away from me and looks at me like maybe she isn't so sure I'm not crazy after all. "Henry," she says slowly, as if I'm stupid. "He goes to trial next month."

I feel like someone hit me in the face with a sledgehammer.

"Wait," I say, trying to catch up. "Henry's going to trial for what happened to me?"

"Of course," Momma says. "His shirt was covered in your blood. You told the police he did it."

I stare at Momma in horror. I don't know what to do. I want to tell her it wasn't Henry, but if I tell her the truth, Elijah will show Daddy the picture, and I'll get stoned in the street or maybe hit in the face with a two-by-four. I imagine Henry, one of my only friends in the world, huddled in some jail cell. I know I should do something. But I'm so scared, I'm frozen. I am afraid if one more awful thing happens to me, I will never be okay again.

"Mara?" Momma asks. "Are you all right?"

"Where is he?" I whisper.

"He can't hurt you, honey. He's in juvie until the trial. And the DA says after that, he'll be locked up for a long, long time."

"Oh, Momma," I say. And I start to cry.

CHAPTER 24

COME IN,' SHE SAID, 'I'LL GIVE YOU SHELTER from the storm.'" Xylia's voice slides out through the morning air, thick and rich. I imagine it has substance. Not solid, like concrete or wood. Not even liquid, like water. But weightless, like fog. It's green, her voice, the color of a lone grass shoot peeking from frosted soil at winter's end.

Inside my head, we're sitting in her room, searching for a way to make sense of my broken heart, of the snakelike gashes slithering over my scalp.

"Mara? Mara Stonebrook?" Ms. Elibee's voice snaps me out of my daydream. It's my first day back at school. I keep forgetting I'm here. I look up at Ms. Elibee. Her skin is freckled, so white and thin you can see her veins.

"What do you think man's purpose is?" she asks.

"What do I think man's purpose is?" I repeat the question, buying time, wondering why she asked it.

Elijah snickers from the back of the room. I can't see him, but I'd recognize that laugh anywhere.

When he saw me this morning, with my white head scarf, he grinned as if he knew he'd won. I just looked away.

My stomach tightens. And I understand that Ms. Elibee asked her question because new teachers always ask questions like that. They still believe that they're shaping minds, not just plodding through an endless string of exhausting days like the rest of us.

Ten years from now she'll know better than to ask those questions. She'll see a picture of herself drawn on a bathroom wall somewhere. She'll have pointed boobs and wild spirals of hair, with some ugly words underneath. It'll dawn on her then that she's not making a difference. Her students may remember her flat chest, her pasty white skin, the way she wheezed when she got excited over her subject matter, but they won't remember what she had to say.

And right then she'll take a black Magic Marker out of her purse and scrawl an even uglier word on the bathroom wall. She'll tell those ungrateful shitheads what she thinks of them. From that day on her grading standards will be tougher. She'll start writing woebegone poetry instead of trying to change the world. She'll die without a thank-you.

I think all of that as I repeat Ms. Elibee's question. I feel so sorry for her that I come up with an answer just to please her. I say, "Man's purpose is to boil things down."

Elijah laughs again.

"Elijah, please," she admonishes, but I guess she doesn't like my answer, because her eyelids droop. Still, she's a good teacher, so she stirs the hope in her heart, lifts her eyelids, and asks, "And what do you mean by that, Mara?"

"We try to boil things down, to make sense of everything that's going on around us, even though nothing really makes sense at all. We try to find the good in the bad, pretend the chaos leads to something meaningful. Something logical."

Ms. Elibee looks very confused, disappointed, like a little girl who got underwear for her birthday when she really wanted a pony. I keep talking.

"When something really bad happens, we try to say, 'Oh, that wasn't so bad.'" I want to tell her about Iggy's brain, about Momma's jaw, about the rape, how I try every day to understand how such horrible things can really happen. I want to tell her too about Henry, about how I stay up every night trying to excuse myself for not telling the truth. Each morning I promise myself today will be the day I set the record straight. And each night I go to bed sick because I haven't done it.

I can't say all that though, so I come up with something else. "Like when we talk about how God gave us this continent, and how the courageous whites subjugated the dangerous Indians. But what was courageous about butchering Indian babies? We boiled what happened down to make sense, so we wouldn't have to feel bad about what we did. Man's purpose is to boil things down."

I glance around at my classmates. They look at me like I am the carrier of some oozing blister disease. I hold my breath, feeling a blush spread over my cheeks. Then I look at Ms. Elibee. She understands what I said. I can see it in her eyes.

"Thank you, Mara," she finally says, full of heartbreak and meaning. "Thank you." I don't just like Ms. Elibee after that. I love her.

This afternoon I walk into the house thinking about the way Ms. Elibee said "thank you" to me. Momma's in the kitchen, rolling out a crust. She smiles, and I smile back.

"Hi, Momma," I say, opening the fridge for the first time in a long time.

"Hi, honey. How was your day?" She wipes flour from her hands onto her apron.

I pull out an apple and bite into it. "The best day in a lot of months," I tell her, and she looks like maybe she'll cry. I run to my room before she can.

Later, I'm standing at the window in my bedroom, running my fingers over the soft stubble of my hair, watching a cedar sway in the wind. The house is quiet. I'm thinking hopeful thoughts about the way my hair is growing back. Maybe I *can* heal.

But then I remember Henry sitting in some cell, waiting to go to trial for what he didn't do to me. I think about the way he picked me up and told me it would be all right. I want to be happy again, but I can't. I can't be happy when Henry's going to spend a long, long time in jail. Momma said they were trying him as an adult. I imagine fragile Henry in a prison full of killers and rapists. Real rapists. Not people like him who got accused of something he didn't do. I feel dizzy imagining what they will do to him. But if I tell the truth, Elijah will tell Daddy what I am, and Daddy will kill me. The thing is, I keep thinking if I don't tell the truth, he'll get off anyway. The hospital did a rape kit. Won't that show he wasn't the rapist?

There's a knock on my bedroom door. "Come in," I say.

"Hey, Sis," Iggy says, smiling.

"Hey, Iggy."

His see-clear-through-you eyes aren't there, which makes me sad, because I need to ask him what I should do. Smart Iggy would know. A voice inside me says, *Smart Mara knows.* I hate that voice right now.

"Knock-knock," Iggy says.

"Who's there," I ask.

"Panther," he says.

"Panther who?"

"Panther no panths, I'm going thwimming," Iggy says, and he laughs so hard, he doubles over.

"Good one, sport," I say, but I don't laugh. I wonder if he is trying to answer my question.

Do what you have to do, no matter what, the voice in my head says.

Shut up, I tell the voice, but it doesn't. Do what you have to do.

"Get it? Go thwimming?" Iggy asks.

"Yeah, Iggy." I touch his face. "I think I do."

I left me by the river. I'm going to find what I lost.

CHAPTER 25

'M NOT SURE I'M READY TO GO "THWIMMING," BUT
I at least have to face the river, so I decide to go fishing
instead. I walk toward my and Xylia's special spot, to
the place where Elijah raped me, thinking if I can stand
there alone, I can make it mine again. If I can stand there
alone, I can find the Mara that I left behind and take her
home.

Carrying my pole and some hooks, I remember the way
Henry talked about a God of love, and moonwalked across
the cafeteria, and told Elijah God would never burn us.

At the river the rocks are the same. The reeds are the
same. The water is the same. But it doesn't feel safe the way
it used to. I walk around, searching for my backpack, which

still must be here somewhere. I'm starting to think it washed away when I find it huddled in the reeds, half buried in the mud. I remember tripping on it, falling, and the memory makes me want to run. But I don't. I look at that backpack until it doesn't scare me anymore.

"Fuck you, Elijah," I whisper. "You took my soul, but you don't get to keep it." I'm not sure if I believe the words when I say them, but I say them anyway. I can't quite touch the backpack yet, so I get my rod ready, dig in the mud for some bait. Soon a wriggling worm is impaled on my hook. I think about Elijah smashing the worm with his boot, and how I cried. I wonder what the difference between me and Elijah really is. He smashed worms. I impale them. Tears don't mean much if I do the same thing he did.

My hook plops in the water, creating little ripples. Even though it's late fall, the sun's warm on my shoulders. I stare into the green water and wait. For what, I don't know. For a fish, I suppose. For something. The top of my head starts to get hot as I wait and reel, cast again, reel some more.

Soon I forget to wait. I forget to think. I forget everything. So it takes me by surprise when there's a sharp tug on my line. I stumble forward, almost losing my pole.

I start to wrestle with a fish that is so strong, I'm panting and sweating and reeling like mad. When his silver back breaks the top of the water, I say, "Holy shit on a stick!" The fish is practically as big as a shark. It's none other than Paul Bunyan himself.

"Holy shit!" I cry again, and I reel harder and faster.

Paul Bunyan fights so hard, he yanks the line back out, but I'm not letting him go. Before long he's flopping in my net on the muddy shore, gasping.

"Holy shit on a stick!" is all I can say.

Paul Bunyan stares at me, desperately. His thick gills lift and close. His skin sparkles like a rainbow in the sun.

I stare deep into Paul Bunyan's eyes. They are like tiny mirrors. I see two miniature me's reflected back. He gasps again.

"Holy shit on a stick, Paul Bunyan."

I hold him against the ground and yank the hook from his jaw. It bleeds something awful, and I feel terrible for what I've done, looking at his small teeth.

"I'm sorry," I whisper. I lift the net and kiss him right on his fishy nose, and then I plop him back into the water. Off he swims, leaving a tiny trail of blood behind him. As he disappears into the murky green, I sink to my knees.

"Did you see that, Henry?" I imagine the way he laughed when he caught the toilet seat. "I caught Paul Bunyan."

I hear Henry say to me, "Paul Bunyan is a piece of God."

Things become clear. It's as if I'm looking down from way above. I don't think I will ever fish again, so I leave my pole there leaned up against the rock. Another worm is dead, and isn't that enough killing for one lifetime? I go back to the backpack. As I bend to pick it up, I notice a bit of metal next to it, glinting in the sunlight. I wipe the mud away from it and gasp. Xylia's ring. It's coated in grime, so I take it to the river and kneel to wash it. Cool water flows over the Virgin's face. When it's clean, I see that it's scraped, but still there, smiling kindly. I close my eyes and slide the ring on my finger, remembering the way I felt when Xylia gave it to me. Like the most precious thing in the world. The ring is proof that I'm not what Elijah made me that day. I'm not an abomination. I'm a girl who is loved.

I walk home quickly, the heavy bag bouncing on my back. I go to my room and lock the door. Unzipping the backpack, I whisper a prayer to Iggy's God of light. "Let the letters be okay." And they are. A little wrinkled, a little faded, but I can read every single word. They are like a math problem with many parts, but when you finally figure out the solution, you get one word: LOVE. When I finish reading them, tears and snot are running down my face. Mara isn't by the river anymore. She's inside me, and she's loved, and she knows what she has to do.

I go to my daddy, who is sitting on the couch watching television. "Daddy, Henry didn't rape me."

"What?" he says, blinking.

"Henry didn't rape me. He saved me." I go to the door and pull on my shoes. "Elijah Winchell raped me. I'm going to tell the police what really happened."

"No!" Daddy jumps out of his seat so fast, I barely know what is happening. He stands between me and the door, holding it shut.

"You can't do this, Mara."

I stare at him. "What do you mean I can't do this?"

"The whole town knows Henry did it."

"Well, he didn't." I finish tying my bootlace and stand up.

"Elijah Winchell couldn't do that."

"Yes, he could." The rock-steadiness of my voice surprises me. "He could, and he did. I was there. And I'm not letting Henry go to jail for it."

"You're not thinking straight," Daddy says. "Everyone knows that little heathen raped you."

I'm stunned. My daddy is too worried about his reputation to care about the truth, to care who really raped me. Sure, Daddy tried to kill Iggy and Momma. But I didn't think he would defend someone who raped his own daughter. He's just like Lot in that story about Sodom and Gomorrah. "Go ahead and take my daughters," he said to the rapists. My daddy is just like him. He's thinking about the way people will look at us in church. He's thinking he will never be able to walk tall through town again. In his book he is the only one that counts. His wife and children are just nameless extras, like in the Bible stories.

But I'm not nameless. My name is Mara, and I matter. I feel strength fill me, from my toes up.

I look Daddy straight in his piggy eyes. "Daddy, I swear to God, I'm telling the truth. Henry's my friend. Henry saved me. If you think I'm letting him go to jail for something Elijah did, you can think again."

Daddy doesn't move. I don't know why, but I'm not afraid of him right now. The worst has already happened to me. What else do I have to lose?

"Fine." I start toward the stairs.

"Where are you going?" Daddy hollers.

"I'm going to climb out my goddamn window!" I yell back. "You think I never climbed a tree before? Then I'll tell the police the truth, and I'll tell them you knew, and you lied, and you'll go to jail for a million years."

I hear Daddy running up behind me. I whirl around. "Don't you fucking touch me!" I scream.

He stops short. He opens his mouth, but no words come out.

"Get out of my way."

He doesn't move, so I push him aside and walk past him, out the door, into the brilliant fall colors and the blazing yellow sun.

CHAPTER 26

M ARA LYNN STONEBROOK!" DADDY'S VOICE
booms with fury through the fog of my sleep.
At first I think it's just one of my bad dreams,
but then I hear it again. I open my eyes. I look at the clock:
12:22. It's been hours since I went to the police station and
told them all about what Elijah did. Is Daddy just now getting pissed enough to do something about it?

Sitting up, I call out, "Yeah, Daddy?" My guts twist with
terror. Whatever made me not afraid of him earlier is gone.
Right now I'm not brave at all. I'm scared shitless.

"Get your little ass down here," he bellows. When I don't
move or say anything, he yells, "Now!"

I'm scared to go to him, but more scared to disobey, so

I step out of bed. The floor is cold, so cold I think I might freeze into one of those ice sculptures they show on the Food Network. I hope I will anyway, but I don't. By the time I get downstairs, my heart's beating so hard, I'm afraid it's going to blow up.

Daddy's standing in the living room with his back to me, looking out the window, holding something in his hand. A paper. The paper is shaking. Daddy's hand is shaking, along with his whole body. He's that mad. My feet want to run, but before they can, Daddy turns, wearing that same devil face he had the day he beat Iggy with the two-by-four.

"What in the name of the sweet Lord Jesus is this?" he asks, holding up the paper.

When I see what's on it, I know I don't need to answer him. He already knows what it is. It's a full-page print of me and Xylia kissing by the river. That's what it is.

"Someone rang the doorbell and left this on the porch," Daddy says. I guess Elijah kept his promise.

Daddy starts toward me, and I know, just know, that after all these years of being the one he never hurt, I'm actually going to be the one he kills. *Told you he'd kill someone,* a voice inside my head says.

"Russ!" Momma's voice comes from behind me. "What's going on?"

"Your daughter is a fucking abomination, that's what's going on." He waves the picture at her. Momma walks toward him. When she gets close enough to see what's on the picture, she covers her mouth with her hands. She moans.

Everything moves slow for a second. The lace curtains rustle in the breeze. Daddy takes two more steps toward me.

"Russ, no!" Momma lunges at Daddy, and he backhands her. She falls, her nose oozing blood. That's when I run. But I'm not fast enough. Daddy grabs the back of my nightgown. It rips all the way down, until it's split in two, like those gowns Momma and Iggy and I had to wear in the hospital. Momma screams, "Russ, you'll hurt her like you hurt Iggy!"

"Shut up, bitch!" She clutches at him, but he pushes her. This time she hits her head on the floor. It makes a loud crack. I wonder if it's broken. It must not be, because she starts crawling toward Daddy. She's gonna try to kill him before he kills me. I can see the fury in her eyes.

"Daddy, I'm sorry!" I scream, but he doesn't hear, or he doesn't care.

"Abomination!" he yells. Something slams into the side of my head. My skull feels like it explodes, and a knife of pain shoots right through my eyes. For a second I'm blind. Then I'm just falling, and everything is blurry.

Then the floor is cold. I'm screaming to wake the dead, waiting for his boot to come down and stomp me, the way Elijah killed the worm in class.

Nothing happens.

I don't know Iggy is in the room until I hear his voice. His words are measured and slow. "Get. The. Fuck. Away. From. My. Sister."

He looms large in the doorway, wearing loose pajama pants and a T-shirt that says, BE ALL YOU CAN BE. His see-clear-through-you eyes are out. He holds the rifle Daddy bought him for his eighteenth birthday. Its barrel is pointed straight at Daddy's face.

Shoot him, Iggy, I think, imagining Daddy's brains spraying all over the sofa the way the rabbit's sprayed all over the grass. The Daddy I loved that day, before the rabbit died, is a million miles away.

Iggy takes a step forward. "I swear to God, I will fucking kill you!" He glances down at me. "Get up, Sis." I'm too scared to move, so he says it again. "Get up."

He looks at Momma, who is frozen on all fours, stunned. "You too, Momma," he says. Momma scrambles to her feet, steadying herself against the wall.

When I try to stand, I'm dizzy. I stumble forward, right into Iggy. The gun clatters to the floor, and Iggy wraps his arms around me tight, kisses the top of my head. He keeps his mouth there for minute, so my scalp gets hot with his breath.

"You okay, Sis?" he asks, and I don't know if I am or not, so I just bury my face in his shirt, breathing the smell of him, loving it, loving him, finally knowing for sure who is whose angel here.

"You fucking punk!" Daddy screams.

Then everything happens so fast. Iggy pushes me to the couch, and Daddy lunges for the gun. Iggy's quick and young, and his hands get to the rifle butt first. Again the gun is pointed at Daddy, and Iggy says, "You will never touch us again."

Daddy's nostrils flare, and he swings at Iggy.

Iggy uses the rifle like a club. The barrel slams into Daddy's skull. Daddy falls to the floor. "Listen, you old, fat fuck," Iggy says. "I told you. You. Will. Never. Touch. Us. Again."

"Oh yeah, retard?" Daddy says through clenched teeth, "What are you gonna do if I do?"

Iggy's eyes glow so bright, so far away, so crazy. He smiles this eerie smile. "I'll kill you, Daddy," Iggy promises. "I'll kill you."

The rifle butt slams into the side of Daddy's head. Daddy falls to the floor. I look at him, hoping he's dead, but he's not. His eyes are closed, but the rise and fall of his chest tells me he's still breathing.

Iggy goes to him, stands over him like a tower. "You're the only abomination in this house."

He marches out of the room, carrying the gun that Daddy gave him, the one that meant he was a man.

CHAPTER 27

AFTER IGGY HITS DADDY WITH THE GUN, ME and Iggy race out the door. We try to get Momma to come too, but she won't leave Daddy.

"Are you sure, Momma?" I ask, and she just nods. We don't have time to wait around for her to change her mind, and we don't have time to call Xylia's mom. We just walk to her house in our pajamas. My shoes were upstairs, so I'm wearing Daddy's, and they make flopping noises on the road. Somewhere far away a coyote howls.

Juliette is wearing her kimono when she answers the door. "Oh, my God. Are you kids okay?"

"Yeah," I say. "I think we are now." It's sorta true. I'm still shaking, and my head hurts, but I'm alive, and I'm so grateful to Iggy, and to Momma. Both of them loved me enough to fight for me.

Juliette leads us to the kitchen. "Do you wanna talk about it?" she asks as she makes us hot tea.

I say I can't just then.

Iggy and me sleep together, curled up in Xylia's bed. It still smells like her, and it makes me miss her so much. When we wake up in the morning, the house smells warm and cinnamony.

We go to the kitchen, and Juliette puts a bran muffin on a plate for each of us. She doesn't even say good morning before she asks, "Should I call the police?" Her forehead is wrinkled with concern.

Iggy and I both say, "No!" Iggy seems normal as he eats his muffin, like he did before the brain injury. He's been himself since last night.

We eat fast, and then I tell Iggy it's time to go. I've spent my whole life keeping Daddy's secrets. The thought of ratting him out terrifies me. And besides, what would the cops do even if Juliette did call them? Probably nothing, and then Daddy would be even madder. I know if we stay any longer, Juliette will keep pushing, not because she's trying to interfere, but because she cares. She doesn't understand though. She doesn't understand Barnaby. She doesn't understand the cops. Most of all she doesn't understand my daddy.

As we walk home, cows low, and I wish I was in their fields with them, petting their soft noses.

We don't say much. I keep trying to tell myself everything's changed. Daddy will be humble from now on, and Iggy will be king. Still, fear gnaws at my belly.

When we get to the door of our house, Daddy steps onto the porch. Momma runs outside after him, wailing. They've obviously been fighting for a while.

"I'm done giving charity to your bastard son," Daddy seethes.

"Please! He's just a boy!" Momma begs.

"If he's man enough to strike me, he's man enough to get out of my house."

I didn't think I could hate him any more than I already did, but it turns out I can.

Daddy lets Iggy inside the house long enough to pack a suitcase. Iggy is surprisingly calm. Normally he'd be crying, but he seems to understand that he has to keep his wits about him. He shoves T-shirts and jeans into his suitcase with his strong hands.

"I'll be fine, Momma," he says, just like the old Iggy would have.

I wonder if last night was a miracle. I wonder if my big brother is back for good. My heart swells with hope. The doctor said Iggy might get better.

Momma folds Iggy's blanket and puts it in the suitcase, telling him all about her cousin Wanda in Albuquerque. I remember meeting her a couple of times when I was little, but me and Iggy weren't exactly close to her. Still, Momma writes her address on a piece of paper and gives it to Iggy.

"When you get off the bus, just find a taxi to take you here," she tells him. "I already called Wanda and told her you were coming."

That scares me. I hope Iggy's better, but what if he's not? He won't know how to get a taxi. He's never even seen one. "Momma, why can't Wanda just pick him up at the bus station?"

She looks at me with desperate eyes. "Wanda doesn't have a car. She's barely sane herself, Mara." She says this as if it's my fault.

"I thought she made forty dollars an hour as a hairdresser."

"She used to!" Momma says. "Years ago." She seems exasperated at my ignorance, like I should know everything about her hairdresser cousin. "She's an alcoholic now."

Great, I think. *Just like Momma.*

"Well, we can't count on Iggy remembering to give the taxi driver the address."

"I'll be fine, Sis," Iggy says. He hugs me, and I inhale the smell of him, feeling so many things. Love. Hope. Terror.

Momma glares at me. "He'll be fine, Mara. Don't even think that way."

Iggy lets go of me and returns to packing. Behind him, the sun casts orange light over the corn plants, setting them ablaze. Iggy has a glow around him.

Daddy stomps into the room. "Time to get a move on."

A few minutes later we stand on the porch. Daddy leans against the railing, eating a pear. He chews so loud, I want to punch him. Pear juice dribbles down his chin.

"What if he forgets where to go, Daddy?" I ask, sobbing.

"That's not my fucking problem."

"Even if I don't live here, I swear to God, if you touch Mara, I will find you," Iggy says. He has that crazy, murderous look again. Daddy walks back into the house without saying a word. I'm starting to like that look of Iggy's.

Me and Momma drive Iggy to the bus station. When Momma goes to buy Iggy a ticket, I tell her maybe we should buy three.

"Where would I get that kind of money? I'm lucky your daddy gave me enough for Iggy's bus fare and taxi," Momma snaps.

Iggy puts his hand on my shoulder. "I'll come back for you. I promise."

We stand by the bus, hugging like crazy, saying "I love

you" over and over. The driver leans against the bus, smoking a cigarette. He throws it on the ground and snuffs it out with the toe of his boot. "You coming?" he asks Iggy.

"Here, Iggy," Momma sobs, pressing a wad of bills into his palm. "Just hail a cab as soon as you get there. Don't forget to show them that address I gave you. Wanda will help you look for a job."

I'm still not convinced Iggy will remember all that when he gets to Albuquerque, but I try to be hopeful. We're due for some good luck. Maybe this is it. Maybe my brother is back, and he's going to get a job and come for me.

"Remember how you told me you were gonna leave this place and be something great?" I ask.

Iggy nods. "I do."

"This is it. This is your chance."

Iggy hugs me hard one last time before he gets on the bus. "We'll be back together soon, Sis."

I sort of believe him. After he comes for me, we can both go to San Francisco.

Iggy climbs the bus stairs. The door closes behind him. As the bus drives away, Iggy waves at me.

When Momma and me get home from the bus station, Daddy is sitting in his chair in front of the TV, watching some talk show. I expect him to attack me, but he just stares.

"Cora, get me a sandwich" is all he says. He pretends I'm not there.

After Momma makes Daddy a BLT, we go to her room and leaf through photo albums. Momma tears up a lot, looking at two-year-old Iggy playing in the snow and six-year-old Iggy swinging on a tire and eighteen-year-old Iggy all dressed up in Daddy's suit for graduation. We talk about the pictures, waiting for Iggy to call. After a few hours the silence starts to feel heavy. It suffocates us. When I stand to go to bed, Momma says, "He'll call soon. Don't worry." Nothing makes me worry more than when Momma tells me not to worry.

As soon as I wake up the next morning, I run to the kitchen, hoping Momma will have good news about Iggy. She's on the phone. "What do you mean he never came?" she sobs. I want to punch her. I want to punch myself. How could we have been so stupid to think that Iggy could handle taking a taxi? Momma hangs up. "I'm going to the cops," she declares, pulling her bathrobe closed.

Momma drives to the police station in her robe. I ride along in my pajamas, not caring what people think. The receptionist tells Sheriff Perkins we're there, and before we know it, we're sitting in his office.

"Coffee?" He smooths his red mustache, which reminds me of the bristle brush Daddy uses to shine his shoes.

I shake my head. The very thought turns my stomach.

"My son is missing!" Momma sobs.

Slouched behind his desk, sipping from a mug with an American eagle painted on the side, Sheriff Perkins tells her to come back in two days. "Iggy's of age," he points out.

"He's not in his right mind!" I say.

"Come back in two days," Sheriff Perkins says again.

In the evening, Momma sits on the porch, watching the sunset crumble. She drinks straight from a vodka bottle. No glass. "I have the sickest feeling, Mara."

I have the sickest feeling too, but I don't tell her. It won't help. I just put her to bed and go to my room and cry. I want to call Xylia, but I don't dare. Iggy's threat will only hold Daddy at bay for so long, and I don't want to provoke him. Outside, an owl hoots. A year ago the sound may have been beautiful to me. But now it sounds like death. Life without Iggy, without Xylia, is uglier than I ever imagined it could be.

Days go by. Momma calls her cousin every morning and night. Iggy never shows up. Momma files a police report. I can't focus at school. All I can think about is Iggy. I keep imagining the things that could have happened to him. None of them are pleasant.

On Sunday, Reverend Winchell gives a sermon about

women burning for women. He reminds us all that God hates abominations. He looks right at me when he says it. Elijah is six rows in front of me, but I still hear him laugh. I look down at my chapped hands. Momma and Daddy stare straight ahead, pretending they don't know Reverend Winchell is talking about me. I want to cry, but I find a round collection plate and stare at it until the tears dry up.

After that, school is harder than ever. Henry never comes back, even though he got out of jail. Rumor has it Henry's dad stormed into Principal Harris's office, squirting people with bleach and shouting that Christians were crazy as canaries in a snake pit. When I hear it, I laugh.

One night, I try to call Henry. I want to tell him how sorry I am, beg his forgiveness for leaving him in jail so long, but his dad answers and says he's in the bath. Maybe he really is. I don't know. But Henry's father sounds distant. I call again and again. It's always the same. Finally, I can't find the courage to call anymore. Martha Pinkerton says Henry switched to public school. Later, Hannah and Keisha claim he went back to the reservation. All in all, people are way more interested in Henry after he disappears than they ever were when he was around.

I thought Elijah would get arrested, but he doesn't. It turns out the hospital lost the rape kit. I throw a fit, but the police say it happens all the time. So I have no proof that Elijah raped me. It's Elijah's word against mine now, and who's gonna believe an abomination like me? Also, Hannah and Keisha have gone to the police and told them that Elijah was practicing singing with them at the church at the time of the rape. Reverend Winchell says that's God's honest truth. He was there in his office studying for his sermon, and he heard those sweet youngsters singing with his own two ears. So it looks like Elijah's gonna get off scott-free, just like Daddy always does. I wonder if someday I'll meet him by the river again. I wonder what he'll do to me then.

So I'm all alone at school, an abomination sitting in the corner, eating mushy peas, wishing for Henry, wishing for Iggy, wishing for Xylia. At night I pray desperate prayers. "Save me" is all I can say. Sometimes, winking stars make me feel like my brother's God is listening. Sometimes, rolling thunder tells me Reverend Winchell's God is waiting, ready with a death blow.

CHAPTER 28

WINTER'S FIRST SNOW COVERS THE world in white, and we get a snow day. I try not to remember the last snow day and Xylia screaming "*Sayonara*, motherfucker!" to the Reverend Winchell snowman.

I get out my sketchbook, wrap myself up in a quilt, and start drawing. I draw every chance I get these days, picture after picture. Most of them are of Xylia. The arc of her neck when it was bent to read something beautiful. The curve of her arm when she was touching my face. The smooth roundness of her belly.

I'm drawing her eyes when I hear someone knocking downstairs. I barely hear it through my closed door, but there it is again. *Bop, bop, bop*. The door squeaks open, and I hear a rumble of voices. I wonder who it may be. Visitors are so rare. I stand to go see who it is. And then Momma screams.

I run down the stairs. Momma is crumpled in a heap on her lilac rug.

"No, no." It's like in the movies, when people die. People in movies always say "no, no" when someone dies. So maybe that is how I know Iggy's dead. I'm not sure that's what tips me off, but I know it before I even notice the sheriff's deputy standing at the door. Before I even hear him saying, "I'm sorry."

My brother's dead. I want to run to my momma and hold her, but I can't. Suddenly I feel heavy, like a bag of rocks.

I sink right down next to Momma. I have the same feeling as that day with Elijah. I'm someone else, watching this scene from far away. Maybe I'm in the sky with Iggy and his God. I reach out my hand to see if that's the case, but all I feel are the fibers of Momma's rug. I'm not in heaven. This is real.

Momma's legs are shaking. I've never heard a person make a gurgling sound quite like that before. She's not saying "no, no" anymore. Now she's repeating "My baby, my baby, my baby."

That man in the uniform is still standing there. He isn't much older than me. His eyes are the same rusty color as Iggy's. I picture Iggy's eyes, and I can't imagine never seeing them again. It doesn't seem real. It feels wrong not to cry, but I can't, thinking any second he'll come walking through the door.

"How did he die?" I ask.

The man looks at his shoes. "He was living under a bridge in Albuquerque. Someone shot him."

And suddenly it's real. I imagine my beautiful brother sleeping under a bridge, his wheat-colored hair sticking up in every direction. I imagine a gun pointed at his head. The image is too ugly, so I move the gun, and it's pointed at his heart. I see a finger pull the trigger, and I see a hole break open in my brother's chest, just like the hole in the coyote me and Henry found by the road.

"Oh, Iggy," I whisper.

And that's when I finally start to cry.

CHAPTER 29

YOU'VE WALKED WITH ME ALL THIS WAY, A million miles it must seem to you. And now you wonder why. Why, you say, did I come so far? I will tell you.

There are names you will remember, like Hitler and Marilyn Monroe and Michael Jackson. But if I hadn't brought you along with me, you wouldn't remember my brother. You'd say, "Who was Iggy Stonebrook anyway?" Maybe now someone will always remember my brother and his beautiful, broken brain.

My brother was my hero. He saved me again and again. He wasn't a spit-shined hero, the kind in comic books with glossy boots and a billowing cape. My brother picked his nose. Still, I loved him with a love that stretches into forever. And now, at least, you know.

I will bury my brother today. I wish it would snow, but it doesn't. I stare out the window, cursing the unseasonably warm weather. Who thought to make it sunny on the day I say good-bye to my brother? The sky cried for Momma's broken face, but it can't make the world pretty and white for Iggy. The patchy remnants of the last snowfall are muddy now, and ugly.

Last night I borrowed Momma's old black funeral dress. She bought a new one, but I think the one I wore for the kittens is good. It's hanging over the chair, as smooth and still as a death shroud.

"Iggy," I whisper, and tears burn my eyes at his name. I go to my bed and muffle my sobs in the pillow. Then I slip into the dress. I run a comb through my hair, which is starting to grow back. I slide on a pair of Momma's fancy shoes instead of my old boots. They hurt my feet, but that's all right with me. I'd do anything to look pretty for Iggy today.

Iggy's dead. A plane flies low over our house. Iggy's dead. Cars speed on by, spraying mud with their tires. Iggy's dead. Chickens squawk. Iggy's dead. By the time Daddy gets dressed, I've been sitting on the couch for hours, watching the sun rise into the pale sky. I stand slowly.

"You ready?" I ask, all business-like. I surprise myself with how cool and calm I seem. You'd think I was on my way to school. Ever since I found out Iggy was dead, I've been going back and forth between numbness and hysteria.

Daddy straightens the lapel on his suit, the one Iggy wore to his graduation, and nods. Momma stands behind him. Her eyes are red. They walk out the door. I go to the change jar on the mantel and dump it in my purse. Then I follow them outside.

As we drive toward the cemetery, I start understanding the sky a little bit. I can't cry right now either. And the worst thing is, I know everyone will expect it. They'll be watching me, thinking, why isn't that girl crying? Doesn't she have any natural affection? I always knew there was something off about her. I try to muster some tears, but they just won't come. Iggy's dead, and me and the sky can't cry at his funeral. What kind of world is this?

At the graveyard rows and rows of white stones are lined up with artificial flowers sprinkled here and there. Black birds squawk and peck. I want to shoo them away, tell them to have some respect for the dead. Ahead, a cluster of people gathers around an open grave. At the center of the people, right next to a pile of fresh, dark dirt, sits a big mahogany box. On top sit sixty billion white roses.

My belly knots up. I stare hard at the box, trying to picture Iggy sleeping there. I imagine breaking open the box, kissing what is left of him, and stealing a little lock of his hair. But the coroner said I shouldn't look at him. He said it wouldn't be easy to see. I agree. I'd rather remember him alive.

I glance around the crowd. I nod to Henry when I see him and smile a little. The grief of my betrayal washes over me, and I half expect him to walk over and slap me. He smiles back. He has new glasses, red ones now. "I like your glasses," I want to say, but he's too far away.

"I'm sorry," I mouth instead, and I think he understands it, because he nods at me, a nod that says lots of things, one of them being, "I forgive you." I wish I could hug him, but his father whispers something, and Henry turns away.

Mr. Farley, who's serving as a pallbearer, whisks us right up front. It's Momma, Daddy, and me, on show in the front row so everyone can get some entertainment from our pain. Trying not to think about all those hot eyes burning into my back, I touch the coffin.

"Bye, big brother," I whisper. Then I step away.

Momma touches the casket too.

Daddy just stares.

I stand with my heels sinking into the soft dirt. The people around me are wearing boo-hoo faces, and I want to break their necks. How dare they pretend to cry, when they're gonna leave this place and go out for a nice lunch, what with the funeral and all? How dare they when today is the last day they'll ever think of Iggy? How dare they when their biggest responsibility is maybe to make a potato-cheese casserole later for Momma? I'll be carrying the memory of this day around forever, like a cinder block.

"You can't share in this," I want to say. "This day isn't yours. It's mine. You people just go home." Like when there's an accident, and folks gather round, the sheriff says, "Everybody move along now. There's nothing more to see here." That's what I want to say.

I think about the way Iggy wanted to be all he could be. The thing I never got to tell him was that he *was* all he could be. He was the best person I ever knew. He deserves a twenty-one-gun salute. Or better, a twenty-one-birdcall salute. In my head, I practice some birdcalls Iggy might like, *caw, caw, whistle, warble,* so on and so forth.

We sit on a row of lawn chairs that have been lined up for the family. A stand-in preacher shipped in from Albuquerque gets up to say a speech since Reverend Winchell couldn't be here—family emergency, he said, though I think it's mostly that he's pissed about me telling the truth about Elijah.

"Ashes to ashes, dust to dust," says the preacher. "God picked one of his flowers, don't you see? He works in mysterious ways."

And I think it's all fine and good that the preacher can explain away my brother's life in one ten-minute speech, but me, well, I'm gonna spend the rest of my life trying to get over this.

I look at my momma. She's staring at the ground with empty eyes, wringing her hands, leaning as far away from Daddy as she can.

And Daddy? He's posing, trying to look like he gives a shit. I want to spit on him, beat him down for all the times he beat Iggy.

A sick taste comes into my mouth. I feel like a coyote must feel when it gets caught in one of those traps. No way out. Panicky. Ready to chew off my own leg if it will do me one bit of good.

The preacher says something about the resurrection of the dead, and I just can't take it anymore. That box. Iggy would never pick a stuffy place like that to sleep. Those white roses too. My guess is, Iggy would've liked a bunch of sunflowers better. This brouhaha has nothing to do with Iggy. I duck my head and stand. When Daddy tries to grab my arm, I jerk away.

"I'll say good-bye to Iggy down by the river, where we played when we were little," I whisper.

"Mara, stop," he hisses.

"Come back here," Momma mouths.

"No." I walk slowly in front of the crowd, feeling their eyes burning into my skin. Let them look all they want. I keep walking.

When I'm safe inside the woods, I finally cry. A breeze plays with my skirt. The smell of river mud dances in my nose. It hurts to feel those things without my brother here. Seems like a sin to enjoy anything at all. I amble along through frozen clay and dead cattails, tasting my tears, thinking all the while about how Iggy would pick a day just like this for fishing or swimming.

When I reach our place, the sight of it nearly knocks the wind out of me. I imagine him sitting there on that rock, reeling in a big one, wriggling his bare toes in the mud, laughing up a storm. But he's not there, and the only thing I can do is sink down on the rock and cry.

"Iggy," I whisper, "I don't know if you can hear me, up there with that God of yours. I'm trying to be happy for you, but I can't. I don't know what I'll do without you."

Dead is forever. Nothing ever lasts. I think about love and leaving, and then I think about Xylia. I stare at her ring, thinking about the letters she wrote me. I think about train tracks and Mexico. I think about the voice in my head that's been telling me to run. I stick my toes in the water, even though it's cold. A branch sloshes against my toes. I pick it up, just for something to hold on to, but this branch has wings. I turn the wood over, and there it is, Xylia's face, waterlogged but beautiful. Slowly I take the angel I carved in my hand, touch the grooves on her wings, kiss the top of her head.

I close my eyes, pretending Iggy's here beside me. He talks the way he did when his see-clear-through-you eyes came out. He talks like Daddy never broke him.

"I'm not afraid, Mara," he says. "The only thing I can't leave behind without crying is you. Sometimes I look around at the clouds, because I figure that's what you're watching too. You always did have your head in the clouds, Sis."

I watch the clouds roll across the sky, over the mountains and away. I don't know if the voice inside me is really Iggy, or if it's only me. It doesn't matter. I stand, staring down at the water as it rushes away from this town.

"Everything beautiful is on its way outta here," I whisper. I close my eyes, trying to find that spark inside me that was strong enough to tell the truth about Henry, the thing that is strong enough to run off alone. Instead I find a cave, so deep and wide, I don't know where the blackness ends and I begin.

"I can't do this alone, Iggy," I say. When I open my eyes, Iggy's face is looking up at me from the water, smiling and sparkling like a million stars. "Iggy!" I call. He explodes in a swirl of liquid light. "Iggy!" I say again. But he's gone.

I keep watching, but the water's just the water, and the only light dancing on it comes from the sun above me. My head hurts so bad now, I think it's gonna explode. I crumple to my knees and sob.

"Help me," I say.

I pray with my eyes wide open, staring up at the billowing clouds drifting across the sun. Bars of golden sunlight fall like slices of heaven. Flurries of dust swirl in the light, and I reach up and touch them. They look like clouds of gold dust. I huddle there, holding a handful of gold dust in my palm, listening to the whisper-whisper of my breathing and the swishing of cattails in the wind. Then I hear it. A shrill whistle comes to me from far away, down the railroad tracks.

"Time to go, Sis," I hear my brother say from deep inside my head.

I stand and put one foot in front of the other. And I begin to walk.

The cedars sway above my head, and the river rushes

along beside me. He's walking with me, my brother. I can almost hear him calling the birds. *Caw, caw, whistle, warble,* so on and so forth.

I got nothing. Nothing but a waterlogged angel, a purse full of quarters, and a handful of gold dust. In the distance the train whistle blows again. If Xylia says San Francisco's pretty, I bet she's right. I'll jump a train. I'll hitch a ride. I'll do whatever it takes to get to her. I remember the words from Ms. Elibee's poem, and the promise I made in the bathroom stall. *I will find out where she has gone, and kiss her lips, and take her hands.*

I can almost see her now, smiling that light-up-the-night smile. "Mara!" she'll say as she opens the door and throws her arms around my neck. I bet she'll smell like flowers. The train whistle blows again.

Iggy and me keep walking.

Acknowledgments

THANK YOU:

To Annette Pollert, Sara Sargent, and the entire Simon Pulse team, who fell in love with Mara, Iggy, and Henry and helped me craft this book into something more beautiful than I ever imagined it could be. To my agent, Andy Ross, who took a chance on an unknown writer and became my first editor, my cheerleader, and my friend. I knew you, and only you, *had* to represent me the first time I saw you standing by a sombrero-wearing donkey. To Mitchell Sommers for your invaluable insights into the juvenile legal system. To my amazing father, Timothy John Hackett, for managing to give me in twenty-one years enough love to last a lifetime. To my beautiful mother, Christine Hackett, who taught me by example what courage was and never lost faith in me. To my beautiful brother, Bryan Hackett, who inspires me every day with his example of what a true follower of Christ should look like. To my babies, Desi and Tim, whose light makes my life worth living. To Eric Auxier for believing in me enough to put your money where your mouth is. Without you, I'd be living in a cardboard box, eating paste. To my angels, Julie Barrett, Polyxeni Angeles, Martine Tharp, Merridith Allen,

Tharp, Merridith Allen, and Jason Hicks. Without you, I'd be dead. To my inspiration, Roger Clyne, for providing the adventures, the magic, and soundtrack that fuel my art. To Jim Dalton, my dear friend who always made sure I was on the safe road. To my brilliant mentors, Amanda and Joseph Boyden, who taught me everything there was to know about writing. To my New Orleans writing family for your support and love, especially Jeni Stewart, Daniel Wallace, Lish McBride, and Kimberly Clouse. And most of all, to God (aka Big Cheese) for giving me the life of my dreams. To my fellow road warriors, who chased the horizon with me and made the highway even more magical: Jessica McDaniel (move!) and Kris Gwynn (buffalo!).